A BLANCO COUNTY MYSTERY

© 2016 by Ben Rehder.
Cover art © 2016 by Bijou Graphics & Design.
Print design by A Thirsty Mind Book Design.

All rights reserved.

This novel is a work of fiction. Names, characters, places, and incidents are either the product of the author's imagination, or, if real, used fictitiously. No part of this book may be reproduced or transmitted in any form or by any electronic or mechanical means, including photocopying, recording, or by any information storage and retrieval system, without the express written permission of the author or publisher, except where permitted by law.

*For Steve Cauley
and Kurt Treadaway*

ACKNOWLEDGMENTS

Much appreciation to Tommy Blackwell, Jim Lindeman, Becky Rehder, Helen Haught Fanick, Mary Summerall, Marsha Moyer, Stacia Hernstrom, Linda Biel, Leo Bricker, Kathy Carrasco, and Pam Headrick. Special thanks to Darrell Crain and Trey Carpenter for their specialized knowledge, and to Rob Cordes, Don Gray, and Martin Grantham for helping me nail down some details. All errors are my own.

I would also like to note the loss of a great talent, Robert King Ross, who brought so many of the Blanco County audiobooks to life with his rich voice. He will be missed.

POINT TAKEN

A BLANCO COUNTY MYSTERY

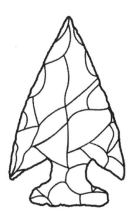

BEN REHDER

1

Brody "Wick" Wickenham was under the impression that the world was his personal toilet, so he asked his fraternity brother Eric to pull to the side of a quiet county road so he could take a massive leak. Four beers in the course of an hour could do that to a guy. But what was a road trip without beer, especially when the trip was in pursuit of a blond hottie named Naomi?

"Jesus Christ, what is that smell?" said Chris, who had stepped up to take a leak on Brody's left.

"Wick ripped one," said Ryan, who was spraying the grass on Brody's right.

That was generally the way it worked. If one guy needed to whiz, they all piled out and took a whiz. Fewer stops that way. Eric was on the other side of the Land Rover, unleashing the beast right in the middle of the road. He didn't even have the decency to move to the grassy shoulder. Didn't really matter. They hadn't seen another vehicle in 20 minutes. They were in the friggin' middle of nowhere.

"Damn tacos," Chris said. "Coming back to haunt us."

"Wasn't me," Brody said. "That smells like one of Ryan's."

"Where are we, anyway?" Chris asked.

"Who the fuck knows?" Ryan said. "Hey, Eric, where the hell are we?"

Eric replied by uncorking an enormous belch. Then he said, "You ladies don't worry about it. I know exactly where we are."

Naomi had grown up in the boonies between Johnson City and Fredericksburg, west of Austin. A rancher's daughter. The good news was, her parents had gone to Abilene for a cattle auction or a rodeo or some shit like that, and Naomi had invited three of her sorority sisters to spend the weekend at the ranch. Just chilling around the pool, basically, drinking margaritas. She'd mentioned it to Brody, who had then badgered an invitation from her.

"Okay, but we can't get all wild," she'd warned him.

"I didn't know ranches had pools," Brody said.

"God, we're not, like, savages living on the wild frontier," Naomi said. "It's just a house with a lot of land around it."

She'd given him the address and told him to Google it. She said it was easy to find. Sure. Maybe if you were Lewis and Clark.

"I'm seriously going to spew," Ryan said when the breeze shifted and the odor got stronger. "That's not a fart. It can't be."

"What *is* that?" Chris said.

The smell seemed to be coming from the other side of the fence, but Brody couldn't see very far, because the land in that direction was thick with cedar trees.

"Haven't any of you retards ever smelled a dead animal before?" Eric said. He'd come around to the rear of the Land Rover.

"Just your mother," Ryan said.

Eric threw a half empty can of Natural Light at him, then said, "It's probably a rotting cow or something. No big deal."

"That's what they do for entertainment out there," Chris said. "Sit around and watch livestock decompose."

Just then, Brody had a great idea.

"Dude, where are you going?" Eric said.

Brody was making his way toward the barbed wire fence. He was going to find the cow—or whatever kind of animal it was—take a selfie with it, and post it on Instagram. Imagine the reaction he'd get. He'd never seen a post like that. What if the carcass was crawling with maggots and stuff? How cool would that be? He had to think of a great caption. He reached the fence and carefully climbed over.

He heard Ryan say, "Bet he has to take a dump."

Brody pushed his way between the lower branches of two cedar trees only to find more cedar trees. It was like weaving your way through a crowded dance floor during a rush party.

"Hurry up, Wick!" Eric called. "Gonna leave your ass out here!"

Brody veered right and the smell faded. So he turned around and went the other way. He could tell he was getting closer now, because the smell was getting stronger—so much so that he had to pinch his nostrils closed.

Up ahead, the cedars gave way to a clearing. He stepped into it and then stopped abruptly, dumbstruck. He saw the source of the smell, and now he wondered why he and his fraternity brothers hadn't considered this possibility.

It was a dead guy. An actual human body, less than twenty feet away. Nude and bloated. The corpse's skin was discolored—purplish black. The stench was almost unbearable. Hard to tell how old he might have been. Brody saw no maggots, but dozens of flies crawled across the man's flesh, swarming his mouth, nose, and eyes, while hundreds more circled and buzzed in the air above. The scene churned Brody's stomach and made him nauseous, but he was also mesmerized. And curious. What had happened to the guy? Was it an accident? How did he get here? Who was he? When did he die? Where were his clothes?

"Wick! Hurry the fuck up!"

Brody began to make a wide circle around the body, and that's when he saw a small pickaxe protruding from the side of the man's head.

2

Sometimes, when Red O'Brien told the story about the trip he and Billy Don Craddock had taken to Las Vegas, he liked to drag it out as long as possible.

He'd start with some background information—telling how he and Billy Don, his best friend and poaching partner, had won $25,000 each in a pig-hunting contest. Then he'd describe how they'd weighed all their options, wanting to do something sensible with the money, and deciding that going to Vegas was the wisest course of action.

Why Vegas?

It turned out—to Red's utter disbelief, since Billy Don was no intellectual giant—that the big cedar chopper was a kickass blackjack player. Frankly, Red had been surprised to learn that Billy Don could even count to 21, seeing as how he had only 20 fingers and toes, but once he saw Billy Don play, there was no denying it.

Then Red would move the story along to Vegas, and he'd describe how Billy Don won more hands than he lost, and how their pile of chips grew larger and larger, and larger still, into tens of thousands of dollars, and then more than a hundred thousand dollars.

It was a goddamn dream come true. This had been their plan, and it had worked. So far.

And then came the final hand.

At this point, when telling the story, Red would share even the smallest details, giving his audience a mental picture of the other players at the table, and the redheaded lady dealer, and the crowd that had gathered around, ready to erupt when the final card was dealt.

Red liked to build the suspense that way. Make them wonder how it had turned out. After all, how many of them had shoved $142,000 worth of chips onto a blackjack table? How many of them truly understood what that felt like? Well, Red knew all too well.

It made you want to puke.

It also made you want to scream "Time out!" and say they wanted to change their minds. Billy Don was the blackjack player, but half of those chips were Red's, and the thought of losing it all made him sweat like a fat guy in bicycle shorts.

And, oh, sweet Jesus, he also knew what it felt like to win.

Because that's what had happened. They'd won that final hand and the crowd around the blackjack table had gone apeshit. Red himself had almost fainted. What a friggin' rush. The best moment of his life, bar none.

But...

Of course there was a "but"—there always was—and in this case, the "but" came in the form of a haunting thought Red had had repeatedly since Vegas:

Having all this money is great, but what if I blow it all?

Red was amazed at the nearly unbearable burden a large sum of money places on a man's soul. Being poor ain't easy, but what about being rich? Nobody ever warned you about that. Having that much cash might sound like a wonderful thing, but what if you were terrified to do anything with it? It kept him up nights. Made him toss and turn. Made him fret to the point of having a sour stomach.

What if I squander it away?

That was the question Red was contemplating yet again, sitting on the front porch of his mobile home, when the unexpected visitor turned off the county road and started up the long caliche driveway on Sunday afternoon.

That question led to so many other questions...

Should he bulldoze his ancient mobile home and put a brand-new double-wide in its place? Hell, for that matter, why not go big and build a frame home on a genuine cement slab? Or maybe even buy a couple acres on a river or lake somewhere, build a small cabin on it, and fish right off the back porch?

At a minimum, before he answered those questions, it made sense that he should buy himself a brand new pickup, right? His faithful red Ford truck had qualified as a classic years ago, and even though he couldn't imagine life without it, it wouldn't hurt to have a more reliable vehicle, would it? On the other hand, why not just drop a new engine into the old truck and see how long she'd go?

See? Too damn many questions.

It weighed on his mind enough that he was actually glad to have a distraction now and then. In this case, it was a gray Toyota Tacoma. Hard to tell from here, but it looked like just one person in the truck. He was halfway up the hill now, which meant he had passed the hand-painted NO TRESPASSING sign, followed by the ARMED RESPONSE sign, then the WE AIN'T KIDDING sign, and finally the SAY YOUR PRAYERS sign. Took a lot of guts for a stranger to ignore all those warnings.

As the truck got closer, Red saw that the driver was hauling something in the bed. Something large, rectangular, and white. What the hell was that? A full-sized freezer? It sure was—the chest type of a freezer with a lid that opens upward.

Red remained seated and let the Tacoma get to the top of the hill—the flat parking area in front of the trailer—where the driver killed the engine.

The driver was on the phone, but he gave a friendly wave. Red did not wave back.

A moment later, the driver ended his call and exited the truck. He looked to be in his late twenties, with long, straight black hair sticking out from under a brown beaver-skin hat with a low crown and a flat brim. He had sharp cheekbones and a dark complexion. Tall, too. Maybe six-three. Lean, with large, capable hands, like a relief pitcher who comes in for the last inning and kicks ass. He was wearing jeans, work boots, and a long-sleeved denim shirt with a logo on the left breast.

Before Red could say anything, the man spoke. "Howdy. Sir, my name is Joseph Lightfoot and I represent the New Mexico Meat Company. I don't mean to bother you, but are you interested in buying some prime-quality beef, fish, or seafood at prices much, much lower than you'd find at your nearest supermarket?"

"You're trespassing," Red said.

"Pardon?"

"You're trespassing, son," Red said.

He could feel the wooden porch vibrating beneath him. Heavy footsteps. *Thud. Thud. Thud.* Billy Don was on his way to the porch from his bedroom.

Red said, "I see you got New Mexico plates, so I'll cut you some slack, but here in Texas, you don't drive past a no-trespassing sign. Not unless you want to deal with a pissed-off landowner. Hell, in hunting season, it might even get you shot."

The man said, "I appreciate the warning. I truly do. I wasn't sure what to do, because once I started up the hill, there was no place to turn around."

"You could've backed up."

"I considered that, but the freezer blocks my view when I go in reverse. I figured it would be easier to come on up. Hope you don't mind."

The front door swung open and Billy Don filled the doorway. He was wearing some enormous cargo shorts and nothing else. His weight had always hovered right at 300 pounds, but lately Red had wondered if that figure had crept upward by ten or twenty pounds. He and Billy Don hadn't been working as regularly, now that they had cash on hand, along with a steady supply of Slim Jims, Moon Pies, and Keystone Light.

"Howdy," the salesman said to Billy Don, who simply grunted in response. He had probably been napping and the voices had woken him up.

Nobody said anything for a long moment.

"While I'm here," Joseph Lightfoot said, smiling, "may I show you some top-quality products?"

Billy Don said, "What kinds of—"

"We're hunters," Red said, interrupting. "We got all the meat we need."

"I bet you do, but does that include grass-fed buffalo burgers? Half a pound each. Great on the grill. Bet y'all like to grill, huh?"

Red had never had a buffalo burger, and he was intrigued, but he didn't like a pushy salesman, especially one who had already trespassed. So he said, "Like I said, we're all set."

"Right now, I have a two-for-one special on anything you buy."

Billy Don said, "Does that include—"

"You need to hit the road," Red said.

Joseph Lightfoot's smile faded. "Just trying to make a living," he said.

"I'm all for that," Red said, "but when you trespass on a man's land, you'd better be ready to take no for an answer."

"Your land?" Lightfoot said.

"Yep."

"You think this is your land?"

"If it ain't mine, whose is it?" Red asked.

"One does not sell the earth upon which the people walk," Joseph Lightfoot said.

Billy Don stepped out onto the porch and the boards groaned beneath his bare feet.

Red leaned forward in his chair. "The hell's that mean?"

The salesman said, "The message is clear for those who will listen."

Red glared at him and the man glared back.

Billy Don said, "We got a problem?"

"That's a good question," Red said, still in a staring contest with Lightfoot. He was ready for trouble, but after another long pause, the salesman turned around, got back into his truck, and started slowly down the hill.

Red's hands were tingling with adrenaline.

"That was weird," Billy Don said. "What was that thing he said?"

"No idea. Can't sell the earth or some such bullshit. Who goes around selling meat door to door?"

Billy Don just shook his head.

"Also, was he an Indian?" Red asked.

"Sure looked like one, but I don't think we're supposed to call 'em that."

"Then what're we supposed to call 'em?"

"Native Americans, I think."

"That don't make no sense," Red said. "Hell, *I'm* a native American, and so are you."

The lower part of the driveway, where it met the road, wasn't visible, but Red could hear the Tacoma turning right to go hassle some of the neighbors in that direction.

"Don't see many Indians 'round here," Billy Don said. "Maybe he was Mexican."

Red didn't reply. He was irked, wishing he'd come up with a better reply to the man's remark about owning land, even though Red was still puzzling out what it meant.

"I'm really getting tired of all this politically correct bullshit," Red said.

"Gotta admit, buffalo burgers sound pretty tasty," Billy Don said. "Wonder what they're made of."

3

"How was the lake?" Sheriff Bobby Garza asked from behind the desk in his office.

When Garza had called John Marlin, Blanco County's longtime game warden, to request his assistance on a new case, Marlin had just finished a long day working with three other game wardens on Lake Travis, west of Austin. Patrolling any of the Highland Lakes on a summer weekend consisted of routine safety inspections, an occasional arrest for boating while intoxicated, and plenty of citations or warnings for minor infractions, such as failing to have enough life vests or creating a wake in a no-wake zone.

But there were usually one or two unexpected encounters or odd occurrences, and yesterday had been no exception. In early afternoon, Marlin and another warden had approached a large sailboat that had been anchored in place for several hours, and they had seen nobody on board the three times they had passed by. Not unusual. Somebody could be sleeping in the cabin. When the wardens passed by a fourth time, they decided it was time for a safety check. Marlin called out to the boat, and a minute later a man popped his head above deck—with a professional-grade video camera propped on his shoulder. He explained with no hesitation or embarrassment that he was shooting an adult film called *All Hands on Dick*. A total of eight people emerged from the small cabin, but they weren't breaking any laws and had all the required safety gear.

"Oh, business as usual," Marlin said, knowing Garza was anxious to dispense with small talk and get to the topic for this meeting, because the sheriff and all of his deputies were swamped with an unusually heavy caseload.

"I appreciate you making time for this," Garza said. "Heard any of the details?"

"Just what you told me on the phone."

Earlier Garza had said a body had been found by a group of Austin frat boys, and it was an obvious homicide. Marlin knew nothing beyond that, but he was always inclined to assist the sheriff's office when asked, and he had proven to be a sharp investigator over the years. Right now, in early August, several weeks before dove season began, Marlin had the time to help.

Garza spoke to the woman in the chair to Marlin's right. "Lauren, why don't you bring him up to speed?"

Lauren Gilchrist—tall, brunette, and a genuine Texas beauty inside and out—was the new chief deputy, replacing Bill Tatum, who had recently retired. Lauren had been a deputy in San Saba County for several years, and had then become the first female special ranger for the Texas & Southwestern Cattle Raisers Association, where she'd investigated livestock rustling cases.

But Marlin had known Lauren long before that—going all the way back to their college days in San Marcos when they'd dated for nearly a year. At first, Marlin had worried it might be awkward working together, but it hadn't been an issue, nor had the fact that Lauren had been dating Marlin's best friend, Phil Colby, all summer. Marlin was glad the transition had gone smoothly, because Lauren made a fantastic addition to the department. She was intelligent and tenacious, and had just the right temperament for law enforcement.

She said, "The victim was nude, but we pulled fingerprints and got a hit on AFIS." She looked down at a notepad in her lap. "His name is Sean Hudson. Twenty-three years old. He's been written up three times for trespassing in Burnet County. Lives in a garage apartment in Marble Falls. His landlord gave me a number for Sean's mother, but I haven't reached her yet. I left a voicemail asking her to call me. Based on the lividity, it was obviously a dump job. The body had to have been carried by hand onto that property, so we're talking about a fairly strong person, or maybe two people working together. No shoe prints going in or out, unfortunately."

"How long had he been dead?" Marlin asked.

"Forty-eight to 60 hours, according to Lem," Lauren said.

Lem Tucker was the medical examiner.

"Any clothing at the scene?" Marlin asked. Sometimes stripping a victim was an attempt to conceal his identity.

"Nope. Hence no wallet and no ID. He had a cell phone, but we haven't found it. We're getting a warrant for his records, so we'll see where that takes us."

The search warrant would include location data for the hours and days preceding Hudson's death, which might help them determine where he had been killed. Also, if they could find the phone itself, it might provide a wealth of evidence—assuming it wasn't password protected. Locked phones were difficult to access, especially if the manufacturer wasn't willing to provide assistance. A battle between the FBI and Apple hadn't resolved the issue one way or the other. Marlin could see both sides of that debate; he respected the power of the courts, but he also valued personal privacy as much as the next person.

"How did Hudson die?" he asked.

"A small pickaxe," Garza said. "Hang on and I'll show you."

He had a laptop on his desk. He clicked a few keys, then turned the laptop around for Marlin to see. On the screen was a photo of the dead man's upper torso and head, along with the murder weapon, which was still embedded in the man's skull. It was L shaped, with a wooden handle about twelve inches long and a long, slender blade that came to a fine point.

"Wiggle pick," Marlin said.

"Wiggle what?" Garza asked.

"That's not just a small pickaxe," Marlin said. "It's a specialized tool called a wiggle pick. It's used to dig arrowheads and other artifacts. And that might explain this guy's three trespassing charges. It might even give us a motive for the killer. Not to jump to any conclusions."

Garza's handsome face lit up. "By all means, jump. Solve this thing for us right now."

He wasn't being sarcastic. Garza valued teamwork and efficiency. He brought Marlin into investigations precisely because Marlin could share a wealth of unique knowledge gleaned from his years as a game warden.

"Okay, stop me if I go into too much detail," Marlin said, "but there are basically three types of people who search for artifacts.

First you've got archeologists and other scientists, followed by amateurs who dig or surface hunt legally. Sometimes there's some tension between those two camps, because the scientists don't like amateurs messing up a site. Then, third, you've got illegal diggers. Looters. Those guys will go just about anywhere, on public or private land, and their goal is to find artifacts they can turn around and sell. When we can catch them—and the good ones are damned hard to catch—we typically file on them for trespassing, and theft, too, when we can. A lot of these guys are willing to take chances because they're meth heads. It's how they pay for their habit. But not all of them, by any means."

"We need to check the details on those previous trespassing charges," Garza said. "Find out if Sean Hudson was a looter."

"I'll do that as soon as we're done here," Lauren said.

Marlin caught himself gazing sideways at her. There were times, even all these years later, that he found himself remembering the curves under her uniform. He couldn't help himself. It was like somebody telling you not to think of a pink elephant. And now he realized Bobby had just asked him a question.

"Pardon?"

"How much are arrowheads worth?"

"It varies a lot. Most of them, probably just 50 or 100 bucks, but I've seen them get into the thousands. I heard about a guy who remodeled his house with the profit from a corner tang knife, so we're talking several thousand, I assume. Then you have Clovis points, Pedernales points, Andice points, which can get into tens of thousands of dollars, in good condition."

"I had no idea," Garza said, shaking his head.

"Of course, like I said, the majority of the pieces aren't worth nearly that much, but it adds up," Marlin said. "A hundred bucks here, a couple hundred there."

"Well, we know any pair of idiots can get into a squabble over ten bucks," Garza said.

"True. Or the last piece of fried chicken," Marlin said.

"I busted a guy once who thought his best friend was making kissy noises at his wife, so he shot the friend in the leg with a twenty-two," Lauren said. "Turned out the victim was calling the dog, which was sleeping at the wife's feet."

"I'm sure alcohol wasn't a factor," Marlin said.

"Of course not. How could you think such a thing?" Lauren said. "Except for the half-gallon of tequila they'd been passing around all day."

"Where do these looters dig?" Garza asked. "Are there particular places that are better than others?"

Garza was hoping to narrow down possible locations for the crime scene.

Marlin said, "Well, I could probably lead you to the best place to dig on a given ranch, but generally speaking, just about any property in the Hill Country is likely to have some decent places to search."

"So Hudson could've been digging just about anywhere," Garza said. "Assuming he was digging when he got killed."

"Pretty much, yeah," Marlin said. "Especially if he was willing to trespass, and he obviously was."

"You can see in this photo that he also had an abrasion on his face," Garza said. "Like maybe he got punched or smacked with some kind of object before he got killed."

"Maybe he was out digging and got into some sort of confrontation," Marlin said. "Could've been with a landowner or a turf battle with another looter."

"How in the world do they manage to dig around here, with all the rock just below the topsoil?" Lauren asked.

"Most of the old Indian camps were near a river or creek, and now the slopes down to the water are covered by a foot or two of soil that isn't nearly as compacted or rocky as in other places," Marlin said. "That's my understanding, anyway. I might sound like I know what I'm talking about, but I'm far from an expert."

"No, this is a great start," Garza said. "Next steps: Notify the family and see what they can tell us. Search Hudson's apartment. Then talk to his friends, girlfriend, boyfriend, whatever. We need to learn everything we can about this guy. When was he last seen and where was he going? Did he have favorite places to dig? Who did he dig with?"

"And where did he sell the stuff he dug up?" Lauren added. "Who were his customers?"

"That brings up another possibility," Marlin said. "Some of these guys have been known to knap new points and pass them off as authentic. You can piss someone off real quick that way. I have no idea if Hudson was into knapping—it takes a lot of skill—but it's something else we need to check."

"Add it to the list," Garza said. "What else?"

"We found Hudson's car in front of his apartment, so wherever he died, he probably got a ride with someone," Lauren said. "Or the killer drove the car back to the apartment. I've got a warrant in the works to search it, and Henry is processing the wiggle pick. Maybe we can get some DNA."

Henry Jameson was the crime scene technician who served a five-county area in the sparsely populated region west of Austin.

"Keep me posted," Garza said.

4

Red enjoyed being a man of leisure. That was something being a thousandaire had done for him—given him plenty of free time. Of course, he had to fill that time, and more often than not, he opted to grab a cold beer and some snacks, kick back in his recliner, and channel surf.

Nowadays, he watched all sorts of weird shit that he wouldn't have watched before. A case in point was the show he was watching right now. It was one of those before-and-after reality shows where the hosts work with common, everyday folks to create something fantastic and wonderful. What were they building? A frigging tree house. Not some kid's hideout, but a large, elaborate tree house built to the same standards as a house on the ground. It had electricity, plumbing, and everything else a person would need. Pretty cool, really.

And suddenly, in a moment that could only be called divine inspiration, Red realized what he was going to do with his money. Or some of it, anyway.

He would build a goddamn tree house!

An actual tree *house*—a full-sized home that he could live in, just like the ones in the TV show. An actual home built into a tree! Or perhaps it would be built in several trees, with covered plank walkways leading from one wing to another. He had a couple of huge oaks behind his trailer that would work great.

It made perfect sense, because Red never felt more comfortable and "at home" than when he was in a deer stand, and wasn't a tree house basically an enormous, glorified, totally kickass deer stand on steroids? A deer stand with heat and a toilet! Cold beer in the refrigerator! A full-sized bed!

Red was just about to holler at Billy Don and explain this

fantastic idea when Red's cell phone buzzed. His phone was a cheap knockoff from a Korean manufacturer, so it didn't always work as well as it should, but that was okay, because most of the calls Red received came from telemarketers who could hardly speak English.

This time, however, it was one of Red's neighbors—one he actually liked and got along with. She was a sweet old lady who lived on a hundred acres a little ways down the road. Unlike some of the other residents in the area, she never complained when he shot varmints in the middle of the night, or when he piled broken appliances down by the road to haul off later, or when his septic tank backed up and cloaked the hillside with a stench that sometimes lingered for weeks. Occasionally Red would do small favors for her, if he wasn't doing something else more important. She generally paid him back with a batch of cookies or a basket of fried chicken.

Red answered the call. "How's it going, Miss Shirley?"

"Oh, I'm doing okay, honey, and I've got a little surprise to thank you for fixing my tractor last week."

"You know you don't have to do that," Red said, "but I sure do appreciate it."

He wondered what she had for him this time. A few weeks earlier, when he'd rounded up one of her stray goats, she'd given him some outstanding brownies. He'd had to hide them from Billy Don.

"Whatever you did, it's running like brand new," Miss Shirley said.

Even at the age of 88, Miss Shirley still liked to get out and mow the pasture in the front of her property. Sometimes Red wondered if he should offer to mow it for her, but that wasn't just a favor, it was more like actual labor, and he wouldn't want it to become a regular thing, at least not without getting paid.

"It wasn't any trouble at all," Red said. "Just needed a tune-up." Truth was, one of the battery cables had come loose, which Red had fixed in less than a minute, but what was the harm if Miss Shirley thought it had taken more effort than it really had?

"Well, I've got an extra-special treat for you this time," she said, obviously quite tickled with herself. "Have you ever had a buffalo burger?"

"He was the nicest man!" Miss Shirley said. "I ended up buying two hundred pounds."

Red and Billy Don were now standing in Miss Shirley's garage, where she kept an upright freezer next to her 1983 Ford Fairmont. The door to the freezer was open and the interior was absolutely crammed with boxes of meat stamped with various labels.

PRIME RIBEYES
MAINE LOBSTER
PORK TENDERLOIN
LEAN HAMBURGER

"That's quite a haul," Red said, because he wasn't sure what to say.

"He was running a two-for-one special," Miss Shirley said, "and I can't resist a deal like that!"

Red wanted to tell her that the man selling the meat was nothing but a slick talker, and that the two-for-one deal had likely been going on for years. Instead, Red said, "Two hundred pounds, huh?"

Miss Shirley grabbed four boxes and thrust them into Red's arms.

He said, "You don't have to—"

"No, take it!" she said. "I'll never eat all of this. In fact..."

She grabbed two more boxes and shoved them at Billy Don, who didn't object at all.

Titus Steele was parked in his favorite spot—high on a hill in his Ford F350—surveying the river below. Keeping watch.

He despised trespassers. They were in the same league as poachers, liars, thieves, and blasphemers. He despised them all, and he had been taught from an early age that you don't let that sort of behavior go unanswered.

He raised his binoculars for another look. A moment earlier, he thought he'd seen a glint of sunlight bouncing off steel or glass. But now he saw nothing. Maybe it had been a reflection off the water.

He put the binoculars on the seat beside him.

Then he said, "Find a buyer for that corner tang yet?"

Three months earlier, Titus had never heard of a corner tang. If you'd described one, he wouldn't have much cared. Then he met Avery, the girl currently sitting next to him. Caught her and a friend digging near the river. Artifact hunters. Trespassers.

"Not yet," Avery said. "The higher the price, the longer it takes to sell."

"How much did you say you was asking?"

"Five grand," she said.

Good. That's what she'd told him last time, so her story was consistent. Wasn't like he trusted her. He realized full well she could sell it for eight thousand and say she sold it for five, but he couldn't think of a sure-fire way to keep her from screwing him. He did take steps to keep Avery and her friend honest, like dropping in unexpected from time to time. The two of them would be focused on digging, and suddenly Titus would be right over their shoulder. Made them nervous, which is what he wanted. That way, they'd be less likely to try to steal any artifacts.

"Maybe you should drop it down to four," he said.

"I think we'll get five, if we're patient. I've had a lot of people ask about it. One guy offered 35 hundred, but that's low-ball."

She was wearing khaki shorts, a light-brown tank top, and hiking boots, grimy from the digging she'd done earlier that morning—but she looked damn good anyway. Pretty face and a hell of a body on her. One particularly hot afternoon the previous week, he'd spotted her swimming in the river, her T-shirt clinging to her tits like a wet Kleenex. At that moment, his high-dollar binoculars had been worth every cent.

He shook the memory out of his head. This was business.

"You get another offer like that," Titus said, "you need to let me know about it."

"How?"

"Huh?"

"How am I supposed to reach you?"

Titus wasn't an old geezer—only 52 years old—but he didn't email or text. Didn't own a cell phone. Didn't care for any of that crap.

"Just call me at the house."

"You never answer."

"Then leave a message."

"I do, but you don't call me back. Do you even check your voicemail? Or is it an answering machine?"

He didn't have a good reply, so he said, "All I'm saying is, you need to keep me in the loop. You don't get to make big decisions on your own, you got me? We ain't partners. You knew that from the start."

He could tell from the look on her face that she wanted to make a smart-ass comment, but she let it go. Wise girl. Why kill the goose that laid the golden egg? Frankly, he didn't understand why she was always so cold to him. Hadn't he given her an enormous break? He could've had her arrested—her and her friend Sean—but instead, he'd given them a sweet moneymaking opportunity.

Now Titus gestured toward Avery's sweat-stained tank top with his thumb and said, "Okay, let's see 'em."

"Excuse me?"

He grinned. "The latest rocks. Show me what you got."

She opened the backpack cradled on her lap and retrieved four small white boxes—about four inches square—with lids taped on. She removed the lid from the first box and revealed a bed of cotton, on which was resting a gray darl blade in outstanding condition. Wasn't that long ago that Titus had never heard of a darl blade. He'd found a handful of arrowheads in his lifetime, most of them just resting on the ground, but he'd never given much thought to what else might lie below. Turned out there was a whole world of tools and artifacts waiting to be discovered, and some of that shit was worth a small fortune.

"This one might bring four hundred, if we're lucky," Avery said.

Four hundred fucking dollars for an old piece of chiseled flint buried in the dirt. Amazing.

"Ask for five," Titus said.

He knew he sounded bossy, but he had to remind her who was in charge.

"It's not worth five. It might not even sell for four."

"Won't know unless you try," he said. "Start at five hundred."

"I don't understand how you think," Avery said. "You want me to drop the price on the corner tang and raise the price on this one."

"Exactly," he said. "That's what I want. That's how our little arrangement works. You do the digging and I'm in charge of everything else. Remember?"

5

LIVE SNAKES! INDAIN ARROWHEADS!
Directly ahead!
Thrill the kids! Its a scientific
and historic wonderland!
(Visa excepted)

The hand-painted sign—typos and all—had been mounted beside Highway 290 on the south side of Johnson City for so many years that Marlin no longer even noticed it. But tourists and random passersby did. The Snake Farm and Indian Artifact Showplace—owned and operated by Junior Barstow—enjoyed modest but steady traffic on the weekends, especially during the summer break. Marlin stopped in once or twice a month just to visit with the colorful old man. This time, however, Marlin was hoping Junior could provide some valuable information.

The Showplace consisted of three dilapidated structures: a garishly colored former fireworks stand (for extra storage space), a Blue Bell ice cream truck (because Junior also butchered deer during hunting season and needed a refrigerated space), and a drooping double-wide mobile home that had been gutted and remodeled, leaving one large room that acted as the showroom—snakes on one side, artifacts on the other. Marlin found Junior in the showroom, sitting behind his desk, reading a magazine.

"Hey, boy," Junior called when Marlin stepped through the door. "Better be careful—I hear the game warden is around here somewhere."

Junior had made the same joke a hundred times, but Marlin always gave him a laugh.

"How you doing, Junior?" Marlin said.

"Same ol'," Junior said.

A middle-aged couple was on the other side of the room, studying a snake in a large glass case. Despite the Showplace's humble appearance, Junior owned more than two hundred indigenous and exotic snakes, from Western rattlers and racers to boas and pythons, and his Indian artifact collection was one of the most interesting and valuable in the Southwest.

"What kind of snake is this?" the man asked.

"Gray-banded kingsnake," Junior said. He rolled his eyes at Marlin, because a small card attached to the front of the glass case identified the snake and provided details about the species, such as the fact that the gray-banded kingsnake is common, but is also very secretive and rarely seen.

"It's pretty," the woman said.

"Sure is," Junior said.

Marlin took a seat on the edge of Junior's desk and talked in a low tone. "Wondering if you might be able to help me with something," he said.

"What's up?" Junior said.

Lauren had texted Marlin earlier, saying she'd reached Sean Hudson's mother and told her what had happened to her son. The mother had not been able to provide any leads other than a short list of Sean's friends. She didn't know if any of them were artifact hunters like Sean. According to Lauren, the mother saw Sean just once or twice a year and didn't seem to know much about his day-to-day life. Sean had no siblings, and his father had died nine years earlier.

Lauren had also checked into the specifics of Hudson's three trespassing charges in Burnet County, to the north of Blanco County, and learned that all three instances were in fact connected to hunting artifacts without landowner permission, as they had suspected.

Marlin said, "You happen to know a guy named—"

"You'd think they'd call it the orange-banded kingsnake," the woman called out, "since it's gray and orange, and orange is prettier."

"That puzzles me, too," Junior said.

"Is it poisonous?" the man asked.

Junior let out a small sigh they couldn't hear. "Snakes aren't poisonous, they're venomous," he said. "And only some of them are venomous. That particular species is not."

"Which ones are poisonous?" the woman asked.

Marlin almost laughed.

"None of them," Junior said. "Venomous snakes inject venom, not poison."

"Are they rare?" the woman asked.

"Venomous snakes or gray-banded kingsnakes?" Junior asked.

"This one here," the woman said.

"Oh, you bet. Probably fewer than a million in the state of Texas," Junior said.

"Wow," said the man, totally missing Junior's sarcasm.

"A million?" Marlin said quietly.

"Hell, I don't know," Junior muttered. "Give or take nine hundred thousand. I haven't done a census lately. What were you saying?"

"You happen to know a guy named Sean Hudson?"

Junior began to nod. "I've seen him online, if we're talking about the same Sean Hudson."

"Artifact collector?" Marlin asked.

"Right. He's been posting a lot on collectors' sites, especially on this one Facebook page where people do a lot pf selling. He's been a busy guy lately."

Marlin explained, very briefly, what had happened to Hudson, although he did not reveal what type of murder weapon had been used. That detail would remain confidential for the time being.

Junior said, "That's a shame. Any idea who did it?"

"Not yet. We're just getting started. Can you—"

"What's this one here?" the man across the room asked.

"That's a Mexican milk snake," Junior said.

"Milk shake?" the man asked, clearly amused.

"Milk *snake*," Junior said. "It's right there on the card."

"Oh, ha. I thought you said milk shake. That's funny."

The woman was shaking her head as if her husband were just the silliest man ever.

"Can you make me a list of those artifact sites?" Marlin asked.

"You bet," Junior said. "That Facebook group I was talking about is pretty small—for collectors in central Texas only—and that's where I saw Hudson posting most often. He's been selling some really nice stuff in the last few months. Or he was, I guess. Kind of making waves, because nobody really knows the guy and he's being cagey about where he's finding it. Guess I can't blame him for that."

"What's he been selling?"

"Just all kinds of stuff—bird points, knives, tangs, you name it."

"All legit?"

"Sure looked that way to me, although some of the fakes are pretty damn good nowadays. I remember that a couple of his higher-end items were papered."

Junior was referring to certificates of authenticity—papers from acknowledged artifact experts—that could enhance the value of a given piece. Many buyers preferred for an item to have a COA before they'd consider spending thousands of dollars on it. There were only a handful of experts in Texas who issued COAs, and only one in the central Texas area. Most collectors didn't bother with COAs for artifacts of lesser value, which were the majority of them.

"You think all of his pieces came from one site or from different sites?" Marlin asked.

Junior frowned. "Top of my head, I don't know. I'd have to take a look back at his posts to tell you that, and then it would probably be a guess."

"Would you mind doing that?" Marlin asked.

"Will do. Keep in mind that he could've claimed just about anything—might say a point came from one county when it was actually found in another."

"Why would he do that?" Marlin asked.

"Some counties are more 'collectible' than others. Something from Gillespie County is likely to be worth more than the same damn point from Blanco County. Never made a lot of sense to me, but what do I know?"

"More than I do, that's for sure," Marlin said. "And I appreciate the help."

"Now I've got a craving for a milk shake," the man across the room said. "Or maybe a Dilly Bar. There's a Dairy Queen in town, right?"

Red woke from an unplanned nap in his recliner to the smell of meat cooking. He went to check the source of the enticing aroma—even though he already knew what it was—and found Billy Don standing on the back porch, beer in hand, while the Weber grill nearby emitted a steady plume of smoke.

"Buffalo burgers!" Billy Don roared, giddier than normal, and then Red saw the seven tall boy empties balanced on the porch railing, which explained it.

"You didn't waste much time, did ya?" Red said.

It was hot and humid out here, but they'd added a roof above the porch a few months earlier, complete with a ceiling fan, so it wasn't too uncomfortable.

"Why wait? Let's try 'em out!"

Billy Don grabbed a metal spatula and opened the lid to the Weber. Five large hamburger patties sizzled and hissed on the grill. Billy Don flipped them one by one and Red's mouth began to water. He couldn't deny that they looked and smelled great, despite the fact that they were sold by a pushy, trespassing Indian who was apparently against the concept of private ownership of real estate.

"You think that guy makes any money?" Red said.

"Who?"

"That Indian dude. The meat man."

"Hell if I know. I guess he must, or why would he be doing it?"

"It just don't make sense," Red said.

"I was gonna ask if you want a double-meat burger," Billy Don said, "but these suckers are too damn thick. Just look at 'em. Give 'em about five more minutes."

Billy Don closed the lid to the Weber. Great grill. They'd bought it for twenty bucks at a garage sale. All it needed was new burner tubes, and now it worked like a champ. Brand new it would've cost $400.

"He said some of his stuff was two bucks a pound," Red said. "Hell, wouldn't he spend that much in gas just driving to the next house? Seriously, how can he sell high-quality meat for two bucks a pound? That's crazy. You can hardly get chicken that cheap, much less beef."

"You want your buns toasted?" Billy Don asked.

"Yeah, sure. Whatever."

Red didn't know why he was letting that Indian get to him so much. Maybe because he didn't appreciate somebody coming onto *his* land and treating him with disrespect. Hell, if anybody could understand that, wouldn't it be an Indian?

He went inside for a beer, then came back outside.

"Billy Don, you see those huge oaks over there?" Red said.

The big man kept watching the burgers. "What about 'em?"

"Imagine a house built into those trees."

"A house built into the trees?"

"Yep."

"A tree house?"

"Well, sort of, but more than that. An actual house. A real full-sized house, with everything a real house has in it. Most of it would be built into that huge oak on the right, but it might stretch over to that other oak beside it, and maybe the one behind it. Don't know yet. I'm in the brainstorming stage."

Red had been contemplating the idea, and he was even more excited than he had been earlier. It was groundbreaking, really. This was the type of innovative thinking that could set him apart as some sort of creative genius. Sure, at first they'd say he was eccentric or maybe even a little nutty, but then, over time, people would begin to appreciate his vision.

"Sounds dumb," Billy Don said.

6

After dinner, Marlin and his wife Nicole adjourned to the living room sofa, where he rubbed her feet and told her about the Sean Hudson homicide and his discussion with Junior Barstow. It wasn't just idle "how was your day?" kind of stuff. Prior to becoming the Blanco County victim services coordinator, Nicole had been a deputy with a keen and creative investigative mind. Marlin always valued her input. At a minimum, she always raised some good questions.

"Did you join that Facebook group Junior mentioned?" Nicole asked.

She had her thick auburn hair pulled back into a long ponytail and was wearing a loose T-shirt and a pair of drawstring shorts. Going for comfort on a hot, humid evening, but she looked gorgeous nonetheless, as usual.

"I did, and he was right that Hudson was very active on it, until four days ago."

"When did he join the site?"

"His first post was about six months ago."

"Was he always an active seller, or had he become more active lately?"

Geist, Marlin's pit bull, was snoozing quietly on her pillow on the floor. The television was tuned to some detective show Marlin didn't keep up with, but Nicole liked it.

"He had definitely become more active in that particular group," Marlin said, "but right now we have no way of knowing what else he was doing online. He could've been using different screen names, or selling on sites I'll never find or know about."

"Did he have a computer?" Nicole asked.

"We'll find out tomorrow, I guess," Marlin said. Lauren and

Deputy Ernie Turpin had gotten a warrant and would be searching Hudson's garage apartment in the morning.

They were both silent for a minute, and then Marlin said, "Junior looked at the pieces Hudson had listed for sale on that group and he said they all could've come from one location. Doesn't mean they did, but they weren't so different that they obviously came from different parts of the state."

"I guess you've considered the possibility that Hudson's murder had nothing to do with artifact collecting," Nicole said. "Maybe that wiggle pick just happened to be handy."

"Yep," Marlin said. "If we're lucky, the apartment will turn out to be the crime scene."

He finished rubbing her feet and moved up to her calves.

"Or," he said, "if we're even luckier, they'll find something that gives us a suspect, because right now, we got nothing. While they're doing that, I'm going to talk to a couple of his friends and coworkers."

"So he had a job outside of selling arrowheads?" Nicole asked.

"He worked part-time on a surveying crew, which was the perfect arrangement for a guy who liked to trespass and dig for artifacts," Marlin said.

"Sort of like the guy who fixes your refrigerator, but he's also planning how to break in later to steal your stuff," Nicole said.

"Exactly," Marlin said.

He couldn't resist moving from her calves up to her thighs. Her eyes were on the TV, but he saw the grin that spread across her face.

"I asked for a foot rub," she said. "Those aren't my feet."

"I might go even higher in a minute," he said.

"Well, what are you waiting for?" she said.

When Red woke up, he wasn't sure what was wrong. But something *was* wrong. Very, very wrong.

It was 2:17 in the morning.

Red's dad used to say that nothing good happened after midnight, and although Red hadn't agreed with that when he was younger, he had begun to appreciate the wisdom of it as he had aged. Generally speaking, he figured it was true, with a few minor exceptions, such as a little late-night poaching. Sometimes that turned out well. In fact, thinking it through, none of Red's arrests had happened after midnight, so maybe it was a wash.

2:17.

What was the problem? What had woken him up? He usually slept like a baby, short of wetting the bed.

He lay silently for several minutes and just listened. Didn't hear anything. No rain. No thunder. No coyotes howling. None of Billy Don's heavy wheezes and snores floating in from the room at the far end of the trailer.

Red had no idea why he'd woken so abruptly.

Then his lower bowels were suddenly hit with cramps more intense than the time he ate a lukewarm shrimp cocktail from a curbside food cart in Nuevo Laredo.

He sprang from bed and hurried down the hallway, clutching his stomach, only to find the bathroom door closed, with a light showing from underneath. And then he heard noises he absolutely did not want to hear.

Red hustled to the kitchen, grabbed a roll of paper towels, then raced out the front door and ran for a nearby cluster of cedar trees.

Ten minutes later, drenched with sweat, he went back inside and found Billy Don sprawled on the couch in his underwear, one foot on the floor, looking somewhat green in the face.

"Jesus Christ," Red said.

"You, too, huh?"

"Those damn burgers."

"How do you know it was the burgers?" Billy Don sounded indignant.

"You kidding me?" Red said. "What else could it be?"

"I dunno. The lettuce? The mayonnaise?"

"It was those damn burgers—that meat. I thought my insides was gonna explode."

"Me, too," Billy Don said. "But you don't know it was the burgers."

"They tasted a little funky," Red said.

"And that's why you ate two?" Billy Don said.

"Hell, I thought it was 'cause they was buffalo. Retroactively, now I know better. They was off. Tainted is what you call it. I just hope it's over with."

"You think there's more to come?"

"I can't see how," Red said. "There ain't nothin' left inside me. That was like a goddamn freight train moving through."

Red put the paper towels back in the kitchen, and while he was in there, he grabbed a large jug of Gatorade out of the fridge and guzzled half of it, because he knew you were supposed to do that in this sort of situation. He took the bottle into the living room and handed it to Billy Don, who downed the rest of it. Then he got a funny look on his face.

Red pointed down the hallway, saying, "You'd better get back in the—"

"No, it's not that," Billy Don said. "I was just thinking about Miss Shirley."

"Oh, crap," Red said.

If that sweet little old lady had eaten any of the bad meat, it would be even rougher on her than it had been on Red and Billy Don.

"We need to go check on her," Red said.

"It's nearly three in the morning," Billy Don said.

"Don't matter," Red said. "Get dressed."

As they neared her house, Red could see light through the window into her bedroom. Not a good sign, but he remembered she'd once told him that she couldn't sleep through the night anymore, and she often ended up watching middle-of-the-night infomercials, which she found oddly interesting.

Red parked in front of her house, and Billy Don said, "Want me to call again?"

He'd tried once on the way over, but Miss Shirley hadn't answered.

Red shook his head and said, "Let's just go knock."

They got out and did just that, knocking several times over the course of three minutes. Red wondered if Miss Shirley was too afraid to answer the door in the middle of the night.

"Miss Shirley, it's Red and Billy Don," he called out.

Nothing.

He turned the doorknob and found it unlocked. Not surprising since Miss Shirley grew up in a time when many country folk didn't lock their doors. Old habit. And out here, there wasn't much to worry about.

Red swung the door open about a foot and said, "Miss Shirley?"

The living room of her small house was almost completely dark, except for the glow from the clock on a VCR resting on top of an ancient RCA console television.

"Miss Shirley?" he called even louder.

He didn't want to rush inside, because even though the old woman didn't lock her doors, she also owned a 12-gauge shotgun. That's how people from Miss Shirley's generation dealt with intruders.

"Miss Shirley?"

Still nothing.

They stepped through the doorway and Red flipped a light switch beside the door.

He said, "Miss Shirley, it's Red and Billy Don. Don't wanna scare ya."

No answer.

"Screw this," Billy Don said, and he went down the hallway to Miss Shirley's bedroom door, which was cracked a few inches open, with light visible from the other side.

"Miss Shirley, we're coming in," Billy Don said. "I hope you're decent."

He swung the door open and Red could see the old woman in her bed, waving one hand feebly. They hurried to her bedside.

"You okay?" Red said.

Miss Shirley shook her head slowly, obviously in great discomfort. Her voice was weak when she said, "I'm so glad to see you boys. I couldn't even get up to answer the phone. I think I need to go to the hospital."

7

Titus Steele first spotted signs of digging on the ranch in late February. Noticed freshly turned soil in a small draw that funneled water into the river when it rained. No tools lying around. No garbage. But he did find prints from hiking boots. Two pairs, one quite a bit smaller than the other. Man and a woman, most likely, as opposed to a man and a child.

Titus wasn't an idiot. He knew exactly what they were digging for. And he knew that this particular piece of property was a good place to do it. There'd been diggers out here before, and Titus wouldn't stand for it. Couldn't abide a thief. Besides, it was in Titus's job description to keep an eye on the place, which included running off trespassers. The boss had never really specified how Titus should go about it, so Titus generally used whatever method would be most effective in a given situation.

Sometimes his methods weren't strictly legal. Like holding a trespasser at gunpoint for several hours while they stood in the rain. Making them strip down to their undies—women included—and hike out without shoes. Taking their possessions—phones, wallets, an occasional rifle or handgun—and tossing them into the river.

What were they going to do? Call the cops?

Judging by the extent of the digging, these new trespassers had managed to slip in and out several times without getting caught. So Titus found a good hiding spot in some cedar trees and watched the same area along the river for three straight days with no luck. Then they showed on the fourth day. Man and a woman, just as Titus had suspected. Young. Mid-twenties. Had all the right tools and other gear, which meant they were seasoned pros at plundering other peoples' property. He let them dig for a while, so when he showed up, they couldn't deny why they were here.

And then he made his move.

"What the fuck do y'all think you're doing?" Titus said, coming up from behind.

Both of them turned to look, and their eyes immediately went to Titus's right hand, which was resting on the nine-millimeter semiautomatic holstered on his hip.

But unlike all of the trespassers and poachers Titus had encountered in the past, these two didn't freak out or try to run away or start spewing lies.

Instead, the guy said, "We're digging. What're you doing?"

"I'm wondering why you're trespassing on this property," Titus said. "And now I'm wondering why you're acting like you belong here."

"Who are you?" the guy asked. The girl simply sat staring. Her pretty face was already covered with sweat and grime.

"I'm the man who's gonna ruin your day if you don't pack your shit and get off this place in about five minutes."

This kid, this punk, actually chuckled. Then he said, "Sorry, but you're being kind of melodramatic, aren't you?"

Titus said, "You're trespassing, moron, and right now, I'm letting you off easy. But that might change."

The woman said, "Sean, let's just go." She stood up, giving Titus a look at her long, toned legs, but Sean stayed where he was.

"She's a smart gal, Sean," Titus said. And now he unsnapped the retention strap on his nylon tactical holster.

"Seriously?" Sean said. "You're gonna pull a gun on us? For digging? You got a tiny dick or something? That's why you carry a gun?"

Titus could feel his face warming as the adrenaline in his system began to kick in.

"I've told you twice that you're trespassing, and every fence on this ranch is marked. Now I have the authority to remove you."

"You own this place?" Sean asked.

"Sean, come on," the girl said. "It's not worth it." She had some sort of tool in her hand. Like a small pickaxe.

Sean was ignoring her, waiting for Titus to answer.

"I'm the manager," Titus said. "Now I'm telling you for the last time—"

"Let me show you something," Sean said.

He reached into his backpack—who knows what he was grabbing?—so Titus drew his weapon. He kept it pointed at the ground, but he was ready for whatever might come next.

"Hey, easy now," Sean said. He came out of the backpack with a Marlboro cigarette box. He opened the lid and extracted an object swaddled in paper towels, which he then unwrapped. "Know what this is?"

"I ain't no idiot," Titus said.

"So you know what it is?"

"Arrowhead of some kind. And it don't belong to you. Put it on the ground. In fact, empty that backpack and let's see what else you got."

"This," Sean said, holding the object carefully, "is a bird point. I can probably sell it for about three hundred bucks."

"*We* can," the girl said.

"Sorry, yeah, 'we,'" Sean said. "It's not the best one I've ever found, but definitely not the worst."

"What's your point?" Titus said. "That you're a thief?"

Now Sean was shaking his head. "I just don't get that attitude. This point has been in the ground for thousands of years. How long was it going to stay right where it was? Forever? Or more likely, 50 years from now, they'll build a subdivision here and this blade would've been destroyed by a bulldozer. Or it would've been covered by a concrete slab for a new home. So what's the harm in me digging it up? Your boss never even knew this blade existed, and he still doesn't, and he never will—unless you tell him."

Titus almost had to laugh, because if this kid knew who his boss was, he wouldn't be making such a dumb argument.

"Bottom line, you're stealing shit that ain't yours," Titus said.

Now the kid made a gesture of exasperation, spreading his hands, like Titus was being unreasonable, which was bullshit.

"You're a letter-of-the-law kind of guy, huh?" Sean said. "Never stolen anything in your life?"

Titus wasn't sure what to do. He didn't want to continue talking to this punk, but Sean wasn't responding the way most trespassers did. So Titus tried the unexpected. He raised the gun, pointed it a few feet over Sean's head, and fired a round.

"Jesus!" the girl said, taking several steps back.

But the damn kid hardly flinched.

"Are you fucking crazy?" the girl shouted.

Titus's ears were ringing. That's what happened when you shot without ear guards.

"Take it easy, Avery," Sean said. "He's just trying to scare us." Then, to Titus, he said, "Okay, dude. We'll take off, if that's what you want. I mean, you're a righteous man and all, so I'm sure you wouldn't want to split the profits with us, right? You wouldn't want an extra chunk of cash every month, tax-free, for letting us dig out here. Not a guy like you. Right?"

As Marlin drove north on Highway 281 toward Marble Falls on Monday morning, he thought about the previous evening with Nicole.

Life is good.

A few months before getting married, she'd brought up the subject of having children, and they had discussed it again last night, lying in bed. Fortunately, they were still in agreement, and their conclusion now as then was that they weren't interested—and they might never be.

"Does that disappoint you?" she'd asked.

"Not even a little."

"You sure?"

"I'd tell you."

"It's kind of odd how everyone just assumes that we will."

Marlin had experienced comments and questions himself. *When are y'all going to have kids? Time is running out. You two would be such great parents.* He agreed that Nicole would be a fantastic mother, if she chose to be a mother, but that didn't mean she *had* to be one.

"It's our business, not theirs," he said.

She'd clasped his hand tightly, then kissed it, and a few minutes later her deep, regular breathing told him she'd fallen asleep.

In her role as Blanco County victim services coordinator, Nicole went to extraordinary lengths to help a range of people in a variety of situations: abused spouses, orphaned children, survivors of all types of violent crimes. She was a tireless advocate, counselor, protector, and educator, and Marlin couldn't imagine anyone else doing the job with the same empathy and patience Nicole brought to it.

Would she be a good mother? Of course she would. And if that never came to pass, the world would have to settle for the abundance of compassion Nicole spread on a daily basis.

8

Thirty minutes later, Marlin was seated at a booth in the world-famous Bluebonnet Café in Marble Falls. Across from him was a young man named Jordan Gabbert, who occasionally worked on a surveying crew with Sean Hudson.

Gabbert said, "Sean was hooking up with a girl named Avery, last I knew. Don't know if they were serious or not. He mentioned her a couple of times."

"Know her last name?" Marlin asked.

"Sorry, man, I don't. I don't even know if they were still seeing each other."

Gabbert was in his early twenties, slender, with eyes that were currently glassy and red. He reeked of pot, which might explain why he had ordered two homemade cinnamon rolls that were roughly the size of a softball. Might also explain why the conversation had a stilted feel to it so far, as if it took Gabbert an extra half-second to process Marlin's questions.

"Got her phone number?" Marlin asked.

"Nah, man, I just know her name is Avery."

"You never met her?"

"Nope."

"Any idea where Sean and Avery met?"

"If he told me, I don't remember."

Marlin was hoping it would be easy to identify Avery once they had Hudson's phone records.

"You and Sean ever hang out?" Marlin asked.

"You mean like outside of work?"

"Yeah."

"We grabbed a beer once or twice, but we weren't tight."

"You like to hunt artifacts?" Marlin asked.

"I'm not sure what those are."

Maybe Gabbert wasn't just stoned. Maybe he wasn't all that intelligent.

"Indian arrowheads and other tools. Old stuff," Marlin said.

"Oh, right. I mean, if I see one on the ground when I'm working, I'll pick it up, but I don't go looking for them. I know Sean was into all that. He talked about it sometimes."

Marlin didn't point out that taking an artifact from private property without the landowner's permission was illegal.

"Where did he like to go?" Marlin asked.

Gabbert was wolfing down one of the cinnamon rolls and he talked with his mouth half full.

"For arrowheads?"

"Right."

"No idea. Sorry."

"Did he ever look for arrowheads when you were on a job site?"

"Not if you mean, like, would he go digging or something," Gabbert said. "He might spend half a minute poking around in the dirt, but that was about it."

"I'm not trying to make him look bad," Marlin said, "but if he ever said anything to you about coming back to a job site later and digging, I really need to know. It might help us figure out who killed him."

"He really didn't, I swear," Gabbert said. "I'd tell you."

"I appreciate that."

"You should talk to his friends."

"Oh, I will." Marlin had another meeting at this same café in two hours. "Who were his best friends, as far as you remember? Who did he mention on a regular basis?"

Gabbert threw out a couple of names, both of which were on the short list provided by Sean Hudson's mother.

"Did Sean ever talk to you about selling the artifacts he found?" Marlin asked.

"I just knew he sold them online and stuff. Some of them were worth a lot of money."

"You know if Sean ever made his own arrowheads?"

Gabbert stopped chewing for a minute. "You can do that?"

"Some people can, and they're pretty good at it," Marlin said. "It's called 'knapping.'"

Gabbert grinned. "I'm pretty good at napping. I'll probably nap right after lunch."

Marlin smiled and nodded. "So did Sean ever do any knapping?"

"He never said anything about it."

"Did he ever mention anything about an angry buyer or anything like that?"

"Not that I remember. You mean like somebody who got mad because Sean sold them a fake arrowhead?"

"I'm not saying that's what happened, but we need to explore that kind of thing," Marlin said. "It's routine."

"I don't remember anything like that," Gabbert said.

"He ever mention any problems with other diggers? Or problems with anybody at all, for that matter?"

"People that would be mad at him?"

"Right."

"Uh-uh. He was a pretty easygoing guy."

"Just one more question," Marlin said, "and I need you to be totally straight up with me. Okay?"

"Yeah, sure," Gabbert said.

"Do you know if Sean ever used drugs?"

Gabbert hesitated. Marlin knew what that meant. Gabbert didn't want to answer, but he didn't want to lie, either. That, in itself, was an answer of sorts.

"What kind of drugs?" Gabbert said, which was an incredibly dumb answer.

Marlin leaned forward to give the conversation a more confidential feel to it.

"Any drugs, including pot," Marlin said quietly. "Speaking of which, it looks like you burned one earlier."

Now Gabbert looked like he'd swallowed a bug.

Marlin said, "As long as you aren't driving, I'm not going to hassle you—because you're cooperating and trying to help us figure out what happened to Sean. But we need to know all the possibilities. The more we know, the more likely it is that we can figure out what happened. You understand?"

Gabbert nodded, staring down at the table.

"So what can you tell me about that?" Marlin asked.

"Sean and drugs?" Gabbert said in a low voice.

"Yeah," Marlin said. "Help me out and then we'll be done here. I'll get out of your hair."

He knew there was a limit to just how forthcoming Gabbert might be, depending on the circumstances. He knew something, that much was clear.

"All I know," Gabbert said, "is that Sean got high now and then. But he wasn't into anything else, as far as I know. If he was, he never said anything about it."

"Just pot, then? Nothing harder?" Marlin asked.

"Uh-uh."

"No meth? No coke?"

"I don't think so. He never said anything. But like I said before, we weren't that tight. His friends would probably know if he was into stuff like that. He didn't strike me that way at all, though. He was too smart for it."

"Where did he buy pot?" Marlin asked.

"Man, I have no idea."

This was an area where Gabbert would remain tight-lipped. He might not know where Sean bought his weed, but even if he did, he wouldn't want to name names.

"How long have you lived in Marble Falls?" Marlin asked.

"About four years. Moved down from Lampasas after I got out of high school. I was dating a girl who lived here, but we broke up about a year after I got here. She kicked me out, so I almost moved back home, but then I decided I liked it here better. There's more stuff to do."

Gabbert was visibly relieved they weren't talking about drugs anymore. He went back to eating his cinnamon rolls.

"When did you meet Sean?" Marlin asked.

"Probably a year ago, when we first worked together."

"Where was that?"

"On a ranch in Lampasas County."

"You ever get down to Blanco County?"

"Not much. I can't remember the last time I was down there. Most of the work we do is in Burnet and Lampasas County."

"Can you think of anyone who might've wanted to harm Sean?

Anybody who was mad at him for any reason?"

"Not at all. No way. He never seemed like the type that would have enemies. He was an okay guy. He didn't deserve what happened."

"Can I count on you to call me later if you think of something that might be relevant, or if you hear any rumors about what happened?"

"Oh, absolutely. Definitely. I'll help however I can."

"You're not driving, right?" Marlin asked.

"I did, yeah," Gabbert said. "Not gonna lie. But I'll walk home and come back for my car later."

"I'll give you a ride," Marlin said. "You can walk back later. Deal?"

"Absolutely. Thanks."

"Somebody needs to teach that sumbitch a lesson," Billy Don said.

"That's for damn sure," Red said.

"He needs a serious ass-kicking, making an old lady sick like that," Billy Don said.

"You got that right," Red said. "And making us sick. And who knows who else?"

They were back home again, after staying with Miss Shirley until dawn in her room at Blanco Memorial Hospital. She had insisted that they go home and get some rest, and she promised to call Red later when the doctors were ready to release her, which should be sometime later that day.

Dehydration could be hell on an old person, apparently. But they'd given her something in one of those IV bags and promised she'd be good as new. "Or good as old," Miss Shirley had joked. Nice to see she could laugh about it.

When Red and Billy Don had revealed that they had been sick too, Miss Shirley felt terrible about the situation and blamed herself. It took Red and Billy Don several minutes to convince her it wasn't her fault. It was that damned meat salesman.

"He's gotta know his meat ain't right, don't ya think?" Billy Don asked now.

"Hell, yeah. Like I said all along. Which explains why it was so cheap," Red said.

"Question is, how're we gonna track him down?" Billy Don asked.

"Wait, what?" Red said.

"We need to get Miss Shirley's money back, but he could be anywhere by now," Billy Don said. "How're we gonna find him?"

Red wasn't sure he wanted to go to the trouble of actually looking for the guy. If they happened to see him somewhere out on the road, fine, but spending the time and effort to conduct a search? Not interested. His gut was already feeling better, so it wasn't that big a deal.

"I would imagine he's long gone," Red said.

"We could at least go into town and ask around," Billy Don said. "See if anybody knows where he is. Spread the word we're looking for him. Warn everybody not to buy his crap."

Okay, maybe Red would be up for that, if they stopped and got lunch somewhere. Make the trip worthwhile.

"Let's grab a nap first," Red said, "and we'll go later."

Billy Don agreed and started down the hallway toward his room.

"Hang on a second," Red said, and Billy Don turned around. "You've got a pretty good imagination, don't you?"

Red was flattering him. Billy Don had all the imagination of an eggplant.

"I guess so," Billy Don said.

"Well, I want you to imagine the best deer blind you've ever seen, built way up high in an oak tree, so you can see for miles, or at least hundreds of yards," Red said. "It has comfortable chairs, a heater, air conditioner, even a working toilet."

"In a deer blind?"

"Yep. And you've got a big TV mounted on a wall, so you can hunt and watch the Cowboys at the same time. In one corner, you got a fridge filled with beer and snacks."

"How do you have room for all that?" Billy Don said.

"Because it's a *big* blind," Red said. "With a room the size of this one. And you could add as many rooms as you want, including a couple of bedrooms, with elevated walkways leading from one room to the other. And you build the whole thing with quality materials, not just a bunch of plywood and scrap lumber. Build it to last for years."

"Sounds pretty awesome," Billy Don said.

"Exactly," Red said. "And now you understand what I meant yesterday about building a tree house."

Billy Don grinned when he realized Red had suckered him, but he was also caught up in the idea. "Never seen nothing like that," he admitted.

"That's right," Red said. "It's what they mean by thinking outside the envelope."

9

Rodney Bauer was putting a new starter into his Chevy truck—a pain in the ass to begin with, but his big belly made it even more difficult to lean into the engine compartment—when he heard a vehicle coming up his long caliche driveway.

Rodney had gotten into the habit of keeping his gate closed at all times ever since his bull had been killed by a couple of incompetent rustlers, but his wife Mabel had left earlier for a grocery run, and she couldn't be bothered to close the gate herself. Oh, sure, she'd gripe at him for leaving the cap off the toothpaste, but if he mentioned the open gate, well, he might as well throw rocks at the wasp nest on the side of the garage. Same result.

Rodney sucked the blood off a busted knuckle as he watched the vehicle emerge from the trees near the county road and break into the open. Gray Toyota Tacoma. Rodney didn't know anybody who drove a Tacoma.

Honeybee, Rodney's yellow Lab, lifted her head and barked once from her spot in the shade, and then went quiet. Rodney didn't blame her. Too damn hot to bark.

The Tacoma got closer, and now Rodney could see a large, white, rectangular object in the bed of the truck. Was that...a freezer?

The Tacoma stopped 20 feet from the rear bumper of Rodney's Chevy, where the driver killed the engine and stepped out.

"Howdy. How are you today?"

It was a young guy. Tall. Had long black hair poking out from a brown beaver-skin hat. He looked like an Indian, with sharp cheekbones and a dark complexion. Wearing jeans, boots, and a long-sleeved denim shirt with a logo over the left breast. Rodney noticed that Honeybee was emitting a low growl, and she never growled at anyone.

"Just fine," Rodney said. "Can I help you with something?"

"Trouble with your truck?"

"Replacing the starter," Rodney said. Then he repeated, "Can I help you with something?"

"Sir, my name is Joseph Lightfoot and I represent the New Mexico Meat Company. I don't mean to bother you, but are you interested in buying some prime-quality beef, fish, or seafood at prices much lower than you'd find at your nearest supermarket?"

Rodney almost laughed. That was the last thing he expected—a door-to-door meat salesman. But that explained the freezer in the back of the man's truck. He must've rigged it up to run on 12 volts. Pretty smart.

"Well, my wife does the shopping," Rodney said. "In fact, that's where she is right now."

The man smiled. "Maybe you should call her before she buys a bunch of overpriced meat filled with hormones and steroids. Ever had a buffalo burger?"

"Don't think so, but—"

"Not only is it all-natural, it's leaner than almost every other kind of meat, including turkey, and it's a great choice if you're looking to lower your cholesterol, because it has less than three grams of fat per 100 grams of cooked meat. Know how many grams of fat are in a comparable serving of beef?"

"Um, well—"

"More than nine," Joseph Lightfoot said. "Nearly four times as much as the buffalo. And despite the low fat content, it makes the tastiest burger you've ever had. I bet you like a nice grilled burger. Am I right?"

"Sure, I—"

"Right now we're running a two-for-one special on most of our products—buffalo burgers, peeled shrimp, pork chops, and all of our steaks, including filet mignon, porterhouse, New York strip, and ribeye. Check out this price list, which is good for today only."

The man produced a flyer and handed it to Rodney.

Rodney pretended to look it over, but he already knew he wouldn't be making a purchase. Why? Because that would be the equivalent of throwing rocks at ten wasp nests. Mabel handled the shopping, period. And Rodney preferred it that way. So, after a moment, Rodney held the flyer toward the salesman and said, "Looks pretty good, but I'd better pass today."

The man didn't take the flyer back. Instead he said, "You don't see anything on there you like?"

"Oh, I like it all," Rodney said, "but my wife takes care of the groceries. If I bought some of this stuff, believe me, I'd be sleeping on the couch for a couple of days."

"Really?"

"Oh, yeah. Big time." Rodney folded the flyer and stuck it into his pocket.

"You can't buy some steaks for her and say it's a surprise?" Lightfoot asked.

"I might as well tell her how to arrange the furniture," Rodney said. "Or how to load the dishwasher. She'd be royally pissed."

Joseph Lightfoot was still smiling when he said, "You aren't much of a man, are you?"

Rodney thought he was making a joke—a harsh joke, but a joke. Then he realized the salesman wasn't kidding.

"Pardon?" Rodney said, because he didn't know how else to respond.

Honeybee hadn't moved from her shady spot, but she growled again.

"You let a woman run your life for you?" Joseph Lightfoot said. "Why would you allow that? I imagine your father is disappointed."

"My father is dead."

"That might be best, to spare him the embarrassment of a son who isn't a man."

It took a lot to make Rodney's temper flare, but that did it. "Who the fuck are you to say something like that?"

"I told you. My name is Joseph Lightfoot."

"Mister, you need to get your ass off my property," Rodney said. "Right now."

"You wanna make me leave? Go right ahead." Lightfoot just stood there, daring him.

Fuming now, Rodney turned and went to his truck, where his .44 Magnum always waited in a holster tucked between the driver's seat and the center console. He kept it handy in case of varmints on the ranch, but it would work just fine in this situation, too. He knew he was being outrageously foolish, but he couldn't help himself. His anger was overwhelming and he couldn't contain it.

When he turned back with the revolver in his hand, Joseph Lightfoot was walking toward his Tacoma. Not rushing. Taking his time. He opened the truck door and faced Rodney. "That's better," he said. "Maybe there's hope for you after all."

Marlin had missed a call from Lauren while he was talking to Jordan Gabbert, so he went out to his truck to call her back at Sean Hudson's apartment.

"Anything from the coworker?" she asked.

He quickly filled her in on his conversation with Gabbert.

She said, "That meshes with what we're finding over here—about an ounce of pot and a couple of pipes, but nothing harder, and no other paraphernalia. Beyond that, we're striking out. As far as we can tell, this is not the crime scene. I won't bore you with a bunch of details, but basically we got nothing. The only thing that might be significant is what we *aren't* finding, and that's artifacts. We haven't found so much as a broken arrowhead in this place."

"That's interesting," Marlin said. "Either he stores them somewhere else..."

"Or somebody took them," Lauren said.

"From what I saw on that Facebook group," Marlin said, "he still had at least half a dozen pieces for sale. And I'm guessing there were others he hadn't listed."

He heard a male voice in the background saying something to Lauren, who laughed. "Ernie's being optimistic. He found a thumb drive and says the key to the entire case is on there. That's the other thing that's missing—a computer. Hudson's got a printer and this thumb drive, but where is the computer? Oh, and the front door was unlocked, so anybody could've been in here."

"Wonderful," Marlin said. That meant the computer could've been taken in a burglary unrelated to Hudson's murder. Maybe somebody had heard he was dead and decided to see what they could score from his place. "Anything from Henry?"

"Every fingerprint he got from the car matched Hudson, which seems unusual, but maybe he cleaned the interior recently. Same with DNA—just one sample, and that's gonna be Hudson. Henry did get three DNA samples from the wiggle pick, so if we're really lucky, one will be the killer. It'll take a while to get those results back, but in the meantime, there is one small bit of good news—what we in law enforcement call a lead. Possibly."

He knew it couldn't be that great or she would've led with it. "Let's hear it," he said.

"I spoke to Hudson's boss—the manager at the surveying company—about thirty minutes ago, and he gave me a list of the last half-dozen sites Hudson worked for him. One of them was a ranch owned by a retired Texas Tech professor. Wanna guess what he used to teach?"

"I have no idea," Marlin said, because he was truly baffled—but then it came to him. "Hang on," he said. "Was it archeology?"

"You're good," Lauren said.

Red and Billy Don stopped first at their favorite hub of social activity in Johnson City—the feed store.

"Don't steal anything," Red said as he opened the glass door.

"Why do you always say that?" Billy Don asked.

"Because it's what my daddy used to say to me, wherever we went. It's funny."

Red's father had been a rodeo clown, and his sense of humor had been every bit as subtle as a big red nose.

"I'm gonna go look at the feeders," Billy Don said.

"Don't get lost," Red said. Another witticism from his dad's extensive collection.

Red went in the opposite direction and soon found one of the store's longtime employees stacking bags of cattle cubes.

"Hey, Cliff."

"Hey, Red. You decided yet?"

Every time the two men had run into each other in the past few months, Cliff had asked Red what he planned to do with all the money from Vegas. Sometimes it made Red uneasy that everybody knew he and Billy Don were rich now, but he also enjoyed the way it had made him somewhat of a local celebrity.

"Still thinking," Red said.

"You need any help spending it, you let me know."

"Will do. Hey, let me ask you something. You heard anything about a meat salesman going door to door in the past few days?"

Red figured Cliff would say no, and then Red would ask the rest of the feed-store employees, who would also say no, and then he and Billy Don would move on to the Dairy Queen, where Red could ask everyone who worked there, too, but only after he'd had a Belt-Buster and a large order of tater tots, followed by a Dilly Bar.

But Cliff said, "Oh, hell, yeah. He suckered Cheryl into buying a bunch of shrimp and it was horrible. Once she thawed it out, the smell was something awful. Goddamn rip-off is what it was. I wouldn't use it as bait."

"You know if he's still around?"

"No idea. Said he was from New Mexico or some bullshit. Why? You're not gonna buy any of his crap, are you?"

Red told him about the whole sorry episode.

"Poor Miss Shirley," Cliff said. "Hope you can get her money back."

"That's the idea, but I don't know if we'll be able to find the guy. He could be in Alabama by now."

"That's true. Hey, he gave Cheryl a flyer with a phone number on it. I tried calling a couple of times, but the scumbag won't call me back. You want that number?"

10

"Yeah, I knew Sean pretty well, I guess, but I always got the feeling he didn't have any real close friends—you know what I mean? I'm one of those guys who's lucky enough to have a circle of buddies I've known since, like, grade school. But Sean didn't have friends like that, as far as I could tell. He was more like the kind of guy who hung out with people that liked doing the same things he did, but that was as far as it went. We never did anything other than riding together. Sometimes I would say, like, 'Hey, I'm having some people over on Saturday night and you should come over,' but he never would. That just wasn't his thing."

The man speaking was 28-year-old Jeremy Shumway, and Marlin could already tell that he was a talker. All Marlin had said was, "I understand you were friends with Sean Hudson." There were some people who got nervous talking to law enforcement officers in any situation, and as a result, they would clam up. But Shumway was the opposite type—hoping to be as helpful as possible, and willing to answer every question at length.

"How long did you know him?" Marlin asked.

They were seated at a table not far from the booth where Marlin had interviewed Jordan Gabbert. Shumway was tall and slender like many of the avid bicyclists Marlin saw pedaling the back roads in central Texas. His eyes were bright and clear. He had ordered coffee only—no cinnamon rolls. Marlin was hungry, but he'd have lunch after he was done talking with Shumway.

"I think we met about three years ago," Shumway said. "He had a flat tire on Mormon Hill Road and I stopped to help him fix it. We sort of became casual riding buddies after that, or we'd ride in a group sometimes. Don't get me wrong about what I said a minute ago—everybody liked Sean and he was a friendly guy, but—I want to explain this right—he was the kind where you reach a certain level of friendliness and then it never goes beyond that. You know how guys will give each other a hard time, just joking around? You'd never reach that level with Sean. He wouldn't open up that much, or maybe he just didn't feel comfortable with it."

"So as far as you know, he didn't have any close friends?"

"Right. On the other hand, he wasn't what I'd call a loner. More like he just wasn't concerned about hanging around with people all the time. It was like he could take it or leave it. He didn't mind doing things by himself."

"Are you an artifact hunter?"

"No, that's not really my jam. One time Sean asked me to go with him, and I did, but I was kind of bored, to be honest. I found one broken arrowhead and that was it. Basically it was like three hours digging in the dirt when I could've been out riding."

None of this background information appeared useful, but sometimes facts that seemed irrelevant could suddenly bust a case open later. Most of the time, however, they didn't. Marlin couldn't help being distracted by the news Lauren had shared earlier. She was trying to arrange a face-to-face meeting with the archeologist she had mentioned.

It was an interesting development because archeologists, paleontologists, and other types of scientists generally held amateur diggers in disdain. Looters like Sean Hudson—or even legal artifact diggers—could damage or destroy the archeological record contained within the strata of a site. Once the soil was disturbed, the research value was lost forever. Had Hudson encountered the archeologist who now owned the land Hudson had earlier surveyed? Had the owner caught Hudson trespassing? It was definitely a lead worth exploring.

"Where did you go to dig?" Marlin asked.

He felt his phone vibrate with an incoming text.

"A small ranch out near Kingsland," Shumway said. "Sean said he had already been there a couple of times, but it was obvious by the time we left that he probably wasn't going to bother coming back again."

Marlin took a quick look at his phone. The text, from Lauren, read: *Nothing on that thumb drive Ernie found at Hudson's place.*

"How long ago was this?" Marlin asked.

"Last year sometime. In the spring."

"Any idea who owns the place?"

"Sorry, no. I think it was just some old rancher Sean met somewhere and he asked if he could come out and dig. He'd do that a lot—just ask people—and every now and then one of them would say yes. Sean would usually take them a small present to say thanks, like maybe a bottle of whiskey or something like that. He was pretty smooth when he wanted to be."

"Was it just the two of you?"

"Yeah."

"Did Sean ever mention having a run-in or argument with anybody? Any other diggers or bicyclists or anybody at all?"

"No, man, not at all. It just seems so weird that somebody killed him. He was like totally chill, you know? A laid-back guy."

Marlin knew that Shumway's assessment of Hudson may or may not be accurate, especially since he freely admitted that they weren't close friends.

"Do you know if Sean used drugs?" Marlin asked.

"Not around me he didn't, but there were times when I wondered if he was a pot smoker. Not that I'd judge him for it. I don't smoke, but as far as I'm concerned, it should be legal. Safer than alcohol. Nothing like having some drunk redneck stop and yell at you for riding your bike on a public road. I've even had beer bottles thrown at me. Potheads don't act like that."

"Do you know Jordan Gabbert?" Marlin asked.

"I don't, sorry. Who is that?"

"He and Sean worked together."

"Sean never mentioned him, as far as I can remember."

"Did you ever meet any of Sean's coworkers or other friends?"

"Nope. He met quite a few of my friends when we'd ride, but I never met any of his," Shumway said.

"Did you ever hear him mention the name Avery?" Marlin asked.

"I don't think so. I'd remember that name. It's kind of unique. Who is she? I assume it's a she."

"We believe Sean might've been dating her, but we haven't tracked her down yet."

"I definitely don't remember him mentioning a girlfriend. It was unlike him to share that sort of thing, so if he'd said anything, I'd remember it."

For the second time in four days, Titus Steele drove his truck down to the river and returned to the site where Sean Hudson had died. He couldn't help himself. He knew better than to think the sheriff couldn't still piece together what had happened, despite the efforts Titus had made to destroy any trace of evidence.

Titus stopped ten feet short of the actual spot and simply surveyed the area.

To the naked eye, there was nothing about the spot under the cypress tree that would catch anyone's eye or draw suspicion. But cops today used all kinds of fancy techniques to figure things out. Maybe not quite as amazing as some of the things they did on those crime dramas, but this sure as hell wasn't the age of Andy Griffith anymore, either.

Titus knew, for instance, that he should be careful not to leave any footprints in the area. They could match those prints to his boots nearly as well as they could match fingerprints. Of course, he had a good excuse for having his boot prints all over this ranch, but why push his luck? He'd use a cedar branch to wipe away any tracks he might leave.

He removed his Stetson and wiped the sweat off his forehead. Too damn hot out here. His armpits were starting to reek.

What about the blood that had once stained the dirt and grass? On his last visit, Titus had hauled gallons of water up from the river and washed it all away, but was that good enough? He had an irrational fear that any blood left under the surface would rise up and stain the dirt again. It reminded him of some short story he'd read in school. A murdered guy's heart kept beating from the hiding spot underneath the floorboards, eventually driving the killer crazy enough that he confessed.

But dealing with facts here in the real world, Titus wondered—could the cops still detect blood in the soil? Could they extract DNA? Could they tell that somebody had died here? He figured it was possible. So how could he stop that from happening? He'd thought about spraying a couple of gallons of bleach around the area, but then he realized just how incredibly stupid that would be. They'd wonder, of course, why the area smelled like bleach. Titus might as well put up a neon sign pointing to this very spot.

Jesus H. Christ, he was letting his nerves get the best of him. The police had no reason to suspect anything had happened on this ranch, and they never would. Why would they? The body had been found miles away. They had no other evidence. No witnesses. Not a clue.

On the other hand...

It wouldn't hurt to take some sensible precautions. That wasn't being paranoid. That was being smart. There had to be some way to get rid of the evidence. Or destroy it. Or contaminate it. Make it useless.

Blood was the problem.

Blood.

Oh, good Lord. It was so obvious now.

Blood was the problem. And blood was also the solution.

"Now that we have his phone number," Red said, "the question is, what do we do with it?"

They were on their way to Blanco Memorial Hospital to pick up Miss Shirley and take her home. She'd have to squeeze between them, as she had on the way over there. It worked fine, because she was tiny.

"We call it," Billy Don said. "That's what we do."

Red always tried to keep in mind that even though Billy Don might've been some kind of genius in blackjack, he came up short in most other departments.

"And then what?" Red said.

They were waiting at the traffic light at Highway 281 and Highway 290.

"What do you mean?" Billy Don asked.

"What're we gonna say to him?"

Billy Don opened his mouth, but nothing came out. He didn't

have an answer. He was starting to grasp the problem.

Red said, "Even if we just called him up without a plan, I doubt he'd answer the phone. It's obvious he goes around selling junk meat, so he's probably got half the county calling him, angry as hell. And if we leave a message asking him to call us back, why would he?"

Red waited for Billy Don to offer an answer, but the big man was obviously stumped.

"What we need," Red said, "is a good lie. We need to con the con artist. Make him call us back. Make him tell us where he is. Or make him come to us. Either one."

"But how?" Billy Don asked.

"I don't know yet," Red said. "Gimme some time."

The light changed and he eased the truck forward.

"Couldn't we tell him we want to place a big order?" Billy Don asked. "Maybe say we want four or five hundred dollars' worth of meat. Bet that would make him call back."

Red blinked, and then he blinked again. Was it really that simple? He couldn't think of a reason why it wouldn't work, but he hated to give Billy Don the satisfaction of coming up with the solution. He said, "That's not very creative, so we'll stick it in our back pocket in case we can't think of anything better."

A few minutes later, Red pulled into the hospital parking lot and found a good spot under a shade tree.

"Let's not tell Miss Shirley we're gonna go looking for the guy," he said. "She'd worry about what we're gonna do to him. She wouldn't want us to get into any trouble on her account. Plus, I don't want to let her down if we can't find him."

"Oh, we'll find the sumbitch," Billy Don said. "Sooner or later, we'll find him."

11

Nicole Marlin was working from home, catching up on paperwork, when she heard Geist bound from the front porch and run barking toward the front of their seven acres. Odd, because Geist wasn't much of a barker, and she'd been taught long ago not to bark at the deer and other wildlife that inhabited the area.

Nicole set her laptop to the side, rose from the couch, and went to the nearest window. From here, she had a good view of their driveway, but trees prevented her from seeing the front gate. She could see Geist, twenty yards short of the road, but standing in place, still barking, and not wagging her tail as she usually did when an unexpected visitor—like the UPS driver—pulled up outside the gate.

Nicole waited. She'd be able to tell from Geist's body language when the visitor, whether it was a person or, say, a wandering dog, moved on. But Geist began to retreat, barking more vigorously than before. And here came a man, emerging from behind the trees, walking along the driveway toward the house.

Nicole didn't recognize him, and the fact that he had ignored the NO TRESPASSING sign on the front fence line was a red flag. She stepped onto the front porch with her phone in hand.

The man, now just 50 feet away, said, "Good morning, ma'am! Quite a guard dog you've got here."

Geist had moved to the man's right and was still barking.

"Sir, I need you to stop right there," Nicole said, using the firm take-charge voice that had served her well for years as a deputy.

The man stopped. "Sorry, I didn't mean to—"

"Geist," Nicole said, and Geist reluctantly stopped barking.

"Cool name," the man said. "Means 'ghost' in German, right?"

The man appeared to be in his late twenties or early thirties. Tall and lean. His complexion and facial features suggested Native American, but Nicole couldn't be sure. He was wearing jeans, work boots, and a long-sleeved denim shirt with a logo on the left side. His black hair was long and straight.

"Sir, may I help you with something?"

Nicole wasn't going to lay into him just yet. He might have a legitimate reason for his visit.

He gave her a big smile. "Yes, ma'am. I represent the New Mexico Meat Company and I was wondering if—"

She raised her hand, signaling him to stop talking, and, wisely, he did.

"You opened a closed gate to try to sell me some meat?"

When he answered, he didn't sound quite as friendly. "No, ma'am. The gate was open. I started to drive in, but I thought you might not appreciate that. So I left my truck out by the road."

Now Nicole knew what type of person she was dealing with. A liar. Thirty minutes earlier, she had taken a short walk around the acreage—something she did several times a week—and the gate had been closed. Not locked, but closed. John had closed it when he'd left that morning. They always kept the gate closed, unless they were expecting company. Was this man really a meat salesman, or was he looking for empty houses to burgle?

"I'm not interested," Nicole said. "And I'm going to caution you against soliciting in this area. Most of my neighbors don't appreciate uninvited guests."

The salesman smiled again, but there was nothing genuine about it.

"Am I breaking any laws?" he asked.

"You're trespassing."

"I didn't see a sign."

"It's on the gate."

"Well, since the gate was open, I didn't notice it."

She wasn't going to argue with him about the gate. It would serve no purpose. Further, the radar she'd developed over the years as a deputy told her she was dealing with something more than a common trespasser.

"Sir, I'm letting you know right now that you're trespassing, and I'm asking you to leave."

He stared at her for a long moment. If he made a run at her, Geist would be on his heels, and Nicole would have time to get inside the house to her handgun. Now she was kicking herself for not grabbing the gun before she'd stepped onto the porch.

Finally, the meat salesman said, "I'll leave. For now."

"What does that mean?" Nicole asked. Had she heard him right?

But the man had turned and was walking away.

Nicole went back inside the house, grabbed a Canon super-zoom camera she used for wildlife photography, and hurried back outside. She made it halfway to the gate, past the trees, where she had just enough time to snap a photo of the man's license plate as he drove away in his gray Toyota Tacoma.

Miss Shirley seemed to be doing much better, so Red and Billy Don took her home and then proceeded toward Red's trailer.

Along the way, Billy Don said, "You got a better idea yet?"

Red had been thinking about it, and the answer was no, he hadn't come up with a better way to make the meat salesman call them back.

Truth was, Red didn't even want to get involved. It wasn't like Miss Shirley had died or anything. She bought some bad meat, made everybody sick, and now they were past it. Lesson learned.

But...

Red knew how Billy Don would react to that. What sort of man lets an old woman get conned by a fast-talking salesman without doing anything about it? Billy Don was weird that way. He might poach, cheat in a pig-hunting contest, get into drunken fistfights, dodge taxes, commit bigamy, and steal just about anything that wasn't bolted down, but that didn't mean he had no personal code of ethics.

"Still thinking," Red said as he turned onto his caliche driveway.

"Miss Shirley can't afford to throw away that much money on bad meat," Billy Don said. "Far as I'm concerned, if he'll give her a refund, I'll spare him an ass-whooping."

Red couldn't resist needling him. "If that's what you're worried about—the money—why don't you just cover her losses yourself?

You can afford it. Hell, you could afford to buy her a brand-new freezer and fill it with prime rib."

He reached the top of the hill and parked in front of his trailer. Now that Red had some money, he couldn't help looking at the trailer with a fresh eye—and there was no denying it was a pile of junk. A man of his status shouldn't be living in a trailer like that.

"It's the principle of the thing," Billy Don said. "He ripped her off and somebody needs to make him pay for it. And if we wait too damn long, we'll never find him. He might switch phone numbers every week or two. Ever thought of that? Maybe he uses one of them phones you set on fire when you're done with it."

"What are you talking about?"

"It's a phone you use for a little while, and then you burn it when you're done."

"Oh, Jesus. You mean a burner phone?"

"Exactly."

Red started laughing, hard. Then he said, "You don't actually set it on fire, Billy Don."

"Pretty sure you do. That's why they call it that."

Red wanted to tell Billy Don exactly how stupid he was, but that was never a wise move.

"That's just a name they give it," Red said.

"I ain't gonna argue about dumb stuff. Point is, that phone number we have might be useless real soon. In fact, let's call him right now and get it over with."

"Billy Don, let's go inside and—"

"I'm tired of talking about it. Either you call him or I will."

Red let out a sigh, then reached into his shirt pocket for the flyer he'd gotten from Cliff at the feed store. He handed it to Billy Don, who surprised Red by reaching into his own pocket and producing a cell phone. Not just a cell phone, but an actual iPhone. Those things were way more expensive than Red's off-brand Korean phone.

"When'd you get that?" Red said.

"Came in the mail Saturday."

"How much?"

"Who cares? I got money now. Might as well buy some nice things. Hang on." Billy Don was fumbling around, trying to figure out how to dial the number.

"Hit the Phone button right there," Red said.

"I can do it," Billy Don said.

"Now hit Keypad," Red said.

"I know."

Billy Don dialed.

"Now hit Speaker so I can hear, too," Red said.

"You're getting on my nerves," Billy Don said, but he did as Red instructed.

The call went straight to voicemail without a single ring.

This is Joseph. Please leave a message.

After the tone, Billy Don said nothing for several seconds. It was obvious he hadn't thought this through at all. Finally he said, "Uh, yeah, I'm, uh..."

Red tried to stifle a laugh, but he let out a snort. Billy Don was totally unprepared.

Billy Don continued, saying, "This is, uh, I'm calling because, uh...I'll call you back."

He ended the call.

"Well, that was smooth," Red said.

"Shut up."

"Silver-tongued devil."

"Shut up."

"How can he avoid such a clever trap?"

"Shut up."

"You're a master of—"

"Shut up. Last warning."

Red shut up.

12

"Ever heard of Hiram Bingham? I'm guessing no. Most people haven't. No reason you should have, I guess—it's not like he's a household name nowadays, and he's been dead since 1956."

John Marlin shook his head, and Lauren, sitting next to him, said, "It's familiar, but I can't place it."

Marlin wasn't sure what a 67-year-old retired archeologist should look like, but Hubert Walz seemed to fit the bill fairly well. Somehow he managed to be vaguely handsome and outdoorsy, but also bookish or even nerdy. He appeared fit and healthy, except for a broken left arm that was in a cast past the elbow. He had the ruddy skin of a person who'd spent a good portion of his lifetime in the sun, dating back to the days when the dangers of ultraviolet rays weren't as well understood. He kept his gray hair short and wore eyeglasses with a thick black frame.

"Surely you've heard of Machu Picchu," Walz said.

"Yes, sir," Marlin said.

"I've been there," Lauren said.

"Oh, you have?" Walz said, plainly excited. "When was this?"

They were seated around a coffee table in a small den with large windows that offered an impressive western view, including a long stretch of the Pedernales River. Walz owned a beautiful hilltop home on 600 acres. Marlin had to wonder if it was possible to build that kind of wealth in the field of archeology.

"About 15 years ago," Lauren said.

"What did you think of it?" Walz asked.

"It was one of the most memorable trips I've ever taken," Lauren said. "I'd like to go back someday."

"Outstanding," Walz said. "However, even though I'm sure it *was* memorable, it appears the name Hiram Bingham must have slipped your mind. He is generally credited for the discovery of Machu Picchu in 1911, and in fact the highway leading up there bears his name now. Stick with me and the relevance of all this will become clear, or at least coherent. Hiram Bingham was this larger-than-life character—some people think Indiana Jones might've been modeled after him. He was an explorer, an historian, a lecturer at Yale, and so on. Later he was elected governor of Connecticut, and eventually became a United States senator. So, yes, he was many things—but one thing he was not was a trained archeologist. And now you can probably see where I'm going with this, as it relates back to your original question."

A few minutes earlier, Marlin had asked Walz if he'd had any trouble with artifact looters on his ranch.

Lauren said, "Some of this stuff about Bingham is coming back to me, and I remember that it's a fascinating story."

"Indeed. Setting aside the question of whether Bingham actually 'discovered' Machu Picchu—and I'm of the opinion he didn't, because locals already knew exactly where it was—there is also some validity to the accusations at the time, and still lingering today, that he and his team inappropriately excavated the site and shipped thousands of priceless artifacts back to Yale. By the time he was done in 1915, the natives in the area were understandably angry. They claimed Bingham essentially plundered the site, and by doing so, he prevented local archeologists from participating in a remarkable opportunity to broaden the knowledge of Incan history."

Walz paused there, waiting for Marlin and Lauren to acknowledge the analogy.

"And you feel that amateur diggers and looters do the same thing around here," Marlin said.

"Oh, there's no question they do," Walz said. "Obviously I'd be stretching the truth if I insinuated there might be another Machu Picchu here in Blanco County. But that doesn't mean there isn't still plenty of valuable information to be gleaned from the artifacts buried just outside our front doors and scattered across our hills."

It struck Marlin as a sound bite from a speech Walz had delivered before, but that didn't make it any less valid.

"Have you ever caught any looters on your place?" Marlin asked, trying to keep the conversation from wandering too widely. And, of course, he was studying Walz closely, as was Lauren, because that was the point of meeting with the archeologist—to ascertain if he'd had any interaction with Sean Hudson. If he had, what exactly had happened? Had there been a violent encounter between the two men? Is that how he got his broken arm?

"I have, yes, on a couple of occasions," Walz said. "When you own a place like this, you catch all types of trespassers. I get a handful of poachers throughout the year, and then in the summer, if there's been any rain, I get people trying to access the river so they can swim or fish or hike. I even get people jumping the fence to collect firewood or pick wildflowers."

"How long have you owned it?" Lauren asked.

"Five years this fall," Walz said. The archeologist paused again, then said, "I have to admit, these questions are making me curious. You said you were looking into the death of a young man from this area?"

"Yes, from Burnet County, just to the north of us," Lauren said.

"But I don't understand why you wanted to talk to me," Walz said.

"The young man was named Sean Hudson," Lauren said. "Did you know him?"

"I don't recall anyone by that name," Walz said.

"He was a looter who'd been caught trespassing several times, and he also happened to work on the crew that surveyed this place last year," Lauren said.

"Oh, I see," Walz said, quickly connecting the dots. "And you're wondering if he cased the place, in a manner of speaking, when he was here surveying, and then returned later."

"That crossed our minds," Marlin said.

Now the expression on the archeologist's face became more serious. "Where did this young man die?"

"We're working on that," Marlin said. "He was found on a ranch west of Johnson City. The body had been moved."

"Moved," Walz said.

"That's right."

"From that I conclude he was murdered—or he was killed accidentally, and the killer wanted to avoid any culpability."

"The former," Lauren said.

Walz took a deep breath. "Well, you've really blindsided me with this. I can assure you I know nothing about it. That's why you're here, right? To see if I make a likely suspect?"

"We're checking every possible lead," Marlin said. "It's fairly routine. We'll be speaking to a lot of people."

"I would never harm a trespasser," Walz said.

"I'm glad to hear that," Marlin said.

"Unless, of course, a trespasser became aggressive," Walz said.

"Has that ever happened?" Lauren asked.

"Never. I don't know why I said that. Usually, as soon as they see me, they take off, just like deer or wild pigs. They don't want any sort of confrontation."

"Usually?" Lauren said.

"Pardon?"

"You said 'usually.' Have there been instances when trespassers haven't taken off?"

"Well, yes, but in those cases, I've simply asked them to leave, and they do, and they usually apologize, or they claim they didn't realize they were trespassing."

"Just out of curiosity, how did you break your arm?" Marlin asked.

Walz began shaking his head. "I got careless on an ATV and took a spill. Completely my fault. But it doesn't look good, does it?"

"How so?"

"I assume you're wondering if I injured the arm in a physical struggle with the young man who died."

"Well, since you mentioned it, is that what happened?" Marlin asked, grinning.

"Absolutely not," Walz said. "I've never laid eyes on him."

"Do you know the names of all the trespassers you've encountered?" Marlin asked.

"Of course not," Walz said.

"Then how would you know if you'd ever laid eyes on him?"

"That's a good point," Walz conceded. "Do you have a photo of him?"

"Hang on," Lauren said. She quickly found a photo on her cell phone and showed it to Walz.

"I can tell you with certainty I don't recognize him," Walz said.

"What was the survey for?" Marlin asked. "Were you trying to sell the place?"

"No, I needed a property line to be marked so I could put up a fence on the west side of the ranch. It was the only side unfenced."

"When was your ATV accident?" she asked.

"Wednesday of last week."

That would be a day prior to Sean Hudson's death, if Lem Tucker's calculations were accurate.

"Where did you go for treatment? Blanco Memorial?" Marlin asked.

"That's right. I can show you the ATV, if you'd like. It's pretty banged up, too."

"That won't be necessary," Lauren said.

Good call. Right now, Walz was mildly flustered, but not yet defensive, and asking to see the ATV—which would indicate a legitimate distrust in his claim—might cause him to shut down the interview.

"Another question out of curiosity," Marlin said. "If you get several poachers every year on this place, I'm surprised I've never heard from you. Or I don't recall hearing from you. Have you ever called me?"

"I haven't, no."

"So what do you do when you find a poacher on your property?" Marlin asked. "I'm talking specifically about poachers, not other types of trespassers."

"Because they're generally armed," Walz said. "That's the distinction you're driving at, yes?"

"It is, yes."

"Well, fortunately, I've only encountered a few face to face, and I've always given them the chance to leave before I call the sheriff's department. That's what they've done each time."

"So you run them off?" Marlin asked.

"I guess you could call it that, but I'd like to stress that I do not get confrontational. I simply instruct them to leave or I'll call the sheriff. More often than not, however, it's Titus who catches the trespassers."

"Who's Titus?" Lauren asked.

"My ranch manager," Walz said. "He takes care of the cattle, maintains the fences, and whatever else it takes to keep this place up and running. Shoots wild pigs, which are always digging up the place. He's out there wandering the ranch a lot more than I am."

"What's his last name?"

"Steele."

Walz was intelligent enough to know that Titus Steele had just become a person of interest in the case. Maybe that's why Walz had mentioned him—to deflect attention away from himself.

"Does he live here on the ranch?" Lauren asked.

"Yes, in the original ranch house," Walz said. "Built back in the thirties. Boy, I've had to spend some money to bring it up to modern standards, but it was that or bulldoze it, which seemed a shame."

"How long has Titus worked for you?" Marlin asked.

"I hired him right after I bought the ranch."

"Is Titus as level-headed as you are when he catches somebody on the property?" Marlin asked.

"I have no reason to think he wouldn't be," Walz said. "He's never told me about any problems."

"Do you and Titus talk every day?" Marlin asked.

"More like once or twice a week. If I need something, I let him know. Otherwise, I'm a hands-off employer. Sometimes I go a week or two without actually seeing him."

"When was the last time you saw him?" Lauren asked.

Walz held his good hand up in a "hold on for a minute" gesture. "Can we please slow down? Two minutes ago, you didn't even know Titus existed, and now you're acting as if he's a prime suspect in the murder of some young man who happened to set foot on this ranch last year."

Marlin thought that seemed like an overreaction on Walz's part.

"Sir, we don't have a suspect at this point," Lauren said. "But we need to ask Titus if he ever saw Sean Hudson. I'm guessing the answer will be no, and that will be the end of it."

"I would hope so," Walz said, "because the tone of this conversation is beginning to concern me, to be frank."

"We didn't mean to rattle you," Lauren said. "This is all very standard. We talk to anybody and everybody who might be able to shed some light on the case. We'll talk to dozens and dozens before we're through. In all likelihood, you'll never see us again after we leave. Same with Titus."

Again, a perfect response. Lauren had picked up the same vibes Marlin had sensed—that Walz was on the verge of asking them to leave, or stating that he'd answer no more questions without talking to his attorney first.

Walz took a deep breath and seemed somewhat reassured. He said, "Titus took me to the hospital about my arm. I haven't talked to him since that afternoon."

"You said that was on Wednesday?" Marlin asked.

"Right."

"You think Titus is here on the ranch right now?" Lauren asked. "It would be great if we could talk to him before we leave. Get it out of the way."

Titus Steele returned to the river, this time with an orange five-gallon bucket bungeed to the inside of his tailgate. He parked and carried the bucket, with its forty pounds of contents, to the spot where Sean Hudson had died.

He set the bucket down and popped the lid off. The stench was incredible. Hard to believe soured corn could create such a stomach-churning odor. He'd had this batch fermenting for nearly a week. Pretty simple, really. Fill the bucket three-quarters full with deer corn, then pour a beer in, and top it off with water. A week later, after sitting in the hot Texas sun, the corn was about as ripe as it could get. You could practically smell it from the next county over.

He grabbed the bucket by the handle and poured the slop in a thick line about ten yards long, nearly retching in the process.

When he was done, he went to the river and washed the bucket out. He was tempted to strip down and jump in the water, because it was damn hot today, but before he could do that, his phone rang. Boss man calling.

Titus didn't know whether he should take the call. He didn't need any more headaches right now. But he hadn't seen Dr. Walz in several days, and he had a broken arm and everything. So Titus answered the way he always did.

"Mornin', sir. What can I do for you?"

Dr. Walz launched right into it, saying he was sitting there with a county deputy and a state game warden, and they were hoping to chat with Titus for a few minutes up at the house.

More headaches? Shit. This was a damn full-on migraine—but not like it was totally unexpected.

Titus needed to stall. Give himself time to prepare for a conversation like that. So he said he was running an errand to San Antonio and the cell signal was weak. When Dr. Walz began to respond, Titus hung up, as if the call had been dropped.

13

As Marlin drove onto his property later that day, he found Nicole using a chainsaw to thin some cedars beside the driveway. Odd. What had prompted that?

When he got closer, he noticed she had her favorite handgun, a Smith & Wesson .38, holstered on her hip. That, too, was weird. Maybe she'd seen a snake.

Marlin pulled up beside her and lowered his window. She killed the chainsaw, removed the foam plugs from her ears, and gave him a grin. She was wearing jeans, an old T-shirt, and protective eyewear. Sweat was streaming down her face. "Hey, there," she said.

"What's going on?" he said. "Decided to trim trees in hundred-degree heat?"

"Oh, I'm just knocking a few branches off so we can see the gate from the house. Been meaning to do that for a long time."

"But why now?" Marlin asked. "And why the thirty-eight?"

The look on her face told him something wasn't right. She said, "How about we go up to the house and I'll tell you what happened."

"A meat salesman?" Marlin said. He was leaning against the kitchen counter with a cold bottle of beer in his hand. Nicole was seated at the table, cooling off with some ice water.

"That's right," she said. "Walked right up the driveway like he owned the place. I'm glad Geist started barking."

Geist, lying nearby, heard her name and thumped her tail on the floor.

"What'd you tell him?"

"I said he shouldn't have come through the gate, but he said it was already open. That was a lie, because I'd walked earlier and it was definitely closed. Not like I was going to argue with the guy about it, so I simply told him I wasn't interested and he needed to leave. Then he said he'd leave—for now."

"Those were his exact words?"

"Sure what it sounded like, but I might've misunderstood. So I asked him to repeat what he said, but he was already walking away."

Marlin took a moment to gather his thoughts before replying. He wanted to scold Nicole for failing to call him when it had happened, but if the situation had been reversed, would he have called her? Probably not. So it wasn't fair to expect her to do something he wouldn't have done.

"What'd he look like?" he said.

"Late twenties or early thirties. About six-two and maybe one-eighty. Long black hair and a dark complexion. Might've been a Native American, but it was hard to tell. Said he worked for the New Mexico Meat Company. I Googled it and they have a horrible reputation. The meat is all junk, apparently, and good luck trying to get your money back. They're hustlers."

"Did he give a name?"

"No, but I got his tag number as he left."

"Nice. What was he driving?"

"Gray Toyota Tacoma with a white freezer in the back."

Marlin took a big gulp of his beer and it felt great at the back of his throat.

Nicole rose to put her empty glass in the kitchen sink. She looked out the window above the sink and said, "It was probably nothing, but it will be good to see the gate from the house."

Not long ago, Marlin's best friend Phil Colby had installed some security cameras at his home. Now Marlin was wondering if he should do the same thing. Depressing thought.

Several hours had passed and the meat man had not returned Billy Don's call. Surprise, surprise. That was fine with Red, because he was about to make an important call regarding his tree-house plans. That was one thing right there—calling it a "tree house"—

that he needed to change, because people would think he was nuts if he said he wanted to live in a tree house. So what should he call it?

Nature-based living? No, that sounded like some tree-hugger hippie bullshit.

Heightened habitation? Would people even know what that meant?

Elevated housing? Hey, that wasn't bad. Good enough for now.

Red settled into his recliner in the living room with a cold beer and dialed the number of Willard Fisk, a Blanco County homebuilder who threw Red and Billy Don some masonry and carpentry work now and then. Of course, it had been several months since Red had done any actual revenue-producing labor, thanks to the nest egg he was sitting on.

Willard answered by saying, "Hey, you rich son of a bitch. Calling to brag about early retirement?"

"It's everything you ever dreamed of," Red said.

"Whiskey and women all day long?"

"And into the night," Red said.

"Well, fuck you very much. Ever gonna work again?"

"Not if I can help it."

"That money's gonna run out eventually."

"That's what I'm calling about," Red said. "I'm thinking about spending some of it on a new place to live and I wanted to get your opinion on it from a builder's standpoint."

"What you got in mind?"

Red described exactly what he was envisioning, but he used his new phrase, "elevated housing."

When Red finished, Willard said, "Am I wrong, or are you talking about a very large tree house?"

"It's a hell of a lot more than a tree house," Red said, getting irritated.

"Don't get me wrong," Willard said, "I've seen some of those tree house shows on TV, and what you're describing sounds pretty damn kickass."

Finally. Someone with some sense.

"Think we can sit down over a beer sometime soon and talk about it?"

"Hell, yeah," Willard said. "I won't even charge you for my expertise."

Red could feel the floor suddenly vibrating, which meant Billy Don was lumbering down the hallway from his bedroom. Sure enough, the big man barged into the living room, saying, "Hey, Red, the—"

But Red held a hand up for silence, and indicated that he was on the phone. Billy Don waited impatiently, shifting from foot to foot as Red and Willard set up a time to meet.

When Red hung up, Billy Don said, "The meat man was cruising Rancher's Estates 15 minutes ago," Billy Don said.

"How do you know that?" Red asked.

"Miss Shirley just texted me," Billy Don said. "She saw it on Blanco County Neighbors."

"On which neighbors' what?" Red asked.

"It's a page on Facebook called Blanco County Neighbors. Miss Shirley says people talk about all kinds of crap on there, and apparently the meat man has been bothering people all around the county for the past week or so, and some other people have gotten sick. But forget about that right now and let's go after him. Hurry, before he's gone."

"Okay, okay, don't get your knickers in a twist," Red said as he reluctantly pushed himself out of the recliner.

When he was pulling his boots on he couldn't help thinking, *Billy Don is texting now? What in holy hell is this world coming to?*

Marlin had just finished loading the dishwasher after dinner when Lauren called to say she'd received Sean Hudson's cell phone records a few hours earlier. Her search warrant had requested calls made and received, any available text messages, and cell-site data, which would provide information on the physical movement of Hudson's phone in the days and weeks before his body was found.

"Bad news first," Lauren said. "He was with AT&T, so there are no texts."

AT&T, like most major carriers, did not retain customers' actual text messages. They did, however, retain a list of every number a particular customer had texted in the past seven years. That might be helpful, although there was bound to be some duplication with the calls made and received.

"Learn anything good from the location data?" Marlin asked.

"I've only scanned it, but you know how it is with rural towers. They cover so much area, you can't really pinpoint an exact location. If you travel down 281 with a cell phone, you're eventually going to ping off every damn tower in the county. But the date and time information might be helpful later. I do know that Hudson's phone was in both Burnet and Blanco County last Thursday, which is the day Lem says he died. The day before, the phone never left Burnet County."

"What about calls coming and going?" Marlin asked.

"I've narrowed it down to the numbers he called or texted more than once," Lauren said. "There are about 12 or 13 from the past 60 days. Tomorrow Ernie will start working on warrants to get the subscriber info on all those, which'll take a couple days."

Once they matched names to the phone numbers, they would research each subscriber extensively. Did he or she have a criminal record? What was his or her association with Sean Hudson? They would want the answers to these questions—and any other pertinent information they could gather—before they made contact with each person.

Marlin said, "In the meantime, it might be worth Googling those numbers. Might get lucky. Want me to tackle that?"

"That would be great. You mind?"

"Not at all. Send 'em to me and I'll start in the morning."

Truth was, Marlin occasionally enjoyed that kind of work—trolling for information online—because it was so different than what he did on a day-to-day basis.

"Will do," Lauren said. "I appreciate it."

"Hey, one more thing," Marlin said. He quickly filled her in on Nicole's encounter with the meat salesman.

"I'm glad you mentioned it," Lauren said, "because we've been getting calls about that guy. Now that we've got his plate number, maybe we can do something about it. Nicole is sure the gate was closed?"

"Absolutely. I remember closing it. We always close it, unless we're expecting somebody."

"Okay, I'll let you know what I find out. As for the implied threat..."

She trailed off.

"Yeah, I know," Marlin said. "She's not positive he said it, and even if he did, he'll say he didn't, or that she took it the wrong way."

"At a minimum," Lauren said, "if we can track him down, maybe we can teach him about trespassing laws, and then convince him to go back home to New Mexico."

"Works for me," Marlin said.

14

By the time Red turned left into Rancher's Estates, a small subdivision inside the Johnson City city limits, the sun was dipping below the horizon.

"What now?" he said.

Billy Don was staring at his iPhone. This was frigging unreal—Billy Don checking for texts on his iPhone. Red wasn't sure whether he should be disgusted or amused.

"Don't know," Billy Don said. "Miss Shirley says nobody has said anything on that thread for 30 minutes."

"What're you talking about—thread?"

"It means a bunch of comments. Different people say stuff. That's how it works."

"That's dumb. Why is it called a thread?"

"Why not?"

"What does it even mean?"

"Who cares?"

"Well, so far," Red said, "that thread hasn't been all that useful. You might even say it's been kind of threadbare."

Billy Don looked at him. "That might be the worst joke I've ever heard."

"'Cause you got no sense of humor. Anyway, this was all your idea, and it's working out like most of your ideas—and that's no joke. So just tell me where to go, genius."

Red hadn't driven through Rancher's Estates in years. None of their friends lived here, and they had no other reason to visit this neighborhood.

"Hang on a second. I'm waiting on the map to load," Billy Don said.

"You know how to do that?"

"It don't take knowing. You just use it."

Red was skeptical. He'd tried to use the map function on his cheap Korean phone a few times, but it kept jumping around all over the place. One minute it would work right, showing exactly where he was, and the next it would suddenly say he was in Amarillo or Baton Rouge.

Red randomly turned west on Diamond X Road, then went south on Liveoak Drive, keeping his eyes peeled for a gray Tacoma.

"Just keep going straight and make a left down here," Billy Don said.

Red went east on Post Oak Drive.

Billy Don said, "This neighborhood ain't very big, so we should be able to check most of it before we—"

"I think this is him," Red said, and sure enough, a gray Tacoma was coming right at them. "Check for New Mexico plates."

"I will."

"Try to get a look at the driver."

"I will."

"Here he comes."

"I know."

Red slowed, and as the gray Tacoma passed, he plainly saw the face of Joseph Lightfoot squinting into the setting sun.

Titus heard them before he saw them—squeals and grunts marking their descent toward the river. A moment later, a sounder of at least 20 feral pigs of all colors and sizes formed a surprisingly orderly line and began to feast on the trail of soured corn.

It would be an easy shot, even in the fading light. Titus was sitting between two scrubby cedar trees with his .30-30 in easy reach. He lifted it, settled the crosshairs on the neck of a black medium-sized pig, and gently squeezed the trigger. The rifle bucked in his arms and the pig dropped dead as a stone. The other pigs scattered and were gone from view before Titus's ears stopped ringing.

Dr. Walz probably wouldn't have heard the shot, but even if he did, it wouldn't matter. He'd given Titus carte blanche to shoot any pig on sight after Titus had stressed how destructive they were, and how they harmed the native animals trying to live off the land. And they dug. The archeologist definitely didn't like that part.

Titus walked over to the pig. The odor from the nearby soured corn was overwhelming, but Titus breathed through his mouth instead of his nose and went to work on the carcass. He rolled the pig onto its back and cut it open from anus to throat, sawing through the sternum, and taking care not to puncture the stomach or intestines. Why taint perfectly good pork?

Then he used a rope and a gambrel to hoist the carcass from a sturdy cypress limb. He made further cuts to connective tissue and let the blood and entrails drop to the ground below—right on the spot where Sean Hudson had died.

Red turned hard into a driveway, backed up, then dropped it into forward gear and went after the Tacoma. It was already out of sight.

"Go straight?" Red asked.

"I think so, yeah," Billy Don said.

"Did he turn?"

"I don't think so."

But just a short distance ahead, Post Oak ended at a T intersection with Miller Creek Loop.

"Left or right?" Red said.

"Right. No, left. Left!"

Red turned left and gunned it. "What if he went right?" he asked.

"Then we're screwed."

"Did he see us?"

"Well, of course he saw us."

"No, I mean did he know we were gonna follow him? Did he recognize us?"

"I got no idea," Billy Don said.

"He might've recognized my truck. It's unique."

"That's one way of putting it."

Red let off the gas as he passed a long driveway on the right. "He coulda turned there."

"Yeah, he mighta."

"Want me to go back?"

Billy Don hesitated.

Red was losing his patience. "This is your deal, Billy Don. I'm just following your orders, so you'd better take advantage of it while you can."

The sun had dropped below the horizon and twilight was setting in quickly.

"Keep going straight," Billy Don decided.

Red sped up for a moment, but then slowed for a 90-degree right turn, followed by a 90-degree left turn. Red knew this road like the back of a can of Keystone Light, so he knew exactly how hard he could push it.

They passed another long driveway on the right, but Billy Don said, "He's gotta be done for the day, right? I can't imagine he'd be turning down driveways and knocking on doors after dark."

"So keep going straight?"

"Yeah," Billy Don said. Then, "There we go!"

Red could see taillights ahead. He gassed it some more, and as he got closer to the vehicle—a dark truck that looked like a Tacoma—he could make out a large white shape in the bed. The freezer.

"That's him!" Billy Don said.

Red was now just twenty yards behind the Tacoma.

"Better ease off or he'll wonder if we're following him," Billy Don said.

But before Red could fall back, the Tacoma suddenly pulled over on the grassy shoulder. Red had no choice but to keep going. After another curve, he couldn't see the Tacoma's headlights in the mirror anymore. "Now what?" he said.

"Just pull over and wait," Billy Don said.

So Red did, and a moment later, here came a vehicle. The headlights were bright in Red's mirrors, but after the vehicle passed, he could see that it was the Tacoma.

"Well, there goes the element of surprise," Red said as he pulled onto the road.

"Don't need it," Billy Don said. "Let's just chase that sumbitch down."

Red slowly caught up with the Tacoma, but instead of driving faster, the meat man surprised him by applying the brakes and coming to a full stop in the middle of the road. Red had to stop behind him.

"What's he doing?" Billy Don said.

"No idea." Red wished he could see Lightfoot through the rear window, but the freezer was in the way.

Billy Don reached over and blasted the horn.

Red revved the engine.

"You be ready if he gets out of that truck," Red said.

Billy Don twisted around, grunting, and removed a 12-gauge shotgun from the gun rack in Red's rear window. "Buckshot or birdshot in here?"

"Buckshot."

"Good."

Red was wishing he'd brought his .45 Colt Anaconda. That big boy could put the fear of God into a lying Indian in no time.

Billy Don opened his door, preparing to step out, but right then the Tacoma began to crawl forward. Red followed.

Then Lightfoot gunned it. Red's old truck couldn't match the acceleration, but Lightfoot didn't know the road well, so he had to slow down at every curve.

"What're you gonna do if we can corner him?" Red said.

"Whatever it takes," Billy Don said.

It sounded like the type of line some tough guy in a movie would say, but Red knew from past experience that Billy Don wasn't just blowing smoke. The big man wanted the meat salesman to give Miss Shirley's money back, and he would definitely do whatever it took to make that happen. Billy Don wasn't by nature a violent or cruel man, but once you earned a spot on his shit list, look out. He was capable of all kinds of crazy stuff.

At one point, Red closed the gap to less than 20 feet, and he saw Lightfoot stick his denim-clad arm out of the truck with a white object in his hand. Beer can. Red recognized it immediately. The man casually flipped it backwards, high in the air, tumbling end over end, and before Red could even touch the brakes, the unopened can of beer thumped hard in the center of Red's windshield, leaving a fist-sized web of cracks right at eye level.

"That asshole," Red said. Those cracks would slowly spread wider and wider over time. Red would have to get the windshield replaced. The man had just cost Red several hundred dollars.

Now Red was pissed. He brought his front bumper closer and closer to the Tacoma, until five feet separated the vehicles. Red's speedometer showed 50, so if the Indian hit his brakes, they were both in for a fairly significant collision.

But, instead, the Indian stomped on the gas yet again, and even with the weight of the freezer in the bed, the Tacoma's four-liter engine generated some impressive acceleration.

The gap widened to 50 feet. Then 100.

Red said, "I'm hoping he'll turn down one of these dead-end side roads. And if he does that, I want you to be ready to—"

"Look out!"

There was a sudden flash of gray hair and antlers as a large buck bounded across the road directly in front of Red's truck.

He stomped the brakes hard and came to a complete stop, somehow missing the deer by no more than a few inches. But now the Tacoma had an even greater lead. Red stomped the gas pedal—

And the engine died.

"Shit!"

"Hurry up, Red."

Red cranked the key, but the truck wouldn't start.

"He's getting away," Billy Don said.

Red pumped the gas and tried again.

"You're flooding it," Billy Don said. "I can smell it."

Finally the engine caught, but it was sputtering and coughing.

"Go, Red. Go."

"If I go now, it'll die. Give it a minute."

"Shit. I can't even see him anymore."

Ten seconds later, the engine was running smoothly, so Red goosed it and went roaring down Miller Creek Loop, rounding curves so hard the tires squealed in protest.

But it was too late. The Tacoma was long gone. They couldn't even see taillights in the distance.

When they reached Highway 281, Billy Don let out a big sigh.

"Not my fault," Red said.

Billy Don slowly shook his head and said, "Know what I'm doing tomorrow?"

"Buying me a new windshield? Because I never woulda been out here if it wasn't for you."

"Hell no."

"What, then?"

"Buying a vehicle that runs worth a damn."

15

"I ran the plate first thing this morning and it comes back to a man named Cody Brock," Lauren said. "Description matches what you gave me yesterday from Nicole. Colorful guy. He has a long record for all kinds of different scams and ripoffs, harassing customers, high-pressure sales, all that. I almost have to laugh at this latest scheme. Apparently, this New Mexico Meat Company that he works for—one of their signature products is buffalo burgers. So what this guy's been doing recently is presenting himself as an Indian. Calls himself Joseph Lightfoot."

"Pardon me?"

Marlin was on the couch with his laptop, preparing to do some online sleuthing. Nicole had left earlier and would be gone all day at various meetings and appointments.

"I'm serious," Lauren said. "I've looked at some of the complaints against him and he wants people to think he's an Indian. Sometimes he flat-out tells them he's an Indian. I guess he thinks that gives him some sort of sales edge. Who would know buffalo meat better, right? Anyway, I'm looking at various mug shots, and it's really quite a transformation. A few years ago he was dirty blond and not particularly dark-skinned. But late last year—when he got booked for doing 110 out near Midland—he had much longer hair, dyed jet black, and it looks like he spent some time in a tanning booth."

"Anything violent in his record?" Marlin asked.

"Three years ago he was convicted on one count of simple assault, which could've been a punch, a shove, or just a threat. If you want, I can have Ernie look into that and find out exactly what happened."

"I appreciate it, but I know he's busy. Let's set that aside for now."

"You sure?"

"Where was the assault?" he asked.

"Trinidad, Colorado."

Marlin had risen off the couch and was now standing near the front windows. With the cedars trimmed, he could see the gate from this vantage point. It was closed. Geist was ten yards from the porch, on the grass, curled up in a patch of sunlight.

He said, "Yeah, let's not bother with it. Lightfoot is probably halfway to Arkansas by now."

"That does fit his pattern," Lauren said. "He hits a particular location for a few weeks or months, then moves along before the heat is on. Tell you what—if I hear anything more about him, I'll let you know. I've seen several people complain about him on Facebook, so I posted that if anybody sees him, they should call the sheriff's office."

"Sounds good. Thank you for checking it out for me."

"You bet," Lauren said. "Okay, let me know if you get anything good from those numbers, and in the meantime, I'm going to call Walz's ranch manager again. If I connect with him, I'll ask him to come in for a conversation. You want to sit in?"

"Absolutely."

The fact that she hadn't heard back from Titus Steele yet was not unusual. Many people would be surprised how little effort their fellow citizens would exert to assist law enforcement, even with something as simple as returning a phone call in a timely manner. And there was a certain percentage of the general public who resisted any interaction with the police under any circumstances, purely out of fear or paranoia.

Marlin and Lauren agreed to touch base later, and Marlin got comfortable again on the couch. He began his research by copying one of the numbers off the list and doing a Google search. It was a pizza place in Marble Falls.

The second number wasn't as quickly identifiable. Only 58 hits, but most of them were click bait for websites that would claim to offer detailed information on any phone number you wanted to enter. All of those sites wanted to charge a fee, and then you'd get almost nothing for it. The ninth hit listed led to an old ad on Craigslist—the Austin edition—from six months earlier. Someone had offered a clothes dryer for sale. Marlin clicked the link, scrolled

past a photo, and read the text:
Whirlpool Electric Dryer
Heavy Duty
Extra Large Capacity
4 cycles
3 temperatures
Auto Dry
Timed dry
Air Fluff
Call anytime and ask for Avery.

"You gotta remember, there ain't many of these beauties left on the road. And I sunk a hell of a lot of money into it myself—body work, fresh paint, rebuilt the tranny, new tires, and about a dozen other things. Now it's a sweet ride. Reliable. Only reason I spent that kind of dough was 'cause I was gonna keep it for myself. But then my wife changed my mind for me."

"So how much're you asking?" Billy Don said.

"Thirteen nine ninety-nine."

"Jesus H. Christ," Red said.

"Worth every penny," the salesman said. "AC blows colder than my mother-in-law's heart."

"Why not just say fourteen grand?" Red said. He was starting to realize that all salesmen—even the honest ones—played stupid games.

"Well, that's a good—"

"I'll give you ten thousand in cash," Billy Don said.

The vehicle in question was a Ford Ranchero. Not just any Ranchero, but one that had previously been owned by Red's cousin, Shelby Roach. Shelby had disappeared a few months back after he and his girlfriend tried to rustle some cattle and she ended up dead. So did a bull. In fact the body of the girlfriend was found under the body of the bull. Weird, but that was exactly the kind of craziness Red expected out of Shelby.

It didn't stop there, either, because the girl's crazy meth-dealing brother decided he needed to kill Shelby, and either he had done exactly that, or Shelby had high-tailed it to parts unknown. Bottom line was, Shelby's Ranchero ended up abandoned and the county impounded it. Then the car dealer bought it at auction and fixed it up. Looked damn good. Engine sounded strong. Stronger than Red's old truck, if he was being honest. Red and Billy Don had both noticed the Ranchero parked on the lot just a few weeks earlier, and Billy Don had talked about checking it out. Red wasn't interested. Any vehicle previously owned by Shelby likely carried some kind of hex. But that wasn't stopping Billy Don.

"Ain't no way I can go that low," the salesman said. "The paint job alone cost me—"

"Don't matter what it cost," Billy Don said. "Only matters what the vehicle is worth. I say it's about ten grand. I checked the book value online."

"I appreciate what you're saying," the salesman said, "and I might could come down to thirteen even, but that's about all I can—"

"You probably got it off the county for five hundred bucks," Billy Don said. "A thousand, tops. Then you spent four or five thousand on it, and now I'm offering ten. You'll make an easy four grand, which'll probably be your best sale of the month."

Red was impressed. Billy Don was doing a hell of a negotiating job. But it was going to be strange if Billy Don suddenly owned a vehicle. For years, Red's truck had served as the only means of transportation for the both of them.

"I'll take eleven thousand," the salesman said. "That's the drive-away price—tax, title, and license included."

"Ten-five," Billy Don said.

"Deal. Let's go inside and get it done."

When the salesman turned, Billy Don gave Red a wolfish grin that seemed to say, *Joseph Lightfoot, I am coming for you.*

What now?

Marlin had learned the number for Avery—Sean Hudson's girlfriend—but he didn't have her last name. None of the other hits on the phone number provided any further information.

He tried a search for "avery" and her phone number, without the area code, and got nearly 4,000 hits. Not helpful. He couldn't wade through all of that, and the handful of pages he checked were totally unrelated to his search objective, such as a part number for an air conditioner that could be ordered from a company in Avery, California.

He tried the number again, this time with the area code, along with "avery." That narrowed it down to roughly 700 hits, but when he scanned the first 30 or 40, he found again that the hits weren't relevant. It was all just unrelated nonsense.

He sat for a moment and thought. What could he do to find Avery's last name? They'd have it soon enough, after they served her cell carrier with a warrant, but how could he learn it before then?

Of course, he could simply dial the number and talk to her, or leave a message—but it was too soon to do that. Before they spoke to her, or anyone else on the list of numbers from Hudson's records, they would want the best possible advantage they could have, which meant obtaining every available scrap of information on that person. A good interviewer spent at least as much time researching a person as questioning him or her.

What if Avery had a criminal history? It would be good to know that beforehand.

What if she had been the last person to see Sean Hudson alive? Had she also been in Blanco County the day Hudson had died? The location data for her cell phone might provide some promising clues. The answers to these questions, and others, would impact how they would approach her.

Marlin was certain Lauren or one of the deputies must've already checked Facebook, but it would only take a few minutes, so he logged on and looked for Sean Hudson. There were, of course, lots of Sean Hudsons, but Marlin narrowed it down by putting "sean hudson texas" in the search bar—and there he was.

Hudson's profile, however, had the tightest privacy settings available. Marlin couldn't see any of his posts or even his friends list. He could see Hudson's cover photo and the resulting four comments, but none were from a woman named Avery.

Marlin went back to the search bar and entered "avery marble falls texas," and he got three resulting names from it, but he was able to rule all three women out. One was fourteen years old, one was about sixty and married, and one had a last name of Marble, rather than being from the town of Marble Falls.

He entered Avery's phone number into the search bar, but got nothing. That didn't mean she wasn't on Facebook. She might not have provided her phone number when she signed up, or she provided it but opted to keep it private.

Marlin moved on to another phone number on the list. A Google search revealed that it was the number for the pharmacy inside the Marble Falls HEB grocery store. Perhaps Sean Hudson had a medical condition that required him to refill prescriptions regularly.

The next number was the landline for the surveying company that employed Hudson on a part-time basis.

The number after that was Jeremy Shumway, the bicyclist. He and Hudson hadn't spoken in nearly three weeks.

The following number on the list generated the same useless come-ons from caller-identification websites. Marlin could tell from the prefix that it was a cell phone. He returned to Facebook, plugged the number into the search bar, and wasn't sure what to think when he saw the result.

Jordan Gabbert. The stoned kid who liked cinnamon rolls.

Marlin hadn't recognized the number because he had only called it once. Interesting. Gabbert had said that he and Sean Hudson had grabbed a beer a couple of times, but they "weren't tight"—so why had he called Hudson eight times in the 30 days before the murder? That was more calls than Marlin would expect from a casual co-worker.

Marlin called a back-door number to the sheriff's office and spoke to Darrell, the dispatcher on duty, and asked him to run a criminal history on Gabbert. Fifteen minutes later, Darrell called him back. Gabbert was clean.

16

"Something occurred to me," Red said.

"What's that?" Billy Don said.

They'd stopped at El Charro for breakfast tacos. They were sitting in a booth with a window looking out on Highway 281.

"Now that you've got your own wheels, you won't need me to tote you around anymore."

"Yeah, I know. That was the point."

"So you can go off and do whatever you want."

Billy Don grunted with a full mouth.

"Or chase whoever you want," Red added.

Now it dawned on Billy Don what Red was saying. He started shaking his head, clearly disappointed, and then he said, "So you're gonna bail on Miss Shirley?"

"Just because I don't want to chase that stupid meat man, that means I'm bailing?" Red said. "How is that bailing?"

"It's bailin' bigger'n shit," Billy Don said.

A well-dressed tourist couple at a nearby table glared at them.

"Why won't you listen to me?" Red said, lowering his voice a little. "The easiest solution is to pay Miss Shirley back yourself, if you're that concerned about it."

"That ain't right."

"Why not?"

"I already told you—it's the principle of the thing."

"Since when do you have principles?" Red said.

Billy Don gave him the look that said he wasn't in the mood for jokes, and that Red was walking on dangerous ground.

"Whatever," Red said.

Billy Don stared out the window.

"Mope if you want," Red said, "but just because you—"

"Holy crap," Billy Don said, rising from the table and rushing toward the door.

Red glanced outside and saw a gray Tacoma with a freezer in the back driving past.

Titus Steele had gotten up at sunrise to repair a stretch of fence on the north property line, and when he took a break, he checked his phone and saw that someone with an unfamiliar number had left a voicemail.

Mr. Steele, this is Chief Deputy Lauren Gilchrist with the Blanco County Sheriff's Office. I believe your employer, Doctor Walz, might've explained why we'd like to speak with you—just a few quick questions. Please call me back at this number as soon as you can. Thank you.

Titus played the message four more times, listening closely for any clues in the deputy's message. Was he a suspect? He couldn't tell. Her tone of voice was neutral. Businesslike.

What now? Call her back? She'd been right that Dr. Walz had explained what the deputies wanted, but Titus had decided to wait and see how persistent the deputies were. He'd been hoping they'd just go away. After all, it was just a routine part of their investigation, according to what they'd told Dr. Walz. They were chasing a lot of leads. But not so many that they'd forgotten about him. He'd have to call the deputy back, but he could put it off until later.

Instead, he dialed a different number—and was sent straight to voicemail.

He said, "Hey, it's me. Listen, the cops came out and talked to my boss, and now they want to talk to me. I'll handle it, but in the meantime, probably better if you don't show your pretty face around here for a while. And don't be surprised if they show up on your doorstep, either. We already talked about that. You have nothing to tell them, right?"

Then it occurred to him, better late than never, that the voicemail he was leaving might not always remain private. Stupid of him to just now realize deputies—or even a jury—might hear it someday. Fortunately, he hadn't said anything disastrous.

So he added, "Maybe they'll be able to find out what happened to Sean. Sure hope so. We deserve to know. Hope you're doing okay. I'll talk to you later."

As Titus hung up, he noticed that his hands were trembling slightly. He'd have to do something about that.

Red managed to jump into the Ranchero just as Billy Don squealed out of the parking lot—but after 15 minutes of searching, they hadn't spotted the Tacoma. Red had offered his opinion that the Tacoma had probably continued south on the highway, leaving town, but Billy Don had chosen to stay in Johnson City, going from parking lot to parking lot, in a semi-methodical hunt for the gray truck. Red felt odd riding in the passenger seat as Billy Don drove, but he could get used to it. Let Billy Don start coughing up more for gas. Make him do all the driving. It was about time.

"You ever see the movie *American Graffiti*?" Red asked.

Billy Don didn't answer. He was too busy winding his way among the vehicles parked in front of the Super S grocery store. Actually, it was a Lowe's Market now, but Red still thought of it as the Super S. Probably always would.

Red said, "Richard Dreyfuss was chasing after this blond hottie in a T-bird, and he kept catching glimpses of her car, but he couldn't ever catch up. Kind of reminds me of you and this guy."

Billy Don didn't reply. Too focused on his search. Now he was driving over by the Subway Sandwiches and the Dollar General. He was looking left, then right, then left again.

"Think about it," Red said. "He was probably knocking on doors all morning, and then he came into town for something to eat, and then he was going back to work. If you'd just gone straight down the highway instead of poking around, maybe we would've—"

Red's head snapped backwards as Billy Don suddenly gunned it, heading for the parking lot exit. He whipped a hard left onto the highway, but then took another immediate left, into the Roadrunner RV Park.

"Jeezus Christ," Red said. "You drive like Jeff Gordon—if he had a stroke."

Obviously, Billy Don had seen something from the parking lot next door, but there was a low metal fence that separated the two lots. He'd had to go around. Now he was progressing slowly down one of the park's narrow lanes, where RVs were parked at an angle in tight slots, with an occasional car or truck squeezed in between two RVs.

Red realized there was a chance Lightfoot could be living here temporarily. He couldn't live out of his truck, right? And paying for a motel every night would be too expensive. And an RV would be a great place to store a large inventory of frozen meat.

Billy Don tooled past several RVs, and then the front grill of a gray truck came into view. It was a Toyota Tacoma, tucked between a small single-axle travel trailer and a much larger fifth wheel trailer. Billy Don stomped the brakes.

"Is there a freezer in the bed?" Red asked. The rear window was tinted too darkly to see through the cab of the truck, and the RVs on either side had prevented a direct view.

"Get out and look," Billy Don said.

But before Red could open his door, an elderly man with a potbelly exited the travel trailer, stepped over to the Tacoma, and opened the driver's side door.

"Good God, ol' Lightfoot has aged a lot since yesterday," Red said. "Hardly even looks like the same guy. I feel sorry for him."

The old man got whatever it was he needed out of his truck, and then, on his way back into the trailer, he paused on the steps and gave a friendly wave—one that seemed to say, *Are you looking for somebody?*

"Well, aren't you gonna get out and kick his ass?" Red said, while he smiled and waved back to the old man. "Look at him. That dude is asking for it."

"Shut up," Billy Don said as he hit the gas.

Marlin had Googled the remainder of the numbers—with little success—when Lauren called.

"We might've just caught a break," she said.

"How so? Titus Steele?"

"No, I haven't heard back from him yet, but I got a call from a man in Kerrville who runs a website where he buys and sells Indian artifacts. He got an email from a man yesterday wanting to sell a couple of pieces, and when he saw the pictures, he knew he had seen them before. Long story short, the man who runs the website—his name is Abel Woerner—is also a member of that Facebook group where Sean Hudson sold some of his items. Members of that group had been gossiping about Hudson's murder, so when Woerner got the email, of course he started wondering who this person was that had those items now, and how did he get them?"

"Legitimate questions," Marlin said. "And who sent the email?"

He was wondering if it might be Jordan Gabbert, or even the girlfriend Avery.

"Sean Hudson's landlord," Lauren said.

Rodney Bauer had always been a Chevy guy, but he was starting to lose faith. After his encounter with the meat salesman the day before, Rodney had finally managed to replace the damn starter in his damn truck, but it still wouldn't start. Damn it.

Time for a Ford? Maybe. Hell, even if he ended up with a Ford that gave him as much trouble as this Chevy, he had a friend in Dripping Springs who loved working on Fords. Had a complete shop, too, with a lift and everything. Give him a case of Lone Star or a bag of homemade jerky and he'd help you out. Bargain.

Rodney was getting ahead of himself. Wasn't quite time to ditch the Chevy. Maybe he could get it running again.

Late the previous afternoon, he'd taken Mabel's car into town to buy a new battery for his truck. Rodney had been convinced the battery was fine, because he'd replaced the battery less than two years ago, but maybe he'd gotten a dud. At least this would be an easy fix, if it did turn out to be the battery.

Rodney hoisted the fresh battery out of the car trunk and carried it to the side of the garage, where his Chevy still sat. He set the battery on the ground, then opened the driver's-side door so he could pop the hood.

Then he stopped.

Something wasn't right. What the hell was it?

He stood there and simply stared at the interior of his truck for a moment. Took him a full 30 seconds to figure out the problem.

Holy crap.

His .44 Magnum was missing.

17

His name was Desmond Langman. Burnet County native. Fifty years old. Manager at a tire store. Married for 18 years. One kid in high school.

Langman's recent record was clean, but eight years earlier he'd been charged with theft by check, and seven years before that, he'd been charged with public intoxication.

He had converted his detached garage into a small apartment several years earlier, and Sean Hudson had lived in the apartment for the past fourteen months, now being two months into a renewed one-year lease.

Of course, the deputies had spoken to Langman several times after Hudson's death, asking various questions about his tenant, but they hadn't had any reason to view him as a person of interest until now.

Langman showed no surprise when he opened his front door, because Lauren had called him an hour earlier to arrange the meeting. He was perhaps six feet tall, with thin brown hair and a barrel-shaped torso. He smelled of cigarettes. He was dressed in cargo shorts and a plain blue T-shirt.

"Morning!" he said, addressing Lauren. Then he turned to Marlin and extended his hand. "Desmond Langman."

"John Marlin. I'm the state game warden in Blanco County."

"A game warden? Interesting."

He invited them in, and they sat on an L-shaped couch in a comfortable living room.

"Glad you caught me on my day off," Langman said. "What's up? Any progress on Sean's case? Oh, hey—you want any coffee?"

It was hard to tell if he was nervous or just a little hyper by nature.

"None for me," Lauren said.

"I'm fine," Marlin said.

"Okay, what's up?"

Lauren said, "Mr. Langman, how well did you know Sean?"

"Not super well. I mean, obviously, we had some interaction, me being his landlord, but that was about as far as it went. He had his own place over there."

"How often would you see him or talk to him?"

"Like I said a few days ago, maybe once or twice a week. But it was usually just a wave."

Now that Langman was a suspect, Lauren would ask a lot of the same questions they'd asked him earlier and see if his answers remained consistent.

"Y'all weren't what you'd consider friends, then?" Lauren asked.

"Not really, no."

"You wouldn't get together for dinner or a few beers—that sort of thing?"

"No. There was the age gap, and honestly, I probably wouldn't want to be friends with any of my renters, because then what happens if a problem comes up? Hard to evict a friend, you know?"

"Was Sean a decent renter?"

"For the most part, yeah. He was a few days late on the rent a couple of times, but no big deal. He always came through with it."

"So you didn't have any sort of ongoing problem?"

"Oh, absolutely not. He was a good tenant, and I don't mind saying I'm a good landlord."

"Any other problems beyond the late rent? Loud parties? Damage to the apartment?"

Langman shook his head. "Fortunately, no. We always worry about that with a young, single guy. But he was hardly ever around, which made him the perfect tenant. You probably already know that he was very active—always out doing something."

Lauren said, "Apparently Sean had been seeing a woman named Avery. Did you ever meet her?"

"I didn't, no, but he rarely had anyone over, male or female. However, there were several times when his car was gone all night, so I assumed he was out doing all the things young guys like to do."

"Like spending the night with a girlfriend?" Lauren said.

Langman grinned. "Right."

"And you don't recall him mentioning a woman named Avery, correct?"

"No, but I don't recall him mentioning *any* girl's name, or any of his friends' names, for that matter. We just didn't have those kinds of conversations."

Langman's characterization was falling right into line with what Marlin had heard from other people.

Lauren said, "Are you by chance an artifact collector?"

"You mean like Sean was, with the arrowheads and all that?"

"Exactly."

"No, that was never my thing. That might be the one topic where Sean and I had a conversation longer than a few sentences, but it was mostly him talking, because I just wasn't that interested. And I really don't have time for hobbies. I usually work 50 to 60 hours a week. The tire game can keep you pretty busy."

The tire game. Marlin couldn't tell whether Langman was being facetious.

"Did you ever see any of Sean's artifacts?" Lauren asked.

Marlin noticed that Langman now had a twitch or tic under his left eye.

"Oh, sure, once or twice," Langman said. "I'd be outside when he'd come back from digging, and so he'd show me what he found that day. I really couldn't keep all of them straight. They all looked like arrowheads to me. And how does he know how old they are just from looking at them?"

"Do you know if Sean ever made his own arrowheads?" Marlin asked. It was a good question to keep Langman off balance. Plus, it would be good to know.

Langman said, "I have no idea. I didn't even know you could do that, but if the Indians could do it..."

"Did Sean ever give you any of his arrowheads? Or sell them to you?" Lauren asked.

Now she was going right at him, and this was the kind of question that Langman should've been able to answer without the slightest hesitation. But he hesitated. It was just a split second, but he hesitated. That's what happened when you had to decide which answer would be more appropriate, rather than simply telling the truth.

"He didn't," Langman said. "As far as I remember."

"Wouldn't you remember if he gave you an arrowhead?" Marlin asked, playing the skeptic.

"You know, really, I might not. If he handed me an arrowhead one day and said I could keep it, I'd probably stick it in a drawer and never think about it again."

Langman was painting himself into a corner. He didn't know what they already knew.

"Would you remember if he gave you, say, five or six artifacts?" Marlin asked.

A longer pause this time. Langman opened his mouth, but nothing came out. His twitch had gotten worse. Finally he said, 'I'm sorry, but what is this all about?"

Marlin gave him a look that said, *Come on, you know the answer to that.*

He said, "You know a man named Abel Woerner?"

"Who? Abel?"

Langman's face had gotten red.

"Abel Woerner," Lauren said. "He lives in Kerrville."

"I don't think so."

There was no mistaking the fact that Langman was lying. Was he covering up a simple theft, or was he a murderer?

Lauren glanced at Marlin, which indicated that she wanted him to continue leaning hard on Langman.

"Mr. Langman," Marlin said, "I want you to think carefully about this situation and some unnecessary problems you might be creating for yourself. What I mean by that is, we have reason to believe that you contacted Abel Woerner in Kerrville by email and offered to sell him some artifacts that belonged to Sean Hudson. We've seen copies of the emails, which were in your name, and if it comes down to it, we can get a warrant and nail down the IP address of the sender. That will identify you further, whether you sent the emails from home or a computer at your tire store. IP addresses are very specific. They lead directly to an individual computer."

Marlin let that sink in for a moment.

Then he said, "What we don't know at this point is why you have those artifacts in your possession and whether you have the authority to sell them. For instance, did Sean give them to you? If that's the case, that's fine, but we need to know that right now. On the other hand, if you took them without permission, either before or after Sean died, I understand why you'd want to cover that up, but if you do, you'll really be putting yourself into a tough spot. Think about it from our perspective. Sean was killed, and suddenly you're trying to sell some of his artifacts. How do you think that looks? If you were in our shoes, running the investigation, wouldn't that make you suspicious?"

Marlin waited for a response, but Langman didn't give one. He was shaking his head slowly and looking down at the carpet.

"Mr. Langman, can you tell me how you came to be in possession of those artifacts?" Marlin asked. "I promise you, now's the time to talk. Don't let it get any worse than it already is. We can work with you to limit the damage. Our chief concern is finding out who killed Sean Hudson, not the theft of a couple of arrowheads."

Langman remained silent.

Marlin said, "Mr. Langman, you need to work with us. Can you explain why you attempted to sell some of Sean Hudson's artifacts?"

Finally Langman lifted his head and looked Marlin in the eye. "I can, yes," he said. "And there was a good reason for it. I'll tell you everything. But before I go any further, I want to talk to a lawyer."

"Thoughts?" Lauren asked when they were back in her vehicle.

Marlin said, "I'd say he stole the artifacts, either before or after Sean Hudson died, but he had nothing to do with the murder. Problem is, he's too scared to talk."

"That's what I was thinking," Lauren said. "And I'm guessing his lawyer will want to cut a deal real quick. Langman admits he stole the pieces, maybe gets probation, and then he can talk freely to us."

"That'll be a lot to ask for, considering the only way we'll benefit is being able to rule him out."

"He mentioned a good reason for having those artifacts," Lauren said. "What do you wanna bet Hudson was behind on his rent? Then Langman rationalized stealing and selling some of those pieces."

"We should check Hudson's bank records and see if he normally wrote checks to Langman, and if so, when was the last one?" Marlin said.

"Think Langman took the laptop, too?" Lauren asked.

"Wouldn't surprise me. It would be a great break if we could get our hands on it. Who knows what we might learn."

"That's his bargaining chip right there," Lauren said. "His lawyer will want him to skate on the theft in exchange for the laptop. I just hope he didn't—"

Lauren's phone—in a mount on her dashboard—rang. "Hang on. That's Titus Steele calling back," she said. "I want to pull over for this."

The fresh battery worked, and now Rodney's truck was running again. But the pleasure of that small victory was diminished by his missing .44.

What now?

Rodney had been mulling it over while installing the battery.

Obviously, any normal person would call the sheriff's department and report the theft. They might even be able to lift some fingerprints from the door handle or somewhere inside the truck.

But Rodney wasn't any normal person, because he was married to Mabel. If he reported the theft, Mabel would have to know about it, too. Which meant Rodney would never hear the end of it.

What kind of idiot leaves a handgun in an unlocked truck?

Why do you need to carry a gun in your truck, anyway? Think you're gonna be some big hero?

Don't even think about replacing it. You already have too many guns anyway.

Was it worth it? Hell, no. Not even close. Rodney decided he'd just take the loss and move on with life.

18

When Red was six or seven years old, his father brought home an enormous treat for Clyde, their hyperactive mongrel of indeterminate breed or origin.

"That there's a femur from a cow," Matt O'Brien said proudly, after he tossed the bone into the yard. "Should keep him busy for a while. Maybe stop him from licking his balls all the time."

The bone reminded Red of something he might see in *The Flintstones*. It was at least a foot and a half long, as big around as a baseball bat, and it flared into a bulb at either end.

Clyde carried that bone around for a solid month, gnawing on it for hours every day, until he broke a couple of teeth and his gums began to bleed. And he kept gnawing after that. He wouldn't stop until Red's dad took it away and hid it in the garbage.

Now Red realized Billy Don wasn't Richard Dreyfuss in *American Graffiti*. He was Clyde with the bone. It was kind of funny, though, since Billy Don was hunting a meat salesman.

Right after they'd gotten back from the fiasco at the RV park, Billy Don had spent a few minutes in his room, and then he'd taken off in his Ranchero, saying he'd be back after a while. Red knew it had to do with Billy Don's obsession, and Red had been tempted to talk some sense into him. But the truth was, Red was enjoying some peace and quiet for a change, having the trailer to himself. He could look forward to more of the same, now that Billy Don had his own wheels.

So now, after a long nap, he was about to watch another one of those shows where they were building an enormous tree house. Red was hoping to pick up some tips on the load-bearing capacity of oak limbs. Was there a formula? A certain amount of weight based on the diameter of the limb? Something like that? Did the age of the tree matter? What about the species? Did the numbers change during a drought or a hard freeze, when a limb might be more prone to snap? Red was knowledgeable about building almost any structure known to man—except a tree house.

Of course, just as Red got settled in, he heard the Ranchero coming up the hill.

A minute later, Billy Don came through the front door carrying a Keystone Light in his left hand and a satchel of some sort in his right. He sank into his regular spot on the sofa, opened the satchel, and placed a laptop computer on top of the cable-spool coffee table.

"Now we're gonna get somewhere," he announced.

"Jesus H. Christ," Red said. "You got that just so you could keep searching for that dude?"

"I can afford it," Billy Don said. "Five hundred bucks. Bought it used from a lady up near Round Mountain."

Red let out a scoff. "You know I ain't no computer genius, but it's not like you can just push a few buttons and figure out who he is. Even I know that."

"Yeah, but just about everything is on the Internet in one form or another. The answer is out there somewhere. The trick is finding it."

"Well, in that case, it probably won't take you more than a year or two," Red said.

Billy Don pushed a button and the computer started up with a loud chime. "Pardon me for dragging you into the 21st century," he said.

Red let out an even louder scoff. "It's the 20th century, genius. That's why the year starts with a two and a zero."

Billy Don looked at Red, started to say something, but then simply shook his head.

"Mr. Steele?" Lauren said.

No reply.

"Mr. Steele, hello?"

Lauren had it on speakerphone. Marlin could see the front of her phone in the dash mount and she had a strong signal.

"Mr. Steele?"

The call ended abruptly.

Lauren reached out and punched a button to dial Steele's number. The ringing sounded clear and strong, and so did the voicemail greeting when it kicked in. Lauren left a message: "Mr. Steele, it's Chief Deputy Lauren Gilchrist calling you back. Guess we got disconnected. Please call me again as soon as you can. I'll be waiting to hear from you. Thanks."

She hung up and looked at Marlin with a skeptical expression.

"Ducking us?" Marlin said.

"Sure feels that way."

She jumped back onto Highway 281 and headed south.

A moment later, she said, "By the way, I overruled you and asked Ernie to call Trinidad, Colorado, about Cody Brock."

The pause afterward told Marlin he wasn't going to like what he heard.

"And?"

"That assault wasn't so simple after all. The deputy who took that call remembered it well, and what happened was, Brock got into an argument with a man in the next room of the flea-bag motel where he'd been staying for a couple of months. It got physical, and Brock ended up knocking the man unconscious. Then he picked him up and heaved him over the railing—this was on the second floor—and the victim landed on the hood of a car below. Ended up with a fracture in his neck. The deputy said the reason for the argument was that the victim had seen Brock's girlfriend walking around with a bruise on her face. He'd heard shouting matches from their room before and figured Brock had smacked her around. So then he called the sheriff's office, but the girlfriend said she'd slipped in the bathroom and hit her face on the sink. Next time Brock saw the neighbor outside, that's when they got into it."

Marlin nodded but remained silent.

"Figured you'd want to know," Lauren said.

"Yeah, I did. I do. Thanks."

"Also, I called Nicole this morning when I found out."

"I appreciate that."

"And I called the New Mexico Meat Company," Lauren said. "At a minimum I want to let his boss know what kind of employee they've got on their hands. Then again, they probably already know. That's the kind of person those sleazy outfits hire."

They drove another mile.

Marlin didn't like what he had learned. Sounded like Cody Brock was the type to hold a grudge, and to settle that grudge when he had a chance. Marlin had encountered those types plenty of times, and it had never ended well.

He tried to think positive. He knew that Nicole would've taken the information in stride. But she also would have taken appropriate measures. She was probably wearing her .38 on her hip at this moment, or carrying it concealed, and she would use it, if necessary. She had no patience with men like Cody Brock. Or women, for that matter. And she knew how to handle herself. But that didn't stop Marlin from worrying.

"Besides, like you said earlier, he's probably halfway to Arkansas by now," Lauren said.

Titus Steele was parked in his favorite spot—high on a hill above the river—with a can of beer in one hand and a bottle of pills in the other.

He'd been dealing with high blood pressure for several years, although he wasn't convinced his doctor knew an ass from an elbow. In fact, it was his opinion that most of the medical "problems" that plagued your average Joe were nothing but bullshit designed to sell medicine or let doctors pad their bills.

High cholesterol? Bunch of crap. Humans evolved from cavemen, who ate meat. That meant Titus could eat all the bacon and brisket he wanted. It was basic biology. End of story.

Erectile dysfunction? For god's sake, either get a boner or don't get a boner. If your junk wasn't cooperating, maybe the woman you were with wasn't all that hot, or maybe you were a secret homo.

The list went on and on. Watch a football game and you might see a dozen different ads telling you to ask your doctor about this or that.

Regardless, Titus's doctor had badgered him enough about his blood pressure—warning him about a possible stroke or aneurysm or whatever—that he'd finally given in and taken the meds, and there was no denying he'd felt better since then.

There was a side benefit, too, according to the way the doc explained it. This pill that Titus took three times a day—something called a beta blocker—made it easier to deal with anxiety by reducing the effects of adrenaline on the body. That's why some performers used it to prevent stage fright. It kept your heart from pounding. No tremor in your voice. No sweaty palms. Ever since Titus had been taking it, he'd noticed that he wasn't necessarily any less likely to get pissed off or worked up, but he didn't *feel* it as much when he did. Weird.

Then, later, Titus came up with a great reason to pop an extra pill or two every now and then. Deer hunting. Take enough beta blockers and goodbye buck fever. Didn't matter if a 12-pointer walked out of the woods, Titus's heartbeat would remain slow and steady, and his hands didn't shake. It was a goddamn miracle of medicine, is what it was.

Titus decided there was no reason the beta blockers wouldn't work equally well when he talked to the cops. After all, he was going to have to deal with them sooner or later, right?

So he took two extra pills, gave them an hour to kick in, then called that female deputy again.

19

Fifty-year-old Hank Middleton had just finished cleaning his shotgun when he heard a knock on his front door. Unusual. Middleton owned 27 acres on a quiet county road, with a closed gate out front, which meant people didn't just knock on his front door. Except maybe the game warden every now and then, because Hank had a tendency to interpret the hunting laws somewhat loosely.

He rose from the table in the kitchen and walked into the living room, carrying the shotgun with him, now with one in the chamber and two in the tube. The top half of his front door was glass, and through it Hank saw a man standing on his porch. Young guy. Tall. Lean. Longish black hair. Wearing boots, jeans, and a denim shirt with a logo on the left breast. A gray truck was parked in front of the house.

Hank opened the door with an expression on his face that said *I sure as hell didn't expect anybody on my porch.* "Help you with something?"

"I think I can probably help you," the man said, smiling, and he launched into a sales routine about meat he was selling. Hank could hardly believe his ears. A steak salesman? That was just weird.

Before the man could finish his pitch, Hank said, "How'd you get on my property?"

"Sir?"

"Did you open my gate?"

"No, sir. It was already open."

"Hell if it was."

The man's smile faded. "I didn't open the gate."

"Well, do me a favor and close it on your way out, then," Hank said.

"Just trying to make a living," the salesman said.

The shotgun was hanging loosely from Hank's right hand.

"Nothing wrong with that," Hank said, "but don't ever open a gate unless you was invited. Just some friendly advice."

"Already told you I didn't open the gate."

"Now you're just lying," and he could feel his face warming with anger. He raised the shotgun and cradled the barrel in his left arm. Not a threat. The gun wasn't aimed at the salesman. Hank was simply making it clear that he wasn't fooling around.

"You always answer the door with a 12-gauge?" the salesman asked.

"Getting ready for dove season," Hank said. "But it comes in handy at other times."

"You prepared to use it?"

"You're trespassing," Hank said. "Get off my property."

"Or what?" the salesman said. He didn't budge. Hank could see that the man's posture had changed. His body was tense. Like he was ready to make a sudden move. How had this situation escalated so quickly?

Hank took one step backward. That would give him more time to react if the salesman did something stupid. Hank believed wholeheartedly in a man's right to defend his home—but did he really want to shoot some guy who was simply trying to sell some meat? Nope. A burglar, sure. But a trespassing salesman?

"Second warning, as required by law," Hank said. "You're trespassing and I'm asking you to leave."

The salesman chuckled. "Maybe instead, just for fun, I'll take that shotgun away from you. How about that?"

Hank swung the shotgun around and aimed the barrel directly at him. He was still angry, sure, but now there was some fear in his belly, too—because what if the salesman rushed him and Hank didn't have the guts to shoot? This was getting out of control.

"Your move," Hank said, daring him, because he had to, right? What sort of country would this be if people like Hank were intimidated by young punks?

Then, finally, thankfully, the salesman blinked first, in a manner of speaking. He raised his hands in a placating manner and gave Hank an unconvincing grin. "Man, I was just messing with you. You Texans are so uptight. Answering the door with a shotgun in your hand just blows my mind. Anyway, hang on, I've got something for you."

"I don't want nothing," Hank said.

But the salesman had already turned and was walking to his truck. Hank noticed for the first time there was a freezer in the bed of the Tacoma.

"Just take off," Hank said more loudly, stepping out onto the porch.

"Hang on," the salesman called over his shoulder. "Got a free set of steak knives."

Hank didn't know what to think about this guy.

The salesman opened his truck door, leaned in, and emerged with something in his hand, and Hank was wondering why the man had had a sudden change of heart.

And then Hank understood all too well, because the salesman wasn't holding a set of steak knives, he was holding a handgun, and as he wheeled and began to raise it, Hank realized he had already lifted his 12-gauge and braced it against his shoulder. The salesman almost had his handgun level when Hank pulled the trigger, too flustered to even aim well.

The shotgun boomed, followed a microsecond later by the roar of the handgun.

An hour after he and Lauren arrived back in Johnson City, Marlin got a call about a missing hiker at Pedernales Falls State Park, but by the time Marlin reached the park, the man had been located. The hiker had wandered off the marked trails and gotten lost for about an hour. He said he'd been too embarrassed to call for help, and he hadn't realized anyone had reported him missing.

Later, while Marlin was driving west on A. Robinson Road back to town, Lauren called.

"Titus Steele is ready to sit down and talk," she said.

"When and where?"

"My office, tomorrow morning, ten o'clock. Can you make it?"

"Absolutely. How did he come across?"

"I could tell he was wanting to do it by phone—to get it out of the way—but overall he was cooperative. I think he's a long shot, to be honest."

Marlin turned right on Highway 281, then took a left on Highway 290. Time to make one of his regular driving loops around Blanco County. It had been several days since he'd made the rounds, and it was good for him to remain visible throughout the year, not just during the prime hunting and fishing seasons. Poachers didn't pay much attention to legal seasons.

"Well, maybe we can at least rule him out," Marlin said. "That in itself would be progress."

"Stop with the positive outlook," Lauren said. "You make the rest of us look bad."

Marlin laughed. "If only you knew," he said, because he was still worrying about Nicole. He'd called earlier and discussed the situation with her, and that had helped him feel better for about an hour. But he kept picturing Cody Brock tossing someone over a second-floor motel railing.

The truth was, Marlin had always been fiercely protective of his friends, family, and other loved ones—sometimes to the point of imagining problems or threats where none existed. He was aware of his tendency to worry unnecessarily, but what about the times when there was a legitimate cause for concern? For instance, not long ago Nicole had donated a kidney to a woman who likely would have died without it, and while Marlin admired Nicole to no end for her compassion, his apprehension about the surgery created perhaps the most stressful period of his life.

"Why don't we meet at nine?" Lauren said. "So we can figure out how we're going to approach him."

"Works for me," Marlin said, and he noticed a gray Toyota Tacoma moving eastbound, toward town. As it passed in the oncoming lanes, Marlin checked the bed of the truck. No freezer. He hadn't been able to read the plate or get a good look at the driver through the tinted windows. Just another gray Tacoma. There were plenty of them on the road.

"You there?"

"Sorry, what?"

"I said I'll see you in the morning."

"Sounds good."

They hung up, and Marlin made a U-turn. Couldn't help himself. The Tacoma was now out of sight, so Marlin gave his truck plenty of gas and had it up to 90 before he had to slow down at the city limits. He followed a hunch and went south on 281. As he curved around the merge lane, he caught sight of the Tacoma just passing the Hill Country Inn.

Marlin had to yield for an eighteen-wheeler, but then he got into the left-hand lane and sped up to catch the Tacoma, which was now a thousand yards ahead, passing the entrance to Lowe's Market.

Waste of time, Marlin was thinking. *But it doesn't hurt to check, does it?*

Marlin goosed the gas again, but by then the Tacoma was taking a left into the Roadrunner RV Park.

Marlin slowed a moment later and made the same left. The Tacoma was easy enough to find, parked in a slot beside a small travel trailer. Marlin cruised past the front bumper slowly, and just as he'd expected, the plate didn't match. Waste of time.

An elderly potbellied man climbing out of the truck gave Marlin a friendly wave.

20

Red had a love/hate relationship with technology, such as his off-brand Korean cell phone. On the one hand, there was no denying it came in handy at times. For instance, Billy Don could hide near the entrance to a particular ranch and warn Red if the owner or the game warden pulled in while he was hunting on the place. Yeah, okay, you could do that with walkie-talkies, too, but walkie-talkies didn't allow you to look at pictures of bikini models while you were sitting in the deer blind, which was another big plus.

On the other hand, Red couldn't help but feel that embracing modern gadgets and gizmos was somehow betraying what it meant to be a small-town Texan. Could you imagine Sam Houston carrying a Kindle around back in the day? Or what about Bob Wills using an iPod? How about Audie Murphy—the most decorated U.S. soldier of World War II—wearing one of those Bluetooth thingies in his ear? Ridiculous. Would never happen. Those legends would probably think today's Texans were no different than a bunch of damn Yankees. Maybe they were right, and that thought made Red sad. Everybody was the same nowadays, or close to it. And it had all happened so damn fast.

Wasn't that long ago that when you'd sit around a beer joint with friends, you'd talk about football or women or hunting or those damned Washington liberals. Nowadays you were likely to hear a bunch of rednecks talking about the latest smartphone or bitching about the lack of a good Wi-Fi signal.

Pathetic. How had it come to this? It left Red with an empty feeling inside.

That feeling got even worse as Red was sitting in his recliner—

minding his own business with a cold beer and some COPS reruns—and he received an email from Facebook informing him that a friend was inviting him to join up.

Oh, for fuck's sake.

Facebook? Really?

And the friend? William Donald Craddock.

Good lord. First Billy Don had gotten an iPhone, and now he was using Facebook.

"Billy Don!" Red shouted.

The big man had taken his new laptop into his bedroom about an hour earlier, because Red had bitched about the noise of his fingers tapping on the keyboard.

"Billy Don!"

Red knew for a fact that Billy Don could hear him at the end of the trailer.

"William Donald!"

"What?"

"Stop sending me crap from Facebook!"

No answer.

"You hear me?"

"What?"

"No more Facebook bullshit!"

Silence followed for a full minute. Then Red received another email, this one directly from William Donald Craddock himself.

The subject line read: *This is awsome.*

The message in the email read: *We shoulda joined facebook year's ago. But Im not just playing around. Gonna find that indian. You should sign up.*

Red couldn't stand it.

"Billy Don!" he yelled down the hallway.

"What?"

"No more emails!"

"I'm going to throw a topic at you," Marlin said. "You won't expect it. So brace yourself."

Nicole gave him a look like, *What on earth are you about to say?*

They were sitting in Adirondack chairs on the back deck, him with a beer, her with a glass of wine. It was still warm and muggy outside, but the ceiling fan overhead generated a nice breeze and kept the mosquitoes at bay. As usual, Geist had found a patch of sunlight in the grass and was lying in it on her side.

"Maybe it's time for us to start talking—in big-picture terms—about retirement."

She was surprised. No doubt about it. He could tell from her expression.

"I don't mean right away," he said. "Just some long-term planning. We've never even discussed it."

"We're way too young," she said. "And, well—"

"You're even younger than I am," Marlin said. "I haven't forgotten. It's obvious when we're in a picture together and I look like a cradle robber."

"I don't think that's true, but thanks."

"I'm eligible, you know," he said. "I have enough years in. We'd have enough to get by."

"What is bringing this up? You're not really ready for retirement, are you?"

"Not at all. That's why I said 'long-term' earlier. Just thinking, I guess."

"I know I'm not anywhere near ready, and I doubt I will be even in 10 or 15 years. I love my job."

"I know you do."

"You love your job, too."

Marlin didn't say anything.

"Don't you?" Nicole asked.

"Absolutely. Most of the time."

She turned to face him more squarely. "Tell me what's going on. This isn't just out of the blue."

Marlin took a big swallow of ice-cold beer and it tasted fantastic. Then he said, "Sometimes I'd just like to be home more, I guess."

Nicole knew as well as anyone that there were times when Marlin had to work 70- or 80-hour weeks. Even in the off-season, being a game warden wasn't just a job, it was a way of life that required an around-the-clock commitment.

But there was more than that to Marlin's comment, and Nicole knew it. Being away from home meant leaving Nicole alone.

"I'll be fine," she said.

He nodded.

She said, "Don't you agree that I have more reason to worry about you on a daily basis than you have to worry about me, considering that you regularly deal with armed people in the middle of nowhere?"

"I will grudgingly admit that."

"And you agree that I am fully capable of taking care of myself?"

"Without a doubt, but that doesn't mean—"

Marlin's phone rang, as if punctuating his point about the demands of his job.

The ring tone told him it was someone from the sheriff's department. He checked the screen and saw that it was Lauren.

He answered, and she immediately said, "Sorry to bother you this late, but can you interview Titus Steele by yourself tomorrow morning? In fact, you might even need to take the lead on that case, if you can. I'm going to be tied up for a while."

"Sure. What's going on?"

"You know Hank Middleton?"

"Not well, but yeah, I know him. I've had to keep an eye on him over the years."

"Well, about an hour ago, a friend of his found him shot to death on his front porch."

21

The following morning, Marlin made Titus Steele wait for 20 minutes inside the small interview room. Let Steele get tense—if he had reason to be tense. Let him worry—if he had reason to worry. And if he didn't, the 20 minutes would be nothing more than a minor annoyance.

Marlin entered at 10:20, introduced himself with a smile, apologized for being late, and then offered coffee.

"No, thanks," Steele said. "I only get one friggin' cup a day. Doctor's orders."

"Oh, yeah?" Marlin said, sitting down across from Steele. "Why's that?"

Steele had a ruddy complexion and deep lines around his eyes and mouth. Not enough sunscreen over the years. He looked strong enough to handle any ranch chore, despite a sizeable belly. He wore a Stetson, blue jeans, and a tan short-sleeved work shirt with a Carhartt tag on the pocket.

"High blood pressure," Steele said. "Got it under control, but damn, it can just about ruin your life. I'm talking about the diet and all that crap. Gotta take it easy on Mexican food, barbecue, anything with salt in it. Jesus, what I'd give for a big plate of chicken-fried venison with gravy, mashed taters on the side."

"You can't have any of that?" Marlin asked.

"Well, moderation is the key, or so they tell me. Can't drink six or eight cold ones watching football on a Sunday. Know what my doctor says? Two. Two beers a day. Might as well not even bother, know what I mean?"

This was a fantastic start to the interview. Normally it was up to the interviewer to try to build a rapport with the interviewee. If you could make a positive connection, most subjects would then provide longer, more detailed answers to your questions. Making the subject feel at ease was key, because even the most outgoing person could be intimidated—and less willing to talk—when having a conversation with a law enforcement officer. That tendency could be even worse if the subject didn't like the interviewer, or if he felt that he was being accused of a crime, even if that wasn't the case.

But Steele didn't appear concerned or anxious at all. At the moment, his body language showed him to be relaxed and comfortable.

"Two beers a day?" Marlin said. "How long have you been dealing with that BS?"

"About three years."

"Man, I feel for you. Surely you say to hell with it every now and then."

"Damn right. Life's too short to listen to a bunch of doctors all the time."

"I hear that. My doctor is always griping at me to get more exercise, but the truth is, I just don't have time for it. Meanwhile, he's about 30 pounds overweight, so I'm guessing he hasn't done a sit-up in years."

"What a hypocrite," Steele said.

"No kidding. On your high blood pressure, is that hereditary or what?"

"I think it can be."

"You have any brothers or sisters?"

"One of each."

"Where are they located?"

"My sister is up in Denver and my brother moves around a lot. He used to be in the military."

"Oh, yeah? Which branch?"

"Army. Four years and out. Never left the States."

"Were you in the service?"

"I never was, no."

"Where are you from originally?"

"Small town in west Texas called Buffalo Gap."

"Oh, sure, up by Abilene," Marlin said.

"Exactly."

"Cool little town. I love the steak house."

"You talking about the new one or the old one?"

"I guess the old one. It had a German restaurant next to it?"

"Right. Deutschlander Garten. The original steak house closed down a long time ago, but I hadn't been there in ages. I left Abilene a few years after school and haven't been back much since."

"What year did you leave?" Marlin asked.

He took careful note of Steele's nonverbal behavior as the ranch foreman tried to remember the year. Steele's eyes went upward and to the left. "I guess that was '92," he said. "My memory isn't the greatest."

"Wait 'til you're my age," Marlin said, grinning.

He continued with the small talk for another ten minutes—asking all sorts of background questions—until Steele finally said, "Dr. Walz said you're wanting to ask some questions about a dead trespasser or something?"

Still no change in Steele's demeanor. Comfortable. Relaxed. Making eye contact.

"That's right," Marlin said. "Last week a young man was killed and dumped on a ranch in the northern part of the county. Of course, in a situation like this, we check all sorts of things, and most of them turn out to be unrelated. But if we're lucky, somebody can provide a key piece of information that will help us figure out what happened. That might even be you."

"I'll help if I can," Steele said. "But I don't know much about it. Was it like a hunting accident or something?"

"You're wondering that because I'm a game warden, right? No, I'm just helping the sheriff's department with the investigation—something I do from time to time."

"Okay, I gotcha. So how can I help?"

"Let me start by asking if you recognize the name Sean Hudson."

"I do, yeah, from the news stories," Steele said. "I've heard his name a couple of times on the radio."

"But you never heard his name before that?"

"Not that I know of."

"You never met him?"

"I don't think so."

"Did Dr. Walz tell you about Sean Hudson's connection to his ranch?"

"He did not. What sort of connection?"

"He was on the survey crew last year out on the ranch."

"Oh, yeah?"

"Him and three other men."

"So that means I probably did meet him at some point," Steele said, "because I ran into that crew once or twice. Earlier, when I said I'd never met him, I didn't know that I had."

"I understand," Marlin said. "Obviously there's no way for any of us to remember every person we ever met."

"Right, and I don't know if I ever even caught his name. I couldn't tell you the names of any of those guys now. Like I said, my memory sucks."

Titus felt pretty good about the interview so far. His voice was smooth and steady. He wasn't hemming or hawing. He didn't sound defensive or reluctant to speak.

"But you ran into them once or twice?" the game warden asked.

Titus had practiced his answer for just this type of question, and he was fully prepared.

"Out on the ranch, yeah," he said. "I always like to introduce myself to anybody that comes out, especially workers. Make sure they know somebody's always around. It's a security issue."

"Smart," Marlin said.

Titus couldn't believe they had a game warden handling a murder case. How dumb was that? This guy was lobbing softballs instead of asking tough questions. Titus would be out of here, and in the clear, in no time.

"It's not like I make a point of saying I'm always watching the place, but I drop hints to that effect," Steele said. "I figure that's part of my job. That way nobody thinks they can sneak out later and do a little hunting or whatnot."

"You run into many trespassers?" Marlin asked.

"Now and then. A few."

"What are most of them doing out there?"

"Poaching," Steele said. "But they usually say they didn't know they was trespassing, or they got mixed up and went to the wrong ranch, or some bullshit like that."

Marlin shook his head, like *Can you believe those people?* He said, "How do you handle 'em?"

"Kind of depends on their attitude," Steele said. "Usually I just tell 'em to hit the road."

"And they do?"

"Yep."

"You ever have to get a little more aggressive with them?"

Steele frowned, puzzled. "Get aggressive how?"

"Well, you know, like maybe have to talk tough with them. Tell them you're about to call the cops. Anything like that?"

Steele shifted in his seat and sat up straighter. "Maybe I had one or two give me some lip, but in general, they just leave. They're happy to get out of there without any trouble. I've never had any of 'em come back."

Marlin nodded. "I run into the same type of thing. Maybe I catch someone who doesn't have enough life jackets on board, but I decide to let them off with a warning. They're generally happy to take off, if I let 'em."

Steele laughed. "Yeah, I would imagine so."

"You ever catch anyone out there looking for arrowheads?" Marlin asked.

And here we go, Titus thought.

Now they were getting to the heart of the matter.

But Titus had expected this, too. After all, Sean Hudson was an artifact digger, and the cops—even a game warden—would know something as basic as that.

"Oh, sure, yeah," Titus said. "This is a great area for arrowheads and all that shit. I've spotted a couple of decent ones sitting right on top of the ground."

"Yeah? You got a nice collection?" the game warden asked.

"Oh, hell, no. I don't pick 'em up. Dr. Walz would be pissed. He always wants me to leave 'em right were they are."

"So you aren't tempted to grab even just one?" Marlin asked. His tone of voice suggested this would be a little secret between him and Titus, but Titus wasn't going to fall for it.

"Nope. Wouldn't risk my job over a rock."

"I don't blame you. Hey, did Sean Hudson ever ask you about hunting for arrowheads on Dr. Walz's ranch?"

Titus Steele's eyes went down and to the right. He appeared to ponder the question for a second or two. Then he said, "Boy, I sure don't remember anything like that. If he did, I don't recall it. But I can guarantee I would've told him no. Ain't no question about that."

"You wouldn't have even passed the request along to Dr. Walz?"

"There wouldn't have been any point," Steele said. "He would've said no, without a doubt. If anyone's gonna do any digging out here, it's gonna be him. That's why he hates the wild hogs so much—they tear up the soil, which ruins what they call the context. Pigs're as bad as looters in some ways."

Looters. Seemed odd that Steele would use that word. Maybe he picked it up from Walz.

"Has Dr. Walz done any digging himself?" Marlin asked.

"Not much. Weird, huh? Him being an archeologist and all."

"Do you know if he had any contact with Sean Hudson or anyone else on the survey crew?"

"Let me think about that," Steele said. His eyes moved down and to the right again.

Marlin wasn't an expert on interrogation, but saying something like *Let me think about that* was typically an attempt to buy time and think about what the answer *should* be, as opposed to the truth.

"I don't think he ever did," Steele said.

"Actually, he told us he had a conversation with Sean Hudson one day about central Texas artifacts," Marlin said. "At least that's what I have in my notes."

"Oh, wait," Steele said. "That's right! I'd forgotten about that." He laughed. "See what I told you about my memory. I remember them talking about arrowheads for a few minutes."

Marlin smiled and nodded along. Only problem was, Marlin had made it up. Walz had never mentioned having a conversation about artifacts with Sean Hudson.

22

Hank Middleton's best friend was a man named Frank Talley, who, understandably, was distraught over Middleton's death.

"Gonna kill the son of a bitch," Talley said for the third time, referring to Middleton's as-yet-unknown assailant.

And for the third time, Lauren Gilchrist said, "Mr. Talley, I really need you to stop making statements like that. Just let us do our job, okay? We'll find the person who hurt your friend."

Right now, Lauren didn't have much confidence that her claims were true. Middleton had been found dead on his porch from a single gunshot to the chest. His 12-gauge shotgun was found near the body, indicating that some sort of confrontation had taken place. But what? With whom?

Henry Jameson, the crime scene tech, was still at Middleton's house, but so far, he had found nothing of value. No shoe prints or tire prints in the caliche. Deputies were currently questioning neighbors to see if anyone had heard or seen anything suspicious—unlikely in an area where homes were hundreds of yards apart and most people minded their own business.

Lauren wondered how John was doing with Titus Steele in the interview room next door.

"Hurt him?" Talley said in response to Lauren's last comment. "The son of a bitch kilt him. And for what? Hank didn't never bother nobody."

"From what I understand, Hank occasionally shot deer on land that wasn't his."

"Well, yeah. A few times."

"And I don't mean to be insensitive, but from what I gather, he had several affairs with married women."

"Wasn't none of them unwilling, though."

"Plus he routinely got into fistfights in beer joints all over Blanco County."

"Aw, that was mostly just a bunch of good ol' boys fooling around."

"Last time he broke a pool stick over a man's head."

"Only 'cause that dude slept with Hank's girlfriend. What kind of man does that?"

Lauren almost laughed, but she managed to hold it in. She said, "Other than the enemies he might've made from the activities I just mentioned, can you think of anyone who would want to harm Hank?"

Talley didn't answer for a long moment. Then he shook his head and said, "Gonna kill that son of a bitch."

Red was comfortable in his recliner when he felt and heard thunder, and then he realized it wasn't thunder, it was Billy Don rumbling down the hallway toward the living room.

"Meat man!" Billy Don yelled, and he stopped for a moment by the front door to pull his boots on. "The meat man is still here!"

Red almost let out a groan of disappointment.

"He's over in Mucho Loco right now!"

"Hell, if he's knocking on doors in Mucho Loco, he's likely to get his ass handed to him."

The populace of that particular rural subdivision consisted primarily of ex-bikers, anti-government zealots, and white separatists.

"I'm going anyway," Billy Don said.

"I'm not coming," Red said.

"Don't care," Billy Don said. "I'll handle it myself."

"Like I said, I'm not coming."

"Better that way."

Red let out a sigh. He was so tired of this meat man business. On the other hand, if there was going to be a brawl, Red didn't want to miss the action. "Okay, I'll come, but only if you promise we give up if we can't find him this time."

"Ain't promisin' nothin'," Billy Don said. He reached for the doorknob.

"Well, goddamn," Red said, popping his recliner upright. "Just hang on a second while I grab some beer for the road."

It was not uncommon for an interview subject to lie or exaggerate or mislead, even when he or she had nothing to do with the crime that was being investigated. Is that what Titus Steele had done?

Marlin sat in his small office within the sheriff's department and simply pondered what he had learned. There were several possibilities.

Steele might have lied because he was worried that Walz was somehow involved in the murder of Sean Hudson, and he wanted to make it appear that any interaction between Walz and Hudson was casual and insignificant. So he played along, saying he remembered them "talking about arrowheads for a few minutes."

But was Steele smart enough to understand the implications of the fictitious conversation, and to decide, on the fly, to lie about it? Marlin hadn't seen anything that would make him think Steele was particularly intelligent or cunning. And would Steele be willing to provide cover for his boss? Didn't sound like they had that type of relationship. Plus, lying to a law enforcement officer could get Steele charged with making false statements or even obstruction of justice.

Marlin woke his computer and began to make some notes about the interview.

A more likely scenario: Steele himself had something to do with Hudson's murder, and he hadn't wanted to admit that Hudson ever had any reason to return to the ranch after the land survey. But when Marlin improvised about the alleged conversation between Walz and Hudson, Steele wanted to appear fully aware of it. *Oh, that? Sure. No big deal. I remember them talking about arrowheads.* That sort of attitude.

But wait. Now Marlin had a different thought.

What if there really had been a conversation between Walz and

Hudson about artifacts?

Walz and Steele might very well have agreed to lie about it, even if neither of them had had anything to do with Hudson's murder. Marlin could imagine Walz saying something to Steele like, "We both know we weren't involved with the murder, so why even mention that conversation? It would only distract the cops from finding the real killer."

That kind of rationalizing happened all the time. Problem was, it could have the opposite affect. Instead of preventing the cops from being distracted, the lies could be more distracting than the truth. What was the truth in this situation? Marlin had continued to push Steele as far as he had dared, talking for an additional 30 minutes, but he had learned nothing more from it.

However, the results of the interview had convinced Marlin that it was time to call the number for Avery, Sean Hudson's girlfriend. He had been on the fence about calling her—adhering to the idea that it was better to know all you could about your subject prior to an interview—but now he felt that the potential benefits outweighed the risks. Perhaps Avery had talked to Sean Hudson about Walz or Titus Steele. Maybe she could fill in some blanks.

Marlin dialed her number. She answered on the third ring.

Red had his right arm braced on the dashboard. "Christ, slow down."

Billy Don didn't reply. Just kept driving with a determined and possibly homicidal expression on his face. In other words, the same as the last two times they'd gone looking for the meat man.

Red tried to sip from a Keystone Light tall boy, but he spilled half of it down his chin as the Ranchero squealed around a curve.

"I said slow down!"

Billy Don was in a world of his own.

They were on A. Robinson Road, now less than a mile to the entrance—the only entrance—to Mucho Loco.

"Smartest thing to do is park near the gate and wait for him to leave," Red said. "Because if you go looking for him, we might miss him."

"I ain't no idiot," Billy Don said.

But sometimes your reasoning skills fall a little short, Red thought. He said, "Just don't let things get out of hand. You wanna get Miss Shirley's money back, sure, and maybe kick this guy's ass, but don't, like, put him in the hospital, okay? You don't need the legal hassles. *We* don't. Just 'cause he ripped some people off don't mean it's open season to give him a beat-down. Not legally."

Billy Don began to ease off the gas as he approached the entrance.

"You hear me?" Red said.

"Unfortunately."

"You know what I think, Billy Don?"

"I rarely do."

Billy Don began to turn left through the rustic stone columns that constituted the entrance to Mucho Loco.

"I think you're taking this thing way too personal. Dude's just trying to make a living."

"Yeah, by ripping off old ladies! Are you serious?"

"What if he didn't even know the meat was bad?" Red asked.

The road into Mucho Loco was a narrow caliche lane with brush growing right up to the sides. They'd need to drive until they could find a decent spot to hang out and wait—maybe somebody's driveway or a place where the brush gave way to an open grassy area.

"Course he knew the meat was bad," Billy Don said. "Otherwise he woulda called us back."

It was a valid point, so Red said, "Not necessarily."

"Here comes somebody," Billy Don said.

And sure enough, there was a vehicle in the distance, roughly 100 yards away. Gray. Looked like a truck.

"Gotta be him," Billy Don said.

At 50 yards, there was no doubt it was a truck. But was it a Tacoma?

At 30 yards, yes, they could verify it was a Tacoma.

At 20 yards Billy Don said, "It's him. Same license plate."

Red noticed for the first time that Billy Don had a Glock semi-automatic handgun tucked between his thighs. A nine-millimeter, it looked like. Another new addition with their newfound wealth.

But it was too late to ask about it, because they were almost nose to nose with the Tacoma, and Billy Don decided to swerve diagonally across the road and try to block its path.

Joseph Lightfoot didn't even flinch. He immediately swung off the road and drove right over several small cedar trees as he went around the Ranchero's back bumper, then jumped back onto the road.

By the time Billy Don made a three-point turn and went after Lightfoot, the Tacoma was out of sight, leaving nothing but a thick plume of dust in the air.

Billy Don gunned it hard, and Red braced himself against the dashboard again.

With each curve, Red could feel the rear tires beginning to slide, but somehow, Billy Don kept it under control. A quarter mile later, there was the Tacoma, just reaching A. Robinson Road, where it turned left, heading east, away from town.

By the time Billy Don reached A. Robinson and turned left, a little sedan had passed and was now between the Tacoma and the Ranchero.

"We're gonna get screwed again," Red said. The sedan was going the speed limit, whereas the Tacoma was well ahead, going at least 80 by now, making a quick getaway.

Trying to pass on this curvy stretch of road would be downright suicidal, so Billy Don got right behind the sedan and began flashing his headlights and laying on his horn. The sedan pulled to the shoulder and let them pass.

Billy Don stomped the gas again, and Red was impressed with just how well the Ranchero responded. Over the next two miles, Billy Don slowly closed the gap between the Ranchero and the Tacoma, until they were 150 yards behind Lightfoot.

Then Lightfoot made a mistake. Understandable, since he wasn't from this area.

He took a hard right—into a ranch entrance. As with most ranch entrances, the gate was set back from the road a considerable distance, so a truck and trailer could pull in and stop at the closed gate without the tail end of the trailer sticking out onto the road. Lightfoot obviously had not seen the gate and had probably mistaken the driveway for a county road.

"Got him pinned in," Billy Don said, opening the driver's-side door with the Glock in hand.

"So you're gonna shoot the guy?" Red said.

"If I have to." He had his left foot on the ground now.

"He's probably got a gun, too," Red said.

Billy Don paused. "You think?"

"Wouldn't you, if you were a traveling salesman?"

That made Billy Don think for a minute, wondering what to do, and while he hesitated, Lightfoot eased his truck up to the gate and began to push it with his front bumper. His rear tires began to spin on loose caliche.

"The fuck is he doing?" Billy Don said.

Red said, "If there's not a lock on the chain, that gate's gonna —"

And just then the chain gave way and the gate abruptly swung open.

"Like that," Red said.

Lightfoot sped through the open gate, leaving the Ranchero behind. Billy Don jumped in, slammed his door, and the chase was on again.

23

"Is this Avery?" Marlin asked.

"Who's this?" Her voice was tentative. Suspicious. Maybe even afraid.

"My name is John Marlin. I'm the game warden in Blanco County."

She didn't reply. There was a lot of noise in the background, as if she were driving with the windows down, or standing somewhere windy.

"Is this Avery?" he repeated.

"What's this about?" She still hadn't acknowledged that he had reached Avery.

"It's about Sean Hudson," he said. "I need to ask you a few questions."

"I don't understand what you want," she said.

"Avery, can I get your last name, please?"

"What for?"

"Ma'am, is there a reason you don't want to give me your last name?"

"Because I don't know who you are. I'm supposed to believe some random guy on the phone? You could be anybody."

"Fair enough," Marlin said. "I'll give you the number for the Blanco County sheriff's office and you can call me back here."

He did, and they disconnected, and he figured he would never hear from her again. But Darrell routed her call through just a moment later.

"Thanks for calling me back," he said.

"My last name is Kingsberry," she said.

The background noise was gone, as if she had just parked or entered a building.

"Thank you," Marlin said. "Has anyone contacted you about

Sean?" There was still the possibility she didn't know Hudson had been murdered.

"About him being killed?" she said.

"Yes, ma'am," Marlin said. "I want to offer you my condolences and to let you know I'm helping the sheriff investigate his death. I'm hoping you and I can sit down and have a conversation very soon. Are you free this afternoon or sometime tomorrow?"

"But I don't know anything about it. I don't see how I could help."

"Well, sometimes people have information that's useful and they don't even know it. If we could talk for—"

"All I know is that someone killed him," she said. "I don't know who or why."

The resistance on her part was almost palpable. Marlin had to resist the temptation to infer too much from that. Many people were reluctant to talk to the police during a murder investigation for fear that the murderer might target them next if they shared any information.

Marlin decided that asking questions right now, on the phone, would be better than no interview at all.

"I understand that it's all very upsetting," he said. "Right now, we don't have a suspect, so we need cooperation from his friends and family if we're going to figure out who did it. I was told that you and Sean were dating. Is that accurate?"

"I don't know if I'd call it dating," she said. "We went out a handful of times. He was a good guy and everything, but I didn't really know him that well, and I don't think I can help you. I'm about to go into work, so I—"

"When was the last time you talked to him or saw him?"

"I can't do this right now," she said.

"When would be a good time to talk?" he said. "Tell me when you can meet and I'll drive up to Marble Falls."

"I don't *know* anything," she said, starting to show some irritation. "How many times do I have to tell you?"

"All I really need is a few minutes," he said. "What time do you—"

"Jeez," she said. "Can I make it any clearer? I don't have anything that will help you. Don't call me again."

The line went dead.

Cows are stupid.

Most people know that. You'd think a meat salesman, of all people, would know that, especially an Indian one. Maybe he *did* know that. Maybe what happened next was just bad luck.

As Billy Don gunned the Ranchero to catch up to the Tacoma yet again, Red could see, 50 or 60 yards in the distance, a cow standing in the middle of the ranch's driveway. The driveway was only about 12 feet across, so the cow was basically acting as a beefy roadblock.

Not a problem, really, because there was a flat grassy area on either side of the road—room to go around—and that's what Joseph Lightfoot decided to do, steering to the right, at a speed of roughly 40 miles per hour, which was way faster than Red would ever pass a cow.

Because in addition to being dumb, cows are unpredictable.

In this instance, the cow saw the truck coming, got spooked at the last minute, and decided to get out of the road. And, being stupid and unpredictable, the cow stepped directly into the path of the oncoming truck.

This all happened so quickly that Joseph Lightfoot had only two options.

Number one: Hit the cow. Not a good option.

Number two: Swerve harder to the right, farther off the road.

He chose the second option, obviously reacting on sheer instinct, not logic, because in that direction stood an oak tree. Not a big oak tree—no more than 12 inches in diameter—but that was more than enough to stop the Tacoma cold when Lightfoot slammed into the tree at full speed, hard enough that the rear tires rose off the ground.

"Whoa," Billy Don said.

"Damn," Red said.

Billy Don eased off the gas and gently came to a stop ten feet from the Tacoma's driver's door.

"He ain't moving," Billy Don said.

The airbags had deployed but were already deflating. Lightfoot was leaning forward, head hanging downward, his torso held in place by the seatbelt. The cow had wandered off.

Red simply stared at the Tacoma for a moment, watching, waiting. He figured it would probably be better for everyone involved if Lightfoot were still alive.

"Think we should haul ass?" Billy Don said.

"We can't just leave him," Red said.

"Sure we can."

"I've been on this ranch before. The owner lives in Austin and hardly ever comes out."

"What about it?"

Lightfoot still hadn't moved. He was either knocked out or already dead.

"If we leave him here, ain't nobody gonna find him for a long time," Red said.

"Sounds perfect," Billy Don said.

"He might be a grade-A sleazebag, but we can't just leave him here," Red said. "He might need a doctor."

"The son of a bitch almost killed Miss Shirley, 'member?" Billy Don said. "And who knows how many other old ladies he's ripped off or put in the hospital. Besides, if he's hurt and we leave him right where he's at, well, that must be what God intended, 'cause everything happens for a reason."

Billy Don didn't reference God often, but when he did, it was usually to justify some fairly questionable behavior on his part.

Red was just about to reply when Joseph Lightfoot—perhaps awakened by God himself—lifted his head and looked around, obviously in a daze, wondering what had just happened. Blood was flowing from his swollen nose.

Red was relieved. He felt the Ranchero shift and realized Billy Don had just opened his door and climbed out. The big man went around the front of the vehicle and approached Lightfoot's truck. Red had no alternative except to get out, too, because there was no telling what Billy Don might do if Red didn't rein him in. By the time Red reached the Tacoma, Billy Don was leaning down to Lightfoot's window, talking to him.

"The hell is going on?" Red heard Lightfoot say. "What happened?"

Red could smell coolant and he heard hissing. Lightfoot had

cracked his radiator.

"You done fucked up, pardner," Billy Don said. "That's what happened. What kind of asshole rips off little old ladies?"

"He okay?" Red asked.

"Loopy as hell, but he's gonna be fine," Billy Don said.

"Call my uncle," Lightfoot mumbled.

"Look at his nose," Red said. "Guess the airbag didn't work all that good."

Lightfoot reached up and touched his face. "Hell's going on?" he repeated. "Where's th' ambulance?"

"Yeah, I didn't say he *is* fine, I said he's *gonna* be fine," Billy Don said. Then he got excited and said, "Oh, hell, yeah. Check it out."

He leaned into the driver's side window—reaching past Lightfoot, into the space between the seats—and when he came back out, he had a .44 Magnum in his hand.

"Now we're talking," Billy Don said, stepping away from the Tacoma. "Look at this enormous sumbitch."

"My head hurts," Lightfoot said.

Billy Don aimed the big revolver at him and said, in his best Dirty Harry voice, "Go ahead. Make my day."

"Put it back, Billy Don," Red said.

"Bet I can sell it and get back every penny he owes Miss Shirley," he said, lowering it.

"You can't just take it," Red said.

"Why the hell not?"

Lightfoot was watching the conversation as if they were speaking in a foreign language.

"It's a felony, Einstein," Red said. "You really wanna commit a felony because of this guy? You gotta leave it."

"Where's my phone?" Lightfoot asked.

"Not in a million years," Billy Don said. "Gonna sell it."

"Sell a stolen gun? Come on, Billy Don. How dumb is that? You're asking for major trouble."

"That's funny coming from Blanco County's worst poacher," Billy Don said.

"Well, that just goes to show—if *I'm* saying it's a bad idea, then it's definitely a bad idea."

"Then maybe I won't sell it," Billy Don said. "Maybe I'll keep it for myself."

"Miss Shirley won't get any money that way," Red pointed out.

"I'll pay her myself. It's like I'd be buying this gun from her. It's not that complicated. We both win."

Now Lightfoot was trying to unbuckle his seatbelt, but he couldn't seem to figure it out.

"Just stay where you are," Red said to him. "You'll be all right." Then, to Billy Don: "Leave the gun and trash his truck instead. That'll make you feel better."

"Look at it," Billy Don said. "It's already trashed. Besides, this settles the score—the price he pays for being a dirt-bag thievin' bastard."

"Search the truck," Red suggested. "Maybe you can find somethin' to take instead of the gun. Somethin' untraceable."

Billy Don pointed at Red with his eyes wide. "Great idea, but if there's anything else, that's just gravy on top," he said. "Miss Shirley deserves a little extra just because this guy is a royal scumbag."

"But taking the gun is just gonna..." Red trailed off, because Billy Don wasn't listening anymore. He was already going around to the passenger side of the truck. The door let out a painful metal-on-metal squeal when he opened it.

At least Red could take consolation in the fact that all of this silly bullshit with the meat man would finally come to an end.

He stepped around to the driver's window to check on Lightfoot. "He's out again. Oh, shit. He's bleeding from his ear."

"Not my problem," Billy Don said from the passenger side, where he popped open the glove box.

"That can't be a good sign," Red said.

"Here we go," Billy Don said, and he showed Red a bank bag he'd found. He unzipped it and let out a whoop.

"Cash?" Red asked.

"Big time," Billy Don said. "There's gotta be three or four grand in here."

"Bullshit."

"Would I bullshit about that?"

In contrast to the .44, Red wasn't bothered at all by the idea of taking the cash. After all, Lightfoot had conned it out of good people. Red figured he and Billy Don could return some of the money to Miss Shirley and other locals who had gotten ripped off, keeping a small commission for themselves, of course. But right now, they had other concerns.

"What're we gonna do about this idiot?" Red asked.

Billy Don didn't answer. Instead he leaned over the truck bed, right where it met the cab, and reached for something behind the freezer.

"What're you doing?" Red said.

Billy Don grinned and showed him the power cord for the freezer. Then, with one quick, powerful yank, Billy Don ripped the cord loose from the back of the unit.

Red grinned and said, "Well, I have to admit that was fun to watch."

"Thanks."

"But what're we gonna do about this idiot?"

"What do you mean?"

"Seems like we should call EMS or something," Red said. "He probably has a percussion."

"You're getting soft, Red," Billy Don said. "This asshole is lucky we don't finish him off and leave him for the varmints."

"He might die."

"Yep," Billy Don said.

Just then, Lightfoot lifted his head and said, "Where are we going?"

Billy Don came back around to the driver's side, reached through the window, and grabbed Lightfoot by the collar of his denim shirt. "Listen up, shithead. Get out of Blanco County. Hear me? This ain't up for debate."

"What?" Lightfoot said.

"Wasting your time," Red said. "He won't remember."

"Remember it!" Billy Don said, shaking him.

"He won't."

"Remember it!" Billy Don said.

"What?" Lightfoot said.

Billy Don gave a frustrated grunt and reluctantly let him go. "Let's get out of here," he said.

Red noticed that Billy Don was taking the gun *and* the cash, but he didn't have the patience to argue about it.

He took one last look at Lightfoot. It appeared the Indian might be okay. Maybe.

24

Now that Marlin had Avery's last name—Kingsberry—he could learn a lot more about her than he'd known before.

She was 23 years old.

She had no criminal record.

Her last traffic citation was two years earlier, when she'd run a stop sign.

She had originally received her Texas driver's license at the age of 19, indicating that she hadn't applied for one before that, or that she had moved to Texas from another state.

She owned an 11-year-old Chevy truck.

She had never been married.

She didn't own any real estate in central Texas.

No Facebook account. No Instagram account. No Twitter account. No social media presence at all, as far as Marlin could tell. Odd for a person her age. Of course, it was possible she used a screen name instead of her real name. Plenty of people did that, despite some sites, such as Facebook, requiring that you use your real name. How could they enforce that?

It was good practice to gather this sort of background on any person of interest, but none of the information was proving particularly useful.

Why had she been so resistant to his questions? Had she and Sean Hudson only gone out "a handful" of times, or was there more to it than that?

Right then, Darrell came over his phone speaker. "John, I've got Jordan Gabbert holding for you."

Chief Deputy Lauren Gilchrist was on her way to Hank Middleton's house—she wanted to take another look around the scene—when she received a call from Ernie Turpin, one of the deputies who had canvassed the area the day before.

"Just talked to Lenore Dalton," he said. "You know Lenore?"

"Haven't met her, but I know she lives to the east of Hank Middleton's place."

"Right. We missed her yesterday because she was in San Antonio overnight, but I left a card asking her to call me, and she just got home 30 minutes ago. Anyway, just before she left town yesterday, she stopped at her mailbox for a minute, and while she was parked there, she heard a vehicle coming down the road way too fast. There is a particular teenager who speeds on that road, so she was preparing to yell at him to slow down, but it was a truck she had never seen before. A gray Tacoma—and she says it was going at least 80. After it passed by, she saw a large white appliance in the bed. She thought it was probably a washing machine."

Turpin knew full well the significance of what Lenore had seen, because, like all the other deputies, he had been made aware of the aggressive meat salesman in a gray Tacoma with a freezer in the bed.

"What time was this?" Lauren asked.

"About 2:45, according to Lenore," Turpin said.

Lem Tucker, the medical examiner, had narrowed Middleton's time of death to a three-hour window between one and four o'clock.

"Did she get a look at the driver?" Lauren asked.

"Nope."

"A plate number?"

"The truck was going way too fast."

"She's sure it was a Tacoma? Maybe it was some other model of truck and it really was a washing machine in the back."

"Her son drives a Tacoma," Turpin said. "She said it was definitely a Tacoma."

Jordan Gabbert's eyes were clear and focused today. He was sharper. More alert. And obviously more nervous. No pot to calm him down.

"I need to tell you something, because you're probably going to find out anyway," Gabbert said.

Earlier, on the phone, Gabbert had asked if they could sit down and talk. Said he could make it down from Marble Falls in 30 minutes. Marlin had readily agreed, and now they were in one of the interview rooms, seated on opposite sides of the table.

"Oh, yeah?" Marlin said. Casual. Friendly. "What's up?"

"I don't wanna get in trouble, but it's something that might help you," Gabbert said. Instead of making eye contact, he was looking at the wall over Marlin's shoulder.

"Help me with my investigation?" Marlin asked.

"Yeah."

"Well, I would definitely appreciate that," Marlin said. "How exactly would the information get you in trouble?"

Gabbert took a deep breath. Marlin waited. He had an idea what was coming.

"I don't think it's a huge thing," Gabbert said. "And it isn't directly related to Sean's murder or anything like that. I don't know who did it. But it might help you figure out who did. I'm sort of hoping I can tell you what I want to tell you, without, like, incriminating myself."

Gabbert paused, but Marlin didn't say anything. Nervous people often filled the gaps on their own.

"Here's what I need to say," Gabbert said. "Sean sold me some pot a couple of times. Just a couple, and not very much." Another pause. Then he said, "I figured you'd want to know that."

Marlin nodded slowly. "You're right. That's helpful, and it says a lot about your character that you'd come talk to me about it. When you say 'a couple of times'..."

"Maybe three or four," Gabbert said.

"This was over the course of how long?"

"The past year or so."

"How much did he sell you each time?"

"Like half an ounce, or even less. Not a lot. It would last me for a long time, because I'm not a big smoker, you know? I smoked the other day because I was nervous about talking to you. I shouldn't have done that. I felt pretty stupid when you called me on it."

"We all make mistakes," Marlin said. "Thanks for being honest about it."

"Sure thing."

"Do you know if Sean sold pot to other people?"

"Honestly, I really don't know. But I started thinking that if he did, maybe one of those people had some sort of argument with him, or something like that."

"Are you thinking of anyone in particular?" Marlin asked.

"No, like I said, I don't even know if he did sell to other people."

"You think anybody else on the survey crew might've bought from him?"

"Probably not, because I don't think any of them smoke."

Marlin nodded again. "Did you ever tell anybody where you got your pot?"

If Gabbert had shared that information with the wrong person, that person might have been tempted to break into Hudson's place and search for pot, money, or both. And if Hudson had happened to catch that person in the act, the thief might've panicked and reacted violently.

But Gabbert said, "No way. I never told anybody. Sean asked me to be cool about it. He was basically doing me a favor. It wasn't like he was a big dealer or anything."

"So you're sure you never said a word to anybody at all?"

Marlin meant what he'd said about Gabbert's character—his willingness to come forward and share this new information—but that didn't mean Gabbert would be totally forthcoming and honest. Sometimes you had to pull the truth out of a person inch by inch, even when that person was trying to do the right thing.

"Not a soul," Gabbert said. "I swear."

"How would you generally reach him?" Marlin asked.

"How would I reach Sean?"

"Right."

"I'd usually text him."

"Did you ever call him?"

Would Gabbert's answer match the phone records?

"Hardly ever," he said, "although recently I was calling him more than I normally did, because my phone was screwing up and I couldn't send texts for a while. Finally got that fixed."

"How many times would you say you called him in the month before he died?" Marlin asked.

"Probably like six or seven," Gabbert said. "Most of those were me getting voicemail and hanging up. Sean was bad about returning calls. Texts, too. Sometimes he wouldn't get back to me at all."

The records indicated that Gabbert had called Hudson eight times in the month before the murder, so his answer was close enough to indicate he was being truthful.

"This is helpful, Jordan," Marlin said. "Thank you."

"It's no big deal. I should have told you all of this the other day."

"While I've got you here—do you recognize the last name Kingsberry?"

Gabbert thought about it, but shook his head. "I don't know that name."

"That's Avery's last name," Marlin said. "Avery Kingsberry. Still doesn't ring any bells?"

"No, sir. If it did, I'd tell you. I'm being straight up this time, I promise."

"I believe you."

"And I'm hoping you won't hold any of this against me," Gabbert said. "Buying the weed, I mean. I could lose my job."

"You're telling me everything you know?" Marlin asked.

"Absolutely. Every bit of it."

"Will you call me if you hear anything that might be helpful?"

"Yes, sir."

"Then we're good."

Miss Shirley's eyes opened wide when Billy Don thrust the wad of cash at her.

"What's this for?" she asked. Red thought she looked good, for an old lady. Fully recovered from the food poisoning.

"We found the meat salesman," Billy Don said, "and—"

"We got your money back," Red said. "Plus a little extra."

Billy Don glared at him for jumping in. "I sure did," he said. He pushed the bills into Miss Shirley's hands.

"My heavens," she said. "How much is here?"

"The amount you paid," Billy Don said, "plus—"

"An extra thousand bucks," Red said. "We insisted he should show some good faith for making you sick."

"*I* insisted," Billy Don said.

"Well, I don't even know what to say," Miss Shirley said, "except thank you. Is that legal, to make him pay extra?"

"Sure it is," Billy Don said. "To cover your hospital bills."

"My insurance covered that," Miss Shirley said.

"All of it?" Billy Don asked.

"Every penny."

"Well, then, you should take that money and buy yourself something special," Billy Don said.

"I will," Miss Shirley said. "I certainly will. How on earth did you track him down? He never called me back."

"I noticed a lot of people were talking about him on Facebook," Billy Don said, "and he was still in the area, so—"

"We found him over in Mucho Loco and talked some sense into him," Red said.

"I sure did," Billy Don said.

"You didn't get rough with him, did you?" Miss Shirley asked.

"No, ma'am," Billy Don said.

"No, ma'am," Red said.

25

When Marlin pulled up to his house early that evening, Nicole was on the porch, crouching beside Geist, with her cell phone in hand.

"I was just about to call you," she said when Marlin got out of his truck.

There was no mistaking the look of alarm on her face. He noticed she was holding Geist by the collar, preventing her from bounding off the porch to greet Marlin.

"She all right?" Marlin said, coming closer. Had Geist encountered a porcupine again? She'd gotten a small number of quills in her snout in the spring, but she was an intelligent dog and Marlin didn't expect a recurrence. He figured she'd steer clear of porcupines in the future.

"She's okay, but I want you to look at something," Nicole said.

Marlin ascended the steps, and now Geist was wagging her tail furiously, as she always did when he came home.

Marlin kneeled down and Nicole held the dog's head steady. Geist's left ear had a round hole in it. Smaller than the diameter of a dime, but larger than the diameter of a pencil. Not an insignificant injury, but it was already scabbing over and Geist didn't seem to be in pain. Marlin would guess that the injury had happened several hours earlier—probably that morning.

"Well, shit," Marlin said.

He knew they were thinking the same thing. It was a bullet hole. Marlin had seen similar holes in deers' ears when hunters had taken a head shot and missed.

"I guess it could be something else," Nicole said.

"Don't know what," Marlin said.

"Maybe she got it snagged on the barbed wire."

It wasn't likely, and Nicole knew it.

He looked at her. "You okay?"

She nodded. "Fine. Just a little shook up."

"When did you get home?" he asked.

"About 15 minutes ago."

He didn't ask if she'd seen anybody leaving their property or lingering in the area, because if she had, she would've mentioned it by now.

"Time for some security cameras around here," he said.

"Agreed."

"I'll talk to Phil about it tonight, and in the meantime, I'll put some trail cameras up."

Nicole studied the wound again, gently cupping Geist's head. "Poor girl. You okay?"

Geist thumped her tail.

"We should call it in," Nicole said.

"Absolutely."

Many women—and men—would have been in a panic by this point. Too frightened to think clearly or make rational decisions. Not Nicole. She was solid as a rock. It wasn't from her experience as a deputy, either. It was simply who she was. She was the type other people turned to in an emergency.

Now she simply said, "I'll make the call, and then I'm going to get some hydrogen peroxide to clean this up." She went into the house. "I don't think she needs to see a vet."

Marlin stood.

Had it been a wannabe burglar? Doubtful. Burglars rarely carried guns.

Stray bullet? All of Marlin's neighbors were responsible gun owners, and a bullet would have a difficult time traveling much distance through the cedars and thick underbrush.

No, the most likely scenario was the one that made Marlin the most apprehensive.

It had been Joseph Lightfoot, aka Cody Brock, making good on his threat to come back later.

The thought made Marlin's face and neck begin to heat with anger.

How would it have played out?

Geist was a friendly dog, but if a stranger appeared at the gate or trespassed onto Marlin's property, she would keep her distance, staying 20 or 30 yards away, barking. The closer the stranger got to the house, the more territorial Geist would become. She would retreat to the porch and begin to growl, refusing to let the stranger advance to the door.

How would Brock respond to that?

If he had any sense, he'd leave at least ten yards between himself and Geist, because a pit bull could move fast. Brock would want a buffer zone. So Geist would be on the porch and Brock would be 20 or 30 feet from the lowest porch step.

He'd probably call out to Geist in an attempt to pacify her, but it wouldn't work.

Brock would assume by this point that nobody was inside the house, but he'd start to worry about the commotion. Would the neighbors wonder why the dog was barking? Was this dog normally quiet? Was the barking unusual enough that it served as an alarm?

Regardless of the reason Brock had returned—whether it was to burglarize the place, or to commit vandalism, or to start a fire, or, God forbid, to confront Nicole again—Geist was ruining the moment.

So Brock would begin to get angry, just as he'd gotten with Nicole. He'd pull out his gun and take aim at Geist. But odds were good that Brock was not a skilled marksman. Most people weren't. Brock probably didn't practice regularly or even know how to hold a handgun properly.

So, when he fired the gun, instead of squeezing the trigger, he yanked it, and as a result, his aim was off by a couple of inches—and that meant Geist survived with a minor wound.

Just one shot, and then Brock had to turn tail and run away. That's what cowards did. Afraid of getting caught.

Marlin descended the steps to the yard and stood where Brock—or some other trespasser—would've been standing. Geist was still on the porch watching Marlin, and wagging her tail. From this spot, the shooter would've extended his arm straight outward. The bullet would've passed through Geist's ear and hit the wall behind her, no more than 18 to 20 inches above the porch.

Marlin climbed the steps again, then squatted down to study the lap-and-gap cedar planks running horizontally on the side of his house. There were natural imperfections here and there—mostly knotholes.

But there it was, two feet to the right of the front door itself. A bullet hole. Easy enough to miss if you weren't looking for it.

Geist was standing beside Marlin now, bumping against him, thinking it might be playtime.

Marlin rubbed her back. "Good girl. Gonna have to stay inside for a few days."

He stood and opened the door. Checked for a hole on the other side of the wall, inside the house. There wasn't one. The bullet had probably hit a stud. With luck, it would have held together well enough to provide some evidentiary value.

He called Darrell, the dispatcher, and asked for a deputy to be sent out, along with Henry Jameson. Best to do this by the book. Keep the chain of evidence intact.

Nail the son of a bitch.

Red was sitting upright in his recliner with a beer between his thighs and a notepad in his lap, in case he got inspired and needed to draw a sketch.

Now that he had watched a dozen episodes of those tree house-building TV shows, he realized he had to make some decisions—not just about engineering and construction, which was a hell of a lot more complicated than building on the ground, but about *concept* and *design*.

Fancy words, yeah, but all of the tree houses Red had seen so far were pretty damn creative. They weren't just boring wooden boxes in the air. Some of them looked like castles or ships or trains. Some were dome shaped, or had eight walls, or four stories. Red had even seen one that looked like a giant eyeball, or maybe it was the Death Star from *Star Wars*. Weird either way. He wasn't going to build anything that wacky, but he wanted his tree house to have some sort of meaning to it. Something that captured a little bit of his personality.

At one point, he got all excited, because he thought he'd totally nailed it. He'd build his tree house in the shape of Texas! How cool would that be? Then he realized it just wouldn't be practical, whether he built it vertically or horizontally. Too much wasted space.

Same thing if he built it in the shape of a deer. Or a deer rifle. Or a longhorn bull. Or an armadillo.

He drank from the can of Keystone Light, and then he wondered: *Why not make it look like a big can of beer?* That was too tacky, even for Red's tastes. It would look like some dumb publicity stunt. But hang on a second. Maybe that was a good thing. What if one of the big breweries would be willing to cover some of the construction costs in exchange for the publicity? Hell, he might even be able to get the tree house built for free. Red was getting pumped about that idea when Billy Don came rumbling down the hallway from his bedroom, carrying his laptop computer.

"Check this out," he said.

Red expected Billy Don to show him something about the meat man—maybe a news report about an accident on a ranch—but that wasn't what happened.

Billy Don stood at the foot of Red's recliner and turned the laptop around so Red could see the screen. Then he punched a button and a video began to play. A young woman with short blond hair was submerged in a river, and from the looks of her bare shoulders, she didn't have a top on. Then she stood up—the river was apparently only about three feet deep in that spot—and yeah, she was totally naked.

"Hellooo," Red said.

"That's what I'm talking about," Billy Don said.

The woman had a smoking-hot body—right up there with the best bods Red had seen on the Internet. Slender, without being all bony. Decent-sized hooters, too. Red had always been a boob man, though he was always reluctant to admit it whenever he was in mixed company. In today's world, you were supposed to admire a woman for her mind or her ambition or some such nonsense, and don't you dare sneak a peek at her rack, even if she was wearing a tight T-shirt. Fortunately, a woman on a computer couldn't catch you gawking.

Red kept watching as the woman began to walk out of the water, toward the camera. Her bottom half was naked, too. Yowser.

She reached the shore, where she had a towel draped over the low-hanging branch of a cottonwood tree, and she began to dry off.

Then she reached down to a small pile of clothes on the ground and began to put some panties on. They were plain beige panties, which was a letdown, but at least they weren't big and baggy. When she put her khaki shorts on, she had to sort of work her hips back and forth, pulling them up a little bit higher each time, and it was just an all-around pleasure to watch.

"Send me a link," Red said. This was a video he'd want to watch several times, even on the small screen of his cheap phone.

"It's not from a website," Billy Don said. "It was on the computer. Whoever owned it must've left it on there by accident."

"I was starting to think the river looked familiar," Red said. "I think it's the Pedernales."

"Yup," Billy Don said. "Somewhere 'round here."

"I'm not usually a fan of short hair," Red said, "but it looks good on her."

"Hell, that gal would look good bald," Billy Don said.

"She'd look good with missing teeth and a lazy eye," Red said.

"Who'd be looking at her face anyway?" Billy Don said.

Now the woman was putting her bra on, doing that thing women do where they clasp the bra in front, then spin it around. Then she lifted the straps onto her shoulders and took a few seconds to adjust her boobs and get them just right in the cups.

Until now, the woman had obviously been unaware that she was being filmed. But now she happened to glance in the direction of the camera and she said, "What're you doing? I told you to stop doing that." But there was a hint of smile on her face. Red suspected that she liked the attention.

A male voice said, "Can't help myself. Just look at you. You're a freakin' goddess."

"I don't need a bunch of videos floating around."

"They won't be floating around. Promise. Someday, when we're both eighty years old, you'll look at this and go, 'Wow, check me out. I was a total babe.'"

"You're sweet, but you need to erase it."

"Yeah, okay. Thought any more about Costa Rica?"

She looked right at him with an expression that said, *Come on, get real.*

"I'm serious," he said.

"We'd just go?"

"Why not? We'll have plenty of money."

"We don't have it yet," she said.

"But we will. And it doesn't have to be Costa Rica. Could be almost anywhere. France. Australia. Just pick a place."

"I wouldn't even know where to start," she said.

"Think about it. I'm up for it whenever you are."

He zoomed in closer on her torso and Billy Don let out a little grunt of approval.

"I know you are," she said with a little laugh. "You always are."

"Come over here," he said.

She knew what he was asking.

"Not on video," she said. "Turn it off."

The picture went all jiggly as he lowered the phone and stopped recording.

"Damn," Red said. "They did it right there by the river."

"Not bad, huh?" Billy Don said.

"She said 'a bunch of videos,'" Red said. "Did you—"

"Nope," Billy Don said. "That's the only one I could find."

"Play it again," Red said.

26

"Just think. Some warrior carved this spear point thousands of years ago. He probably sat under a tree somewhere along this river—maybe right over there—and worked on it all afternoon. He was an artist. A true craftsman. Now it's ours, and the edge is just as sharp as the day he created it. Isn't that totally awesome? It's a piece of history, dude—right here in our hands."

Titus didn't care about any of that shit. Wasn't it just as likely that some caveman handled one of the rocks in the riverbed? So what? It was just a goddamn rock.

"But what's it worth?" Titus asked.

"This one? Probably about a million dollars."

Wait a fucking second. That couldn't possibly be right. This little fucker was jerking Titus around. Joking or something.

"A million dollars?"

"Some warrior carved this spear point thousands of years ago."

"You already said that."

"Well, it's important to remember. Who cares about the money?"

"How are we gonna sell it?"

"Oh, we're not going to sell it. Didn't you hear me?"

"What? Why?"

Titus knew he should leave before something bad happened. All he had to do was open his eyes.

"That's not what it was made for. You want to know what it was made for?"

"I don't know what you're talking about."

"You never have, Titus. That's the problem. And you're always staring at Avery."

"So?"

"You think I don't notice that? How old are you, anyway? Like, forty?"

"Come on, now. I can't control the thoughts I have about her. You know how it is."

"You want to know what it was made for?"

"I don't even know what you're—"

Sean suddenly jumped at Titus, slashing downward with the spear point, and Titus could feel it slamming into the crown of his head—

—and now Titus bolted awake, sitting upright.

Heart pounding.

Sheets soaked with sweat.

He reached upward to remove the spear point that was lodged in his skull, knowing it wasn't really there, and of course it wasn't.

It had seemed so real.

He sat still for a moment and let the dream recede into his subconscious. The small TV mounted on the wall above his dresser was still on, showing some old movie starring George Kennedy. Titus always had weird dreams when he fell asleep with the TV on.

After a moment, he swung his legs onto the carpeted floor and stood up. Went into the bathroom and took a long, slow piss.

The dream hadn't meant anything. Just a strange dream, that's all.

He finished up, shook it, and flushed.

Went into the hallway. Stopped at the closed door on the right, the only other bedroom in this small house, which had been built during the Depression.

He knocked, got no answer, and opened the door anyway.

Cody was sprawled across the bed, still on top of the bedspread, just as Titus had left him hours earlier. If he had moved an inch, Titus couldn't tell.

Crazy fucking kid.

When Cody had called, he could hardly string a sentence together. Took Titus a good while to figure out where Cody was and what had happened. A run-in with a couple of local rednecks. Wrecked his truck and smashed his face on the steering wheel. Had a swollen nose, possibly broken, and probably a concussion. For a minute or two, Cody would make sense—but then he'd say something completely fucking nutty. At one point he'd called Titus

"Carey." Titus hadn't corrected him, because Carey was Cody's brother who had died seven or eight years ago in the oil fields.

Titus moved over to the side of the bed to make sure the kid was still breathing. Funny that Titus almost wished the answer was no. Might make things easier around here.

27

"Wanna hear something interesting?" Lauren asked over the phone.

"Always," Marlin replied.

A full day had passed since Nicole had discovered the hole in Geist's ear, and now it was late in the afternoon on Thursday.

Marlin had spent time that morning reaching out to game wardens and deputies in neighboring counties, hoping one of them might've encountered Cody Brock, or had heard about an aggressive meat salesman. No immediate leads, but they all agreed to keep eyes and ears open. After that, Marlin had simply driven for hours, all around Blanco County, highways and back roads, looking for a gray Tacoma. He had seen several, but not the one he was looking for. He had returned home dejected.

Now he was hoping Lauren had a break in the case.

She said, "Henry just called, and he's pretty sure the bullet he dug out of your door frame matches the bullet used to kill Hank Middleton."

Marlin stopped what he was doing—mounting a security camera in the eaves under his porch—and let that sink in. Phil Colby was on a ladder at the other end of the porch. The previous evening, when Marlin had told Phil what had happened, Phil had offered to run into Austin and buy the same security system he had installed at his place. Eight cameras total.

"Pretty sure?" Marlin said in response to Lauren's comment.

"Both of the bullets were beat up pretty good," Lauren said. "But Henry says there was enough left over from each that he could see similarities—enough so that he's about 90 percent sure of the match."

Marlin sat down on one of the nearby porch chairs. "If it *was* Cody Brock who shot Geist..."

"Then he's now a suspect in the Middleton homicide," Lauren said. "How's your pup doing, by the way?"

"Good. Thanks for asking."

Geist was stretched out nearby, in the Sphinx position, gazing out at the yard, or "surveying her queendom," as Nicole often put it. Her ear was going to be fine.

"At this point, to be honest, if it's Brock, I'm a little worried about what he might do next," Lauren said. "If he shot Hank Middleton on Tuesday afternoon, maybe now he figures, what the hell, he might as well go after someone else who pissed him off. Someone who wouldn't listen to his sales pitch, or who called him out for trespassing. So he came to your place yesterday morning or early afternoon."

Marlin agreed that there was cause for concern—but they also needed to keep in mind that Brock might've had nothing to do with either of the crimes. And, of course, there was the chance that Henry was simply wrong about the possible bullet match, in which case the crimes were likely unrelated. Maybe Brock was responsible for Geist's wound, but he hadn't shot Hank Middleton. Henry's 90 percent certainty was pretty solid, but the remaining 10 percent—meaning the bullets didn't match—was too significant to ignore.

Marlin hadn't replied, so Lauren said, "You doing okay?"

"I'm pissed off. I don't like looking over my shoulder."

"I don't blame you."

"Shooting a dog is about as low as it gets," Marlin said.

"We'll figure out who did it," Lauren said. "And make him pay for it."

"Hope so," Marlin said.

"In fact, I think it's time to bring the media in," Lauren said. "Get Brock's photo out there. Get some calls coming in."

"Name him as a suspect?" Marlin asked.

"You know what? I think we should call him a potential witness. He doesn't know we've got a match between the two bullets, and—"

"Possible match," Marlin said.

"Right. So if we call him a potential witness, maybe he'll think we figured out he visited Hank Middleton's house and need to know why. On the other hand, if we call him a suspect, he'll take off for parts unknown. You okay with that plan?"

"Absolutely," Marlin said.

"Here's the other thing I called about, and hang on, because this is about to get even more interesting. Henry just told me the crime lab ran those three DNA samples from the wiggle pick through CODIS. One sample was from Sean Hudson, which we expected, and another was from an unknown female—probably Avery Kingsberry, which wouldn't be a surprise, since she was out there digging with him. The third sample matched an unidentified male suspect from an unsolved burglary that went bad five years ago."

CODIS was the Combined DNA Index System maintained by the FBI. It included DNA profiles of offenders convicted of various felonies, such as sexual assault, homicide, or indecency with a child. It would have been nice if the database had named a specific suspect for them, but at least it gave them a potential link between two crimes, and that might eventually help them identify a suspect.

"What's the story?" Marlin asked.

"An old man came home and caught two men in his house. One of the scumbags punched him in the face before they left. No reason to do that except being mean. Fractured the old guy's cheekbone. They'd busted a window to get in, and the techs were able to pull some DNA off some of the shattered glass that remained in the frame, like one of the burglars scraped his arm when he reached in to unlock the window."

Phil had finished with the camera he was installing. He stopped at the front door and made a drinking motion with his hand. *Want a beer?* Marlin nodded and Phil went inside.

"Any suspects?" Marlin asked.

"Unfortunately, no. It was dark and the old man couldn't provide a decent description. Just two youngish guys, maybe white or Hispanic. That's all he could say."

"Where was the burglary?" Marlin asked.

"Sanders, Arizona," Lauren said, "which is on Interstate 40, about twenty miles west of the New Mexico border." Before Marlin could speak, she added, "Yeah, I know. Cody Brock is from New Mexico."

"And he seems to travel to neighboring states a lot," Marlin said. "He's been here, and he had that incident at the motel in Colorado."

They both remained silent for a moment. The implication was clear: Perhaps Cody Brock was responsible for all three of the recent crimes in this area—the murder of Sean Hudson, the murder of Hank Middleton, and the hole in Geist's ear. A one-man crime wave.

Marlin said, "That time he got busted in Colorado—that wouldn't have gotten him entered into CODIS?"

"Not for simple assault, no," Lauren said.

That was unfortunate. If Brock had been required to provide a DNA sample back then, now they might be able to connect him to the murder of Sean Hudson and the burglary/assault in Arizona. Or rule him out.

"Did we ever hear back from anyone at the meat company?" Marlin asked.

"Nope, and I left some very firm voicemails," Lauren said. "You know how those outfits operate. There's no upside to calling a cop back, so they won't. If we ever reach them, they'll say they never got the messages."

"What's the connection between Brock and Hudson?" Marlin asked. "Think Hudson was just another customer who pissed Brock off?"

"It's a good theory. He obviously doesn't handle rejection well."

Marlin didn't say anything.

"You don't buy that scenario?" Lauren asked.

"Maybe, but that would have happened at Hudson's apartment, right?"

"Probably."

"So why didn't Henry find any blood? And would Brock really hassle with moving the body?"

"He might if he was afraid there would be witnesses who would remember him being in the neighborhood," Lauren said. "And it's not entirely impossible that he could've cleaned the scene well enough that Henry couldn't find anything."

Phil came back onto the porch with two bottles of beer. He handed one to Marlin, then went back to the other end of the porch, giving Marlin some privacy.

"Sounds like we need to talk to Hudson's neighbors," Marlin said.

"Agreed. Team up on that tomorrow morning?"

Marlin knew that Nicole would be gone with appointments the next day, which was good, because he wouldn't want to leave her home alone. They set a time to meet at the sheriff's office in the morning for the drive to Marble Falls.

When Marlin hung up, Phil wandered over with his beer. "You've been spending more time with Lauren than I have lately," Phil said, taking a seat in a nearby chair. "Starting to wonder about you two."

Marlin gave him a weak grin.

"Not in the mood, huh?" Phil said. "Don't blame you."

Marlin took a long swig of beer. "Thanks for helping with the cameras."

"No problem."

Marlin could hear a neighbor's horse whinnying in the distance.

"Listen," Phil said. "I know I have to be careful what I say—you being a law enforcement big shot and all—but I think you know that if this guy is stupid enough to cause you any more problems...if you need my help with anything...or even if you don't..."

Marlin knew exactly what Phil was insinuating. Like Cody Brock, Phil had a temper, but his generally flared up at appropriate—or at least understandable—times, such as being pushed too far by a punk like Brock. Phil had a stubborn streak and he was committed to doing what he thought was right, even if the law wasn't always on his side. It had caused him some trouble in the past, but nothing he hadn't been able to work his way out of.

What he meant was, he had Marlin's back.

And what *that* meant was, if Cody Brock seriously hurt Marlin or his family, Phil would track him down—whether it took a day or a year—and make him pay dearly for his transgressions.

Marlin held his beer bottle out and Phil tapped it with his own. They each took a swallow, and then Marlin said, "Let's get the rest of the these cameras up before it gets dark."

It was almost midnight Thursday when the kid finally came out of the bedroom, after more than 40 solid hours of sleep. He was moving slowly. Still wearing the same jeans but now shirtless and shoeless. He had one hand on his forehead, obviously still in pain.

"Feel like I got kicked in the head by a mule," he said.

Titus was in his usual spot on the couch, watching boxing on ESPN. Couple of Mexican middleweights he'd never heard of.

"You drove plumb into a tree," he said. "Fucked your truck up good. Busted the radiator."

"Holy hell," Cody said, lowering himself slowly into an upholstered chair to Titus's right.

He looked pretty good, considering. His nose was still somewhat swollen.

"You remember anything?" Titus asked.

"Not much. I remember the two assholes chasing me."

"Remember calling me?"

"Nope."

"Me coming to get you?"

"Nope."

"You weren't making a lot of sense," Titus said. "First I thought you were drunk."

Cody turned and watched the fight for a minute or two. "Where's my truck now?" he asked.

"Still out there."

"Shit, really?"

"Didn't really have a lot of options at the time. Don't worry—I hid it under an oak tree. Didn't hurt to drive it a couple hundred yards before it heated up. It's fine out there for now, but we'll need to go get it pretty soon. Maybe tomorrow, if you're up to it."

"What about the radiator?" Cody asked. "We can't drive it like that."

"We'll tow it. We'll just have to take the back roads."

Cody nodded, and even that seemed to give him some pain. A minute later, he said, "Got any painkillers? Vicodin?"

"In the bathroom cabinet. Second shelf, in a brown prescription bottle. But hang on a sec."

"What?"

"I saw your picture on the news earlier. Why is the sheriff looking for you? What's the deal between you and this guy Hank Middleton?"

28

Friday morning. Nearly two full days since that idiotic meat salesman had slammed his truck into a tree.

Red had spent the entire day yesterday—between naps and trips to town for Mexican food—trying to come up with a design for his tree house. He hadn't made much progress. Why?

That damn video.

He found himself stopping what he was doing every ten or fifteen minutes to watch the blond woman emerging naked from the river. And when he wasn't actually watching it, he was thinking about watching it. There was just something about that girl. The body, obviously, but also the way she carried herself.

Red could view the video on his cell phone now, because Billy Don had posted it on YouTube.

"That gal's gonna be pissed when she finds out it's online," Red had said.

"She ain't gonna find out," Billy Don said. "I set it where the only people who can see it are me and you."

Red hadn't known what to say to that. How in the hell had Billy Don rigged it so nobody else could see it? Was he pulling Red's leg? Red damn sure wasn't going to reveal that he didn't understand the Internet as well as Billy Don did.

Red was no expert, but he was pretty sure if you put something "on the Web," as they called it, everybody could see it. That's why, when some young actress accidentally stepped out of a limo the wrong way and revealed that she wasn't wearing underpants, the photo would make it around the world in about ten seconds.

But back to the blond.

Now that Red had watched the video at least 50 times, he had some questions.

For starters, who was she?

And who was the guy with her? Husband or boyfriend? Had to be one or the other.

Another important question: Would a woman like her be willing to live in a tree house?

Red knew it was stupid to be wondering such a thing. He'd never even met the gal. Maybe, in person, she was a flat-out crazy woman. Or maybe she'd put on 20 pounds since this video was shot. Either would be a deal breaker, as far as Red was concerned. But it was fun to daydream.

He was about to watch the video for the 51st time when he felt the familiar rumbling again. Billy Don was coming down the hallway.

Red waited. He could tell from the hurried pace of the rumbling that Billy Don was on a mission—coming to tell Red something he considered important.

Yep, and here he came, into the living room, carrying his laptop yet again.

"Check this out," he said, sounding all urgent, as he showed Red a photo on Facebook. Red studied it for a moment. A photo of the meat man. Not just any photo, but a mug shot. No surprise that he had been arrested at some point. Who hadn't?

"So what?" Red said.

"Everybody's looking for him," Billy Don said.

"Yeah, we already knew that."

"But it ain't just about the meat anymore," Billy Don said. "The sheriff posted this. They wanna talk to the meat man about Hank Middleton."

Red blinked twice. "They think Lightfoot killed Hank?"

Word had spread a few days earlier that Hank had been shot dead on his front porch, and nobody knew who did it. Red and Billy Don weren't running buddies with Hank, but he had always seemed like a decent enough guy. Usually hung out with a man named Frank. Drank Budweiser. Drove a Ford. Told good jokes about Mexicans and gay people.

Hank lived no more than four or five miles from Red's place, as the crow flies, but there was a big ranch between them. The one time Red had been to Hank's place, it had taken 30 minutes to drive there, going around that ranch.

"They don't come right out and say the meat man killed him," Billy Don said, "but when you read between the lines, yeah. The sheriff says he's a 'potential witness,' and they wanna know if anybody's seen him in the past few days. Plus, his name ain't really Joseph Lightfoot, it's Cody Brock. Weird, huh?"

Red didn't reply right away. He was thinking things through. The situation was getting complicated.

"We gotta call the sheriff," Billy Don said, getting impatient.

"Hang on," Red said.

"What's there to hang on about?" Billy Don asked.

Red pulled the wooden lever on the side of his recliner and sat up straight. "Think about it for a second," he said. "If we tell 'em what happened the other day, that's gonna open a can of worms."

"I know, but—"

"That cash you took," Red said. "And the gun. I told you not to take it."

"*We* took it," Billy Don said.

"*You* took it," Red said.

"You were right there with me," Billy Don said. "And I gave you half the money, after we gave Miss Shirley her portion."

"Whatever. No point in arguing. I just don't see any reason we should talk to the cops about it. It's been two days since we saw him. Old news. Surely somebody else has seen him since then."

Billy Don shook his head. "You ain't getting it, are you?"

"Getting what?"

Billy Don gestured toward his bedroom at the far end of the trailer. "That gun in there might've been the one he used to shoot Hank."

Oh, shit. That was so obvious now, but it hadn't occurred to Red.

"Well, duh," he said. "That's why I told you not to take it. I knew nothing good could come of it."

"But at the time, you didn't know—"

"The important thing is, what're you gonna do?" Red said.

"You mean *we*. What are *we* gonna do?"

"Yeah, okay," Red said. "I was just screwing with you."

Billy Don set his laptop down on the cable-spool coffee table and lowered himself into his regular spot on the sofa, where he sunk so low that his knees were nearly as high as his chest.

"Gotta come clean," Billy Don said. "It's evidence. Can't hide something like this." Then, after a pause, he added, "Can we?"

Good question. Red was willing to ignore a lot of laws—most of which were a serious intrusion on his liberty as a sovereign citizen—but concealing evidence in a murder case? That was some serious shit. Even if Red was positive they'd never get caught, he wasn't sure he wanted to cross that line. Besides, if the meat man did kill Hank, he deserved to rot in prison for a while, and then get the needle. But without the possible murder weapon, would the cops be able to prove what had happened?

Red rose from his chair. "I need to lubricate my brain. Want a beer?"

"Dumb question," Billy Don said.

"A door-to-door meat salesman? That's just odd."

"Yes, ma'am, I agree," Marlin said. "He's from New Mexico. Driving a gray Toyota Tacoma with a white freezer in the bed. Sometimes he uses the name Joseph Lightfoot."

The woman who'd answered the fourteenth door Marlin had knocked on was perhaps 30 years old, wearing sweat pants and a T-shirt. A stay-at-home mom. Or maybe not. Why make assumptions? Maybe she was a high-powered financial wizard who traded on the international markets, and she happened to work from home. Of course, none of that mattered.

All that mattered—with this woman or anyone else who was home at mid-morning on a Friday—was how they answered the key question.

Have you ever seen this man?

Accompanying the question was a photo of Cody Brock. A recent photo, in which he had long black hair and a deep tan. Several people had actually asked if Brock was an American Indian.

"Who would buy meat that way?" the woman asked.

Marlin said. "Got me. I take it that means you haven't seen him?"

Officers from the Marble Falls Police Department had already spoken to many of Sean Hudson's neighbors in the days after his body had been found—but the questions they'd asked at the time had been much more general. They hadn't been looking for a particular person.

"Nope," the woman said, "because I would definitely remember a salesman like that. I wouldn't have answered the door anyway. I only answered for you because of your uniform, and because of your truck."

Marlin's green Dodge Ram had the Texas Parks & Wildlife logo on both doors, with GAME WARDEN in small, discreet letters below that. The newer game warden trucks were dark-brown Chevy Silverados with STATE POLICE in large letters on the back and a light bar with red and blue strobes mounted on the roof. Slick, modern law enforcement vehicles. Too conspicuous, in Marlin's opinion, which was why he'd opted to stick with the Dodge, with its flashers tucked behind the grill. He'd drive it until the bosses said he couldn't.

"Thanks, anyway," Marlin said. "Let me give you a card with my cell number on it, in case you hear anybody else talking about him."

Marlin was leaving when the woman said, "Hey, what did he do? Sell some bad meat?" She was smiling at her own joke.

"Actually," Marlin said, "we think he might be a witness in a homicide in Blanco County."

Her smile evaporated. "Oh."

Marlin returned to his Dodge. He was working the streets to the west of Sean Hudson's garage apartment, while Lauren worked the streets to the east. They were staying in touch via text, but so far, both of them had struck out. Likewise, Darrell, the Blanco County dispatcher, had promised to let them know if anything good came in as a result of the media push. So far, all they'd gotten was a lot of angry residents who'd bought questionable meat. None of the callers had seen Cody Brock since Tuesday, and today was Friday.

He got a text from Lauren: *Dead end over here so far.*

He replied: *Same.*

29

"I got it!" Red said, lowering the volume on the TV. "I think I got it."

"Let's hear it," Billy Don said.

They'd both had several beers, followed by several more beers.

"That wreck was pretty bad, right? When he hit the tree. I'm pretty sure he busted the radiator, which means he couldn't drive it out of there. And, think about it. If he killed Hank Middleton, wouldn't he want to keep, you know, sort of a low profile?"

"I guess."

"So he wouldn't call a tow truck, would he?"

"I guess not."

"Of course he wouldn't, because the tow truck driver would remember him later. So what would he do?"

"The tow truck driver?"

"No, Billy Don, not the tow truck driver. There is no tow truck driver. I'm talking about Lightfoot. What would he do?"

He gave Billy Don a moment to ponder that question. A moment went by, and Red realized Billy Don was watching Jerry Springer on TV.

"Hey, Skeezix," Red said.

Billy Don snapped out of it. "Huh?"

"What would he do? I'm talking about Lightfoot."

"Maybe instead of calling a tow truck, he'd call a friend to help him tow the truck somewhere so he could fix it?"

"Where?"

"Don't know."

"We got no reason to think he has any friends around here," Red said. "So let's presume he don't."

"You know what happens when you presume?" Billy Don said. "You make a pre out of Sue and me."

"Stop joking around," Red said. "We've gotta figure this out."

Billy Don grunted, drained the last of his beer, and flung the can in the general direction of the kitchen.

"What would *we* do in that situation?" Red said. "If my truck broke down on some ranch where we didn't have permission to be?"

Red gave Billy Don a moment to think about it, except this time, Red grabbed the remote and turned the TV off.

"Who cares?" Billy Don said. "This is dumb. Why're we trying to figure out where his truck is?"

"Because," Red said, "if we can find the truck, we can put the gun back where it came from."

Perfect solution. That's why Red was the brains of this outfit.

"You serious?" Billy Don asked.

"Sure. Why not? No need to call the cops. We won't get in trouble that way."

"But if the cops don't find Lightfoot's truck, that means they won't find the gun."

"As you said the other day, that ain't our problem. We're just putting things back the way they was before we chased him. Beyond that, we don't have to—"

"Nope," Billy Don said. "They need to find the gun, so they can arrest the sumbitch all proper. So we either gotta give it to the cops ourselves—"

"Not doing that."

"Or put it back in the truck and then tip 'em off somehow."

Red took a long drink of beer. He needed to think. Five minutes passed. Deep down, he had to agree that it would be best if Lightfoot was caught with the gun. But how would they find Lightfoot's truck? Where was it right now?

"Turn the TV back on," Billy Don said.

Red ignored him.

Billy Don got up to get another beer.

Red tried to think logically—and it was difficult. If he were in Lightfoot's situation, what would he do? Tough call. Couldn't just leave the truck there. What about installing a new radiator, so he could drive it out of there? That might be an option, assuming a new radiator would make the truck drivable again. But how long would it take to get a radiator? Probably have to drive to Austin or San Antonio to get one, and how would Lightfoot get there? Red was stumped.

Billy Don came back from the kitchen with two beers, one of which he handed to Red. Then he said, "Okay, if it was us, we'd want some time to figure out what to do next. So the first thing we'd do is hide the truck somewhere, so the owner wouldn't see it. We know he don't live out there, but he might show up anytime, right? So we'd move it. Even if the radiator is busted, we could drive it for a minute or two without hurting anything. Then we could come back later and fix it, or tow it, or whatever, once the heat is off. That's what we'd do. Which means the truck would still be out there. If it was us."

By now Red was nodding vigorously. "Everything you just said is exactly what I was thinking."

Damned if Billy Don wasn't exactly right, so Red said, "We were right."

The meat man's Tacoma was hidden off a lesser-traveled caliche road running east from the main road through the ranch. Weeds grew high in the center of this road, so it was obvious it wasn't used much—probably only during hunting season. The truck was tucked beneath the low-hanging canopy of an enormous oak tree. Hard to spot in the shadows.

Billy Don found a place to turn his Ranchero around, and then he stopped not far from the big oak tree. He nodded toward the glove compartment and said, "Hand it to me."

"Oh, hell no," Red said. "I ain't touching it."

"You really are turning into a pussy in your old age," Billy Don said. He leaned over, popped the glove compartment, and removed the .44 Magnum. Then he began to wipe it down with a Dairy Queen napkin he found on the floorboard.

"Better get 'er good," Red said. "Otherwise, they'll pull your DNA off there in a heartbeat."

They both realized they were obliterating any fingerprints or

DNA left by Joseph Lightfoot, but there was no getting around that. Maybe the cops could get something off the bullets or casings in the chambers. Billy Don hadn't touched those.

Now the big man climbed out of the Ranchero—still holding the revolver with the napkin—and walked toward the Tacoma, ducking under a limb to get closer. Suddenly he stopped abruptly and cupped his nose with his free hand. He obviously smelled something bad. Now the idiot was using his other hand—the one with the revolver—to swat at flies that were buzzing around his head.

Oh, God. Was Lightfoot dead inside the cab? Maybe he'd moved the truck, then passed out again and never woke up. A body would get ripe real quick in this heat.

Then Red figured out what the smell was. Probably.

"The meat in the freezer," he called out. "That's what you're smelling."

By now, it would be rotting away.

Billy Don didn't look convinced. He approached the truck slowly and peered inside. He didn't freak out, which was a good sign. No dead body in there. He opened the driver's door, leaned inside for a few seconds, then exited and closed the door. He used the DQ napkin to wipe the spot he'd touched on the door.

Back in the Ranchero, he said, "Good lord, that stinks to high heaven."

"Where'd you put the gun?" Red asked.

"Under the seat," Billy Don said. "Out of sight."

Smart. When Lightfoot had regained his senses, he had probably searched the truck from top to bottom, and he knew that the gun and his bank bag were missing. If he came back for the truck, he'd have no reason to think the gun had been returned to the truck.

"Okay, then let's hit the road," Red said. When they reached the highway, Red said, "Guess I'll close the gate. Keep the riff raff out until the cops get here."

Two more hours and Marlin and Lauren had gotten nowhere. A surprising number of Marble Falls residents had been home to answer their doors, but none of them remembered a visit from Cody Brock. The theory that Sean Hudson had been one of Cody Brock's customers, and that the solicitation attempt had somehow turned violent, was looking increasingly unlikely.

Lauren sent a text: *Hang it up and grab some lunch?*

As Marlin was typing a reply, an incoming call popped up on his screen. Marlin didn't recognize the number, but plenty of Blanco County residents and landowners had his phone number, so he answered.

"This is John Marlin."

"Hey, there, Mr. Marlin. Red O'Brien. How're you doing today?"

Marlin had dealt with O'Brien many times over the years. If there were a Poachers Hall of Fame, he and Billy Don Craddock would both be in it. They'd earned various fines and suspensions of their hunting licenses over the years, but what they really deserved was a lifetime hunting ban. Marlin hadn't been able to make that happen.

"Just fine," Marlin said, remaining courteous but professional. "How can I help you?"

"Well, I wanted to talk to you about the meat man that's been in the news. I got some information you might be able to use. Hey, that rhymed."

"Let's hear it," Marlin said.

"Okay, but first, I gotta stress that I can't personally verify whether or not this particular information is truthful, as far as being accurate or whatnot. I'm just passing along something I heard. But I'm pretty sure it's on target."

Hemming and hawing like that was an O'Brien trademark. He rarely ever stated anything clearly or directly. Many times he was hardly coherent.

"Go right ahead," Marlin said.

"Okay," O'Brien said. "From what I'm led to believe, based on a comment I heard from a reliable resource—someone who may or may not have firsthand knowledge of this particular set of facts—I'm pretty sure I know where the meat man's truck is."

30

"Where?" Marlin said.

"It's supposably on a ranch off Miller Creek Loop," O'Brien said. "Reason the truck is sitting there is because it's in disoperable condition. The meat man might've hit a tree, or something like that. What I heard was the truck is parked under an oak tree, about a hundred yards east of the main road."

"Which ranch?" Marlin asked.

O'Brien told him where the gate was. Marlin knew the place, of course, because he was familiar with virtually every ranch in the county. The owner was a dentist from Austin named Ruben Granado. He didn't visit the place often, except during deer season.

"Who told you this?" Marlin asked.

"It was part of a conversation I heard around town," O'Brien said.

"So it was basically gossip?"

"No, it was more than that."

"Who was involved in the conversation?"

"Honestly, I can't even remember. I didn't think it was important at the time, but then this morning I heard y'all were looking for him because of Hank Middleton."

"If you don't remember who said it," Marlin said, "then how do you know it was a reliable source?"

Silence followed for several seconds.

Then O'Brien said, "Well, that's just the class of people I hang out with. Reliable types."

Marlin wasn't fooled in the least. There was no source. O'Brien had been on the ranch himself. Maybe he'd been poaching. Or maybe he'd had some sort of dispute with Cody Brock and followed him over there. With O'Brien, it could be just about anything.

"Ever been on that ranch?" Marlin asked.

"Couple of years ago, yeah. I delivered some firewood to the owner's cabin. Can't remember his name. Good guy."

"Was Brock injured in the accident?" Marlin asked.

"Who?"

"Cody Brock. Also goes by Joseph Lightfoot."

"Oh, right. I think so, yeah. Got a concussion or something. Banged his head on the steering wheel. That's what I hear."

"Have you ever met him?"

"Who, this Brock guy?"

"Yes."

Another pause, and then O'Brien said, "Hang on a second."

Marlin heard a noise—like a hand covering the phone. O'Brien was buying time, trying to decide how to answer the question. A guy like O'Brien wouldn't want to lie when he didn't have to, chiefly because the more lies he told, the more likely it would catch up with him later.

While Marlin was waiting, he sent a text to Lauren: *On phone. Might have something good. Will call shortly.*

Finally O'Brien came back on the line, saying, "Sorry about that. Got something cooking on the stove. Anyway, yeah, he stopped at my house to try to sell me some meat. I said no thanks, and that was the end of it."

"That was the only time you saw him?"

"Yep."

"When was that?" Marlin asked.

"When he stopped at my house? Oh, that was this past weekend. Either Saturday or Sunday."

"How long was he at your trailer?"

"No more than five minutes. I sort of ran him off. Warned him about trespassing." There was pride in O'Brien's voice.

"How did he react to that?" Marlin asked.

"Well, he—I'm not sure what any of this has to do with the current location of his truck."

"I need to know everything I can about this guy," Marlin said. "You want to help, right?"

"Course I do."

"So how did he react when you ran him off?"

"He was a little snotty, but he left."

"Snotty how?"

"Back talk and such. Said something about my land not really being mine."

Marlin figured that was part of Brock's Native American angle—pursuing it even after his sales pitch had been rejected. Weird. Maybe he was starting to believe it himself.

"Where is Brock now?" Marlin asked.

Titus knew that the owner of the ranch didn't live on the place, but that didn't mean they could just drive in and out like they belonged there. They had to be careful that nobody saw them, just as Titus had been two days earlier when he'd picked Cody up.

Titus wouldn't even be helping Cody with this bullshit if Cody hadn't satisfactorily answered his question about Hank Middleton. Last night, when Titus had brought it up, Cody said that Middleton had left him a voicemail bitching about some meat he'd bought. Demanded an immediate refund. Pushy as hell. Middleton's attitude had pissed him off, so Cody then left a voicemail telling Middleton to go straight to hell. "That's why the cops're looking for me," Cody had told Titus. "No big deal. They've got to check something like that out."

Titus had taken Cody's word for it, because it sounded reasonable. Then, this morning, Cody said he'd called the cops and gotten it all straightened out. Fair enough. If it was true. Titus hoped it was.

"Ever been towed before?" Titus asked now.

Cody had been silent all day, but that was generally his nature, unless he was trying to sell something. Now he shook his head at Titus's question.

"It ain't real difficult," Titus said, "but you gotta keep the strap tight, which means working the brakes just right. A light touch. Don't stomp on 'em."

Cody nodded.

"It can be tricky when we're going downhill," Titus said. "You've gotta keep some pressure on the pedal or you'll be riding my bumper."

"Yeah, I got it," Cody said, with some edge to his voice.

When it came right down to it, being totally honest, Titus had never liked the kid much. Arrogant. Smug. Disrespectful. But he was kin, so there was a certain amount of obligation there on Titus's part. That's why, three weeks earlier, when Cody had called to say he was making a sales run through Texas and needed a place to stay, Titus had offered his extra bedroom. Sort of had to, right? And it hadn't taken long for Titus to remember why the kid rubbed him the wrong way. Just like he was doing right now.

"I'm just sayin', there's a particular way you gotta go about it," Titus said.

"And I said I got it."

They rode in silence for another mile, and then Titus turned onto Miller Creek Loop. A few minutes later, as they approached the entrance to the ranch, Titus was glad to see no vehicles behind him and none coming from the opposite direction.

"Let's make this quick," he said.

Cody didn't reply.

When Titus pulled off the pavement and stopped at the gate, Cody got out, taking his sweet time.

"No idea," O'Brien said. "I got to say, it's almost like you don't believe me or something."

"Why was he on that ranch?" Marlin asked.

"Don't know that either."

Marlin decided to remain silent for a few minutes. Let O'Brien squirm. And it worked.

"Maybe one of the people he ripped off was chasing him," O'Brien offered. "Just a guess. A lot of people were mad at the guy, right?"

Marlin kept quiet.

O'Brien said, "And if there was a chase, they was probably driving kind of fast. Maybe Lightfoot swerved to miss a cow or something, and then he lost control. That's when he hit the tree."

Marlin waited. O'Brien said nothing more.

Marlin said, "So when we catch up to Brock—and we will, sooner or later—he won't tell me that you were the one chasing him? You and Billy Don Craddock?"

Marlin would've been surprised if O'Brien had thought that far ahead. It wouldn't have occurred to him that Brock might identify his pursuers to the police.

"Hang on a second," O'Brien said. Again, the phone was covered. A full 20 seconds passed. Then O'Brien said, "Chili was boiling over. Anyway, what was your question?"

"Will Cody Brock tell me that you were the one chasing him?"

O'Brien made a scoffing sound, as if he were offended that Marlin would ask such a question. "If he does, he's a damn liar," O'Brien said. "Of course, we already know that, don't we? That he's a liar? He's been lying to people all over Blanco County, trying to sucker them into buying garbage meat. He's a con man."

Marlin didn't reply.

"So I got no idea what he'll say," O'Brien said. "Can't trust a guy like that. Might as well be a lawyer or a politician. But I'll tell you this much—we *wasn't* the ones chasing him. I just heard some information and I'm passing it along, wanting to be helpful, if I can. You can take it or leave it, far as I care."

Marlin waited again.

"Might be that none of it's even true," O'Brien said. "Guess you'll have to drive out there and find out."

"I will, if the landowner gives me permission," Marlin said.

"Oh," O'Brien said. "He can keep you off?"

"Well, sure. In that case, I'd need a warrant, and I can't get one if all I have is second-hand speculation."

"You think the owner's gonna be a problem?"

"I have no idea."

"Well, I hope not."

"Me, too."

"Because I bet you'll find something good in the meat man's truck," O'Brien said.

"Like what?" Marlin asked.

"I don't know, but Hank Middleton was shot, right? Maybe the gun's in there or something."

Which meant the gun *was* in the truck, no question. O'Brien and Craddock had chased Lightfoot, causing him to wreck, and now

O'Brien was tipping him off. Trying to do the right thing, which wasn't always O'Brien's standard operating procedure.

So Marlin said, "Thanks for the call. I might have more questions later, which means I'll need you to be available. I can reach you at this number, right?"

"Oh, yeah. Sure. I'm always around. Where'm I gonna go?"

A fucking flat tire.

Titus should've known this wouldn't go smoothly.

When they'd first approached the truck, they'd gotten hit with the smell of rotting meat—and then Titus noticed a flat rear tire on the driver's side. He must've picked up a thorn when he'd moved it two days earlier. What a pain in the ass.

"Got a spare?" Titus asked.

"Yeah."

"In good shape?"

"How the fuck should I know?" Cody asked.

Titus was reaching the end of his rope.

"Really?" he said. "That's your answer? You depend on that truck to make a living, but you don't even know if the spare is good? Does it at least have air in it?"

"Last time I checked."

"Which was when?"

"Couple of months ago," Cody said, and that probably meant a year or more.

"Got a jack?" Titus asked.

"Of course I've got a fucking jack," Cody said.

"Then get busy changing the goddamn tire," Titus said.

For a moment, judging by the look on Cody's face, they were about to get into a serious beef. Maybe even something physical. Titus was ready for it. Then Cody shook his head and got out of the truck, muttering something Titus couldn't make out.

31

Just after one-thirty, Marlin and Lauren got back into Johnson City, but instead of stopping at the sheriff's office, Marlin turned right on Highway 290, and then left on South Avenue F, which eventually became Miller Creek Loop.

Marlin was hoping this was the break in the case they'd been waiting for, but he wasn't getting his hopes up just yet. The fact that the tip had come from Red O'Brien meant—well, there was no telling what it meant.

Then again, O'Brien was an enigmatic character in some ways, and so was his running buddy, Billy Don Craddock. Marlin could never figure them out. They would quite happily break hunting and fishing laws, and then, in different circumstances, they might go out of their way to do the right thing. This could be one of those cases.

Marlin had been lucky enough to reach the ranch owner, Ruben Granado, on his first call, and, after Marlin had explained the situation, Granado had readily granted permission for Marlin and any of the deputies to search the place. All he wanted was a report later. Granado had mentioned that he'd been meaning to get a lock for the gate, but he hadn't gotten around to that yet. He figured a lock wouldn't keep out a determined trespasser anyway, and Marlin tended to agree. The gate had been chained, but that was all.

When they were less than a mile from the gate, Lauren said, "The place is basically a rectangle—twice as long as it is wide." She was looking at the ranch on Google Maps. "I can see two smaller roads branching off from the main road, one running east and one running southwest."

"They probably lead to deer blinds," Marlin said.

"If O'Brien's information is right, Brock's truck is somewhere along that road going east. That road is only a few hundred yards long, so it shouldn't take long to check."

Marlin pulled into the ranch entrance and Lauren hopped out to open the gate.

"What's the problem?" Titus asked, getting antsy.

It was obvious from the delay that something wasn't right. Titus was standing beside the Tacoma while Cody was lying on the ground under the bed of the truck.

"I can't get this fucker loose," Cody said.

Cody had a full-sized spare, but it wouldn't do any good if they couldn't get it down from its storage bay underneath the truck. Earlier, Cody had connected the jack handle and two extensions into one long piece, and then inserted it a hole in the rear bumper, but the handle wouldn't turn.

"I understand that," Titus said, "but why not?"

"'Cause it's fuckin' stuck, that's why," Cody said.

"Oh, well, that's a lot more specific, then," Titus said.

Cody mumbled something that might've been *Fuck you*.

"What exactly is stuck?" Titus asked.

"The fucking lowering screw," Cody said. "And you can't get to the damn thing. It's blocked."

"Can you spray it with some WD-40?" Titus asked.

Cody made a noise then. It wasn't much of a noise, but at the same time, it meant so much. *Stupid old man. You don't know what you're talking about. Why don't you shut your mouth?*

Titus wouldn't be able to stand much more of this farce. It was too damn hot out here. That, and this kid's mouth were going to make Titus do something rash. Something he'd regret later.

Maybe he should just get back into his truck and drive away. Let Cody solve his own problems.

Tempting.

"Try it now," Cody said.

Titus didn't like the bossy tone in the kid's voice, but his desire to get this over with and hit the road was even stronger, so Titus didn't object. Instead, he inserted the jack handle extension into the hole and tried to turn the screw.

"Still froze up," Titus said. "You let it get rusty."

And that set the kid off. He came out from underneath the truck and said, "It ain't rusty, it's a bad design, and if you'd climb under there yourself, you'd realize you're full of shit. I need a fucking hammer."

He opened the driver's side door, popped the seat forward, and began to root through all the junk on the small bench seat in the back.

What kind of idiot doesn't keep his spare tire in proper shape? Titus wondered. *Especially when he spends so much time on the road?*

"Pretty sure I've got a hammer in my truck," Titus said, although he couldn't imagine how a hammer would help the situation if the lowering screw was really blocked.

"Don't worry about it," Cody barked, on the verge of totally losing it, because now he was throwing shit around like an angry toddler. He emerged from the cab, slammed the driver's seat backward, and began to look underneath it.

"Guess I know what I'll be getting you for Christmas, huh?" Titus said, trying to lighten things up.

And here came Cody out of the cab again, turning toward Titus, his face twisted with anger, and Titus realized that the stupid kid had a huge revolver in his right hand, pointing it directly at Titus's head.

"Hang on a sec," Titus said, raising his hands, and he could feel the sudden warmth of urine running down the inside of his pants leg. "I was just—"

Then there was an explosion.

Lauren had the gate halfway opened when she suddenly stopped and stood still, her head cocked. She looked at Marlin through the windshield and made a gesture toward her ear. *Hear that?*

Marlin hadn't heard anything over the noise of the air conditioner. He rolled down his window.

"Heard a shot," she said. "I think."

"Yeah?"

"Sounded fairly close."

They both knew, however, that sound could carry for a great distance in these hills. Likewise a nearby shot could be muffled by a strong wind.

"Rifle or handgun?" Marlin asked.

"Not sure. I'm not even positive it was a shot, to be honest."

They waited a full minute. No more shots. That likely ruled out anybody target practicing.

Lauren opened the gate fully, so Marlin could drive through. He did, and she closed the gate behind him. Then she came to his window and said, "Got a padlock?"

Smart. Thinking ahead. They'd lock the gate behind them, just in case there was a trespasser on the ranch.

Now that the meat man craziness was a thing of the past, Billy Don had gone back to his regular routine—which consisted of a post-lunch six-pack, followed by a two-hour nap. Red decided to take advantage of the lull by watching one of his favorite movies, *The Alamo*. Not the silly 2004 version with Billy Bob Thornton and Dennis Quaid, but the original, released in 1960, starring the one and only John Wayne. A big-screen classic that truly brought the story of Texas's battle for independence from Mexico to life!

As he watched, he simultaneously contemplated his tree house. Frankly, he was starting to lose his enthusiasm for the project, simply because he couldn't come up with a good idea for the design. It needed to be—what was that word he'd heard on the radio the other day?—iconic! That's what he wanted. Something iconic. "Iconic," if Red understood correctly, meant that something had a lot of importance. For instance, *Bob couldn't go home early, because he had an iconic meeting to attend.*

So...what was important to Red, as a Texan?

He had already exhausted many of the possibilities—whitetailed deer, longhorn, hunting rifle, armadillo, bluebonnet—because the shapes wouldn't work. But there had to be something he was overlooking. Something that would work perfectly. A building, maybe.

But what kind of building would represent Texas? It had to be something everyone around the world would recognize, unless they were living in a jungle or in Kansas or something.

Red was still mulling it over when Billy Don woke from his nap and came into the living room. He grabbed a beer from the kitchen, sank down into the couch, looked at the TV, and immediately said, "There's your tree house idea right there," Billy Don said. "Make it look like—"

"The Alamo!" Red said, struggling to maintain a poker face, despite the overwhelming sense of excitement he could feel all the way to his toes. Of course! It was so obvious! The Alamo! "Obviously I already thought of that. Why do you think I'm watching the movie again? The idea came to me while you was asleep."

The caliche road on the Granado ranch was in decent shape, but Marlin drove slowly, so he and Lauren could scan the wooded areas as they passed. Their objective—to determine whether Cody Brock's truck was on the property, as Red O'Brien had said—hadn't changed. But now they were also keeping an eye out for a possible trespasser.

Lauren was still checking Google satellite photos on her phone, and now she said, "The cabin is at the end of this road, on the north fence line. But we'll be turning east about two hundred yards before that—unless you think we ought to check it out first."

"The cabin?"

"Right. If we look for Brock's truck first and there's someone at the cabin, they'll have a chance to slip out."

Which was true. They'd locked the gate, but that wouldn't stop someone with a pair of bolt cutters.

Marlin was wishing they'd had some rain in the past few days. As it stood now, the caliche was dry and hard, hence no tire tracks, and no way of knowing how many vehicles had driven this road recently.

He kept easing along the road, weighing the two alternatives, and studying a thick cluster of oak and cedar to his left.

Finally, he said, "I think we ought to—"

"Truck coming," Lauren said.

Marlin looked directly ahead, and there, perhaps 70 yards away, just this side of a small crest, was a white Ford F-350 with a chrome grill guard. The truck had come to a stop.

"Looks like Titus Steele's truck," Marlin said. He'd gotten a good look at it when Steele had come to the sheriff's office for his interview two days earlier.

Strange. Was there a connection between Cody Brock and Titus Steele? If Brock's truck was out of commission nearby, and the oncoming truck was in fact Steele's, what did that mean? On the phone earlier, Marlin had asked Ruben Granado if he knew Cody Brock—or Joseph Lightfoot, or a traveling meat salesman by any other name—and the answer had been no. Marlin had had no reason to ask Granado if he knew Titus Steele.

Lauren was now holding a pair of binoculars, studying the Ford. "Can't make out the plate. Looks like there's mud on it."

Marlin tapped the brakes and came to a stop with the F-350 50 yards away. "Let me make a quick call."

He grabbed his phone, went to the list of recent calls, and dialed Granado again.

Lauren said, "Looks like it's just the driver. Nobody else that I can see."

Could be someone crouched down on the passenger side, or several people in the rear seats, if it had a dual cab, or there could be people riding in the bed of the truck.

A voice came over Marlin's phone, which was set to hands-free. "This is Ruben."

"Mr. Granado, it's John Marlin again. Hey, do you know a man named Titus Steele?"

"I'm sorry, I didn't get that," Granado said.

Marlin began to repeat his question, but the F-350 suddenly began to move. Not slowly, either. The driver gunned it, and the big Ford came roaring at Marlin's truck head on.

Marlin dropped the phone and grabbed the steering wheel with both hands.

32

Everything was black, and then the smallest bit of light began to creep in around the edges.

Same with sound. Nothing. Absolute silence. Then Titus heard something. A soft roaring from a great distance. It rose and fell. Rose and fell. Louder, softer, louder, softer. He realized it was all in his head. Not imaginary, but coming from *inside* his head.

He tried to move his hands and found that he could. But just his hands and fingers. Not his arms. They were too heavy. Like sleeves filled with concrete. Same with his legs. He could move his toes, and that was some comfort.

Why wasn't he dead? Where was Cody? That son of a bitch. Titus would kill him when he got the chance. No question about it. Cody Brock—kin or not—was a dead man walking.

Now Titus heard something else. A cardinal calling from somewhere nearby.

And now he felt a sensation on his neck. His shoulder. His chest. His stomach. And now all over his groin and down his thighs. Crawling.

Oh, God, and now they were biting.

Titus was lying in a bed of fire ants.

Homer Griggs had known Rodney Bauer going back to first grade, and they got together every now and then for a cold beer or a plate of brisket. But today Homer was acting in his official capacity as a reserve deputy for the Blanco County Sheriff's Office. Taking a report on a theft, according to the dispatcher.

Homer parked his unit in front of Rodney's house, and just as he was getting out, the front door began to swing open.

Please don't let it be Mabel, Homer thought. *Please, please, please, not Mabel.*

The door opened wide and there was Mabel.

"Well, hey, there, Mabel!" Homer called as cheerfully as possible.

Mabel, on her best day, was unpleasant. On her worst day, Satan himself would duck and run the other way.

"How ya doing today?" Homer added, because Mabel hadn't responded. And now here came Rodney out the door behind her, looking like a kid who'd been scolded by his mother.

Mabel still hadn't replied when Homer met her and Rodney near the front of the cruiser. Then, without so much as a hello, Mabel said, "This genius here got a gun stolen out of his truck earlier this week and never called it in."

"Oh, yeah?" Homer said. "What kind of gun, Rodney?"

"It's a .44 Magnum," Rodney said. "Smith and Wesson."

Damn. That was a big son of a bitch. The "Dirty Harry" caliber. That's how most people remembered it.

"Makes him feel macho carrying it around in his truck," Mabel said.

"They make the .44 in several different models," Homer said. "You happen to remember which—"

"Model 629," Rodney said. "Stainless steel. Synthetic grip. Six-inch barrel."

"I dug up the receipt," Mabel said. "We're talking about a thousand-dollar gun, and the only reason I found out it's missing is because we had a rattlesnake in the weeds beside the garage this morning. I went to get the pistol out of his truck, but it was gone."

She gave Rodney a glare that would have killed some lesser men.

"You remember when you last saw it?" Homer asked, taking notes.

"The snake?" Rodney asked.

"No, Rodney, not the snake," Mabel said, shaking her head. Then, to Homer, she said, "He said it was Monday, but he didn't figure out it was gone until Tuesday."

"So tell me about Tuesday," Homer said.

Mabel kept quiet, except for looking at Rodney and saying, "Well, go ahead."

"Okay," Rodney said. "I was working on my truck. Putting a fresh battery in it. I go around to pop the hood and...it was gone."

"The battery was gone?" Homer asked.

"No, the gun. From inside the truck where I normally keep it."

"Just...gone?" Homer asked.

"Yep. Gone."

Homer noticed that Mabel was fidgeting impatiently, and he wondered how long she would keep her tongue.

"Did you notice anything else missing?" Homer asked.

"Nope."

"No other guns?"

"Nope."

"Was there any ammo with the gun?"

"Just the rounds in the cylinder."

"Was it fully loaded?"

"Yep."

"Any idea who might've taken it?"

Homer could tell from Rodney's reaction that he did have a theory, but before Rodney could answer, Mabel said, "That meat salesman everybody's talking about came by on Monday afternoon."

"Yeah, we're looking for that guy," Homer said.

"Because of my gun?" Rodney said.

"No, Rodney, not because of your gun, obviously, because they didn't know it was missing until now," Mabel said, rolling her eyes. Then, to Homer, she said, "It's because of Hank Middleton, right? I heard about it."

"Yes, ma'am," Homer said. "And this makes me wonder...Rodney, did the meat man happen to see your gun?"

The answer was written all over Rodney's face. "He was pushier'n hell. Saying some pretty nasty stuff. So I went to the truck and—"

"You pulled your gun on him?" Mabel asked, fixing Rodney with an angry glare. He had obviously kept that part from her until now.

"Sure as hell did, because it's my right as an American," Rodney said, finally showing a little spine. "And it scared him so bad he took off."

"Yeah, Rodney, and then he came back and stole it from you," Mabel said. "And then he went and killed poor Hank with it." She turned toward Homer. "That's what you're saying, right?"

"I'm afraid it sounds like a possibility," Homer said.

"Ah, crap," Rodney said.

"So Hank was killed with a .44?" Mabel asked.

"I'm afraid I can't share that specific detail with you," Homer said, "but go ahead and assume the answer is yes."

"Ah, crap," Rodney said.

"Well, isn't this just a fantastic state of affairs," Mabel said.

33

Marlin slammed his Dodge into reverse, but before he could even touch the gas, the Ford had closed the distance between them, seemingly intent on ramming them head on, and just as Marlin braced for the impact, the F-350 swerved to the right, plowing through the tall, dry grass on the side of the caliche road, passing within inches of the Dodge.

Marlin left it in reverse and cut the wheel hard to the left, backing into the grass the Ford had just trampled. Then Marlin jammed it into drive, cut the wheel right, and stepped hard on the gas. Even with just a few seconds' head start, the Ford had already opened up a sizeable gap, trailing a thick curtain of caliche dust in its wake.

"Didn't get a good look at him," Lauren said, "but it was just the one guy."

Marlin nodded at his radio and said, "Let's get some back-up."

Lauren grabbed the microphone and asked Darrell, the dispatcher, to send any available units to Miller Creek Loop—ideally a unit on each end.

Marlin pushed the Dodge as hard as he dared, but he couldn't get any closer to the Ford, which was at least 80 yards ahead.

The Ford crested a hill, then dropped out of sight. The gate was not far on the other side of the hill.

"No way is he gonna stop," Lauren said.

Four seconds later, Marlin's Dodge topped the small rise, just in time to see the Ford smash into the gate. Of course, the chain and lock provided no resistance at all, and the gate swung open violently on its hinges. The Ford took a squealing right turn—just in front of a slow-moving white truck with a set of flashing yellow lights mounted on its roof.

"Oh, crap," Lauren said. "Oh, no."

The white truck was a pilot vehicle, and following along behind it—lumbering along at no more than 30 miles per hour—was a tractor-trailer towing a mobile home.

Marlin covered the 50 yards to the open gate in less than four seconds, but he was too late. The tractor-trailer was just passing the ranch entrance. Marlin turned in behind it, but he didn't bother flipping on the red-and-blue strobes tucked behind the grille. The big rig had nowhere to go. The shoulders along the road were too steep for the driver to pull over, and likewise Marlin couldn't use them to skirt around the tractor-trailer. For the moment, they were stuck, with no chance to catch the F-350.

Lauren grabbed the microphone again and informed Darrell of the situation.

"Already got unit 102 on the north end of Miller Creek Loop," Darrell said. "And unit 103 is en route, currently on 281, four miles north of Blanco."

That meant unit 103—Ernie Turpin—could reach the south end of Miller Creek Loop, where it intersected US Highway 281, in about three minutes. Turpin would beat the Ford, because it had a similar distance to travel, but it would have to travel much slower.

Marlin said, "In about a quarter mile, the shoulder will level out and I'll have a chance to pass."

Lauren nodded. She had likely grown to know this road as well as Marlin did, considering that Phil Colby's ranch was up ahead.

It was a long, slow, quiet 30 seconds. When Marlin finally reached the level shoulder, he goosed his siren, activated his strobes, and edged over onto the left shoulder to pass the big rig and then the pilot truck in front. The road was all clear ahead—the Ford long gone—but sharp curves prevented Marlin from reaching much more than 50 miles per hour on the straightaways.

Ernie Turpin's voice came over the radio. He had just reached the south end of Miller Creek Loop and would wait there until further notice. That was the smart thing to do. If Turpin proceeded northward on Miller Creek Loop, there was a chance the Ford could be hidden on some small side road, and once Turpin passed, the Ford would have an opportunity to reach the highway and make an escape.

Marlin and Lauren passed the entrance to Phil Colby's place, then Blue Ridge Drive, then the entrance to the Diamond X Ranch. Still no sign of the Ford. By the time they passed Hidden Valley Ranch Road, Marlin began to suspect they were out of luck.

One minute later, Marlin could see the highway ahead, and then Turpin's unit parked on the side of the road. He pulled up beside it, driver's door to driver's door.

Turpin said, "You sure he didn't have time to reach the highway before I got here?"

"Not a chance," Marlin said. "He pulled off somewhere."

"So we got him bottled up."

Marlin pondered what to do next. There were a lot of "ifs" in this situation.

If Red O'Brien was right about Cody Brock's truck being crashed and out of commission on Ruben Granado's ranch...

And if Cody Brock really did kill Hank Middleton, and possibly Sean Hudson...

And if that wasn't just some random trespasser in the Ford F-350...

And if that shot had come from someplace on the ranch...

Then it would be worth making some fairly major efforts to find the driver of that Ford F-350.

"Maybe we should call Jacob Daughdril," he said.

Daughdril was a friendly man of about 55 who lived just south of Round Mountain, in the northern portion of Blanco County. More important, Daughdril owned a helicopter—a Robinson R-22 two-seater. Daughdril was retired from some sort of job in finance, and now he occasionally conducted deer censuses for ranchers in the area for a small fee.

"Sounds like a good plan," Lauren said.

Daughdril could cover the surrounding area fairly quickly and let them know if he spotted any vehicle that might be a white Ford F-350.

Marlin said, "Ernie, you mind calling him while Lauren and I go back to Ruben Granado's place? We never got a chance to see if Brock's truck is really there or not."

"Will do," Turpin said.

"If you reach him and he's available, have him stand by for the moment. Just give us 15 minutes. Then we'll know whether we need him in the air."

After all, if Brock's truck wasn't on the ranch, that meant the person in the Ford might very well have been a random trespasser, in which case tracking him down wouldn't be as crucial.

As Marlin drove onto the ranch, past the crumpled gate, Lauren checked in with the deputies on either end of Miller Creek Loop. Still no sign of the Ford F-350.

Again, Marlin drove slowly, giving them both a chance to survey the countryside as they went. Perhaps the person in the Ford hadn't been alone on the ranch. Maybe he had dropped someone off, and that person was now on foot.

Marlin still wondered if it had been Titus Steele's Ford. Had it been Steele behind the wheel? And what about the gunshot? If the shot had come from someplace on the ranch, who had fired it and what had been the intended target?

There were no answers at the moment, and nothing that looked out of place as they drove.

Marlin turned right on the lesser-traveled caliche road that ran to the east, keeping his speed at no more then 10 miles per hour.

Around a thick grove of oak and cedar trees.

Across a dry creek bed.

Over another small rise.

And there was movement.

"Up ahead," Marlin said.

"I see him."

A man was in the road, 40 yards away, moving unsteadily toward Marlin's Dodge. He was wearing nothing but a pair of blue boxer shorts—no shirt, no pants, no footwear or socks. He wasn't so much walking as he was staggering, and holding both hands in front of him, as if groping his way in the dark, although he would occasionally use one hand to rub his torso or thighs.

"Looks like blood all over his chest," Lauren said.

Marlin stopped 10 yards away.

"Oh, man," Lauren said. "Look at his face. What happened to

him?" She grabbed the microphone, saying, "I'll get medical rolling."

Marlin nodded, stepped out of his truck, and hurried forward, calling out, "State game warden," so the man would know who was approaching.

He had plainly been grotesquely injured—perhaps beaten. He face was so severely swollen that his eyes were totally closed, and there was blood on the right side of his head, running onto his face and down to his chest and abdomen. Was this man Titus Steele? If so, he was unrecognizable. The man tried to speak, but what came out was unintelligible.

Marlin reached him and touched one of the man's arms—an effort to reassure him—and then Marlin saw that he had several fire ants crawling on him. Marlin immediately began to swat some of the ants off, at the same time asking, "Can you breathe?"

The man nodded.

"No trouble at all?"

He tried to say something, but what it was, Marlin could only guess.

"A little trouble?" Marlin asked.

The man said something else.

"Your tongue is swollen?" Marlin asked.

He nodded.

"Are you allergic to fire ants?"

Another nod.

Was the swelling all from anaphylactic shock? Possibly, but that didn't explain the blood.

"Sir, did you hear a gunshot?"

The man nodded even more emphatically, and then he gently lifted the thick hair on the right side of his head. Now Marlin saw it—a furrow wound running horizontally above his ear.

Lauren joined them now and said, "EMS will be here in about ten minutes."

The man nodded and grunted, pointing again at the side of his head, plainly worried about the extent of his injury.

"Looks like it grazed you," Marlin said, "but we need to get you checked out as soon as possible." Even if the bullet hadn't entered the skull, there could be fractures at the point of impact. For now, the bleeding appeared to have stopped.

"Sir, where are your clothes?" Lauren asked. Marlin knew she was hoping to find the man's ID, in case his condition took a turn for the worse and they needed to identify him.

He made a vague gesture back behind him. No time to pursue that right now. Same with Cody Brock's truck. It would have to wait again.

"We should meet them at the road," Marlin said. Time was critical when a victim's airway was compromised.

Lauren grabbed the man's other elbow and they began escorting him toward the Dodge.

"Who shot you?" Marlin asked.

The man shook his head. Either he didn't know or he wasn't going to say. Or maybe he simply couldn't remember right now.

Lauren opened the passenger door and quickly climbed in the rear seating area. As Marlin helped the man into the front seat, he said, "Are you Titus Steele?"

The man nodded.

34

"The Alamo?" Willard Fisk said. "Gotta say, I had no idea what to expect today, but that right there is pure genius."

"I appreciate that," Red said, beaming with pride. "Seeing as how I'm a native Texan and all, the Alamo has special meaning to me. I've studied up on it over the years, and now you might say I'm sort of an expert."

Billy Don let out a small snort.

"Is that right?" Willard asked.

"Yep, and proud of it," Red said. "I was just watching the movie again earlier today. The John Wayne version, of course."

It was five o'clock on Friday afternoon and Red was finally meeting with Willard, the homebuilder, to talk about Red's tree house design. They were in Red's living room—Red in his recliner, Willard on the end of the couch that hadn't been destroyed by the crushing punishment of Billy Don's sizeable hindquarters. Billy Don was sitting to Willard's left, sunk down in his usual spot, eyes on his laptop.

They were on their first beer, but there would be plenty more to come as they nailed down—no pun intended—all the details for building Red's dream home.

For the moment, Red had managed to stop thinking about Joseph Lightfoot's truck, and the revolver inside it, and wondering whether the owner of that ranch would let the cops check it out.

Red realized Willard had just asked him something.

"Pardon me?"

"That's a pretty good flick," Willard said. "It's a shame they got so much of the story wrong."

"Huh?"

"The way they butchered some of the details," Willard said. "Too bad they took so many liberties."

"That's true," Red said. "But that's Hollywood for ya."

"Did you know that two of the historical advisors—J. Frank Dobie and Lon Tinkle—demanded that their names be removed from the credits?"

"I did, yeah," Red said, starting to wonder if Willard was pulling his leg, because what kind of name was 'Lon Tinkle'? That sounded made up.

"Anyway, if you want it to look like the Alamo, I guess you're talking about the chapel, without the barracks or any of the other structures," Willard said.

Red wasn't sure how to answer that—because he didn't know what the hell Willard was talking about. Barracks? What barracks? So he said, "Yep. You got it."

"Okay, but you want it to look the way it looks today, not the way it looked during the revolution. Right?"

Again, Red was stumped, so he said, "I want it to be authentic."

Willard made an expression, like *You sure?*

So Red said, "Authentic, meaning it's gotta look like the Alamo you see on postcards and key chains and such."

"Oh, okay," Willard said. "I was confused there for a second, because the way it looked back then—without the humped gable on top of the parapet—well, most people wouldn't even recognize it. But you probably already know that."

"Well, yeah, of course I do," Red said, making a mental note to look up the word 'parapet' later.

"Because the U.S. Army added the gable in 1850, along with the outer windows on the upper level," Willard said.

"Right. Exactly."

"Most people don't know that," Willard said.

"Amateurs," Red said.

"And they don't know that it was originally called the Mission San Antonio de Valero," Willard said. "It wasn't called the Alamo until later."

"Basic stuff," Red said.

"And the legend about William Travis drawing a line in the sand," Willard said. "I can understand why everyone loves it..."

Red loved it, too. It was probably the best Alamo story. The men who stepped across that line were facing certain death, but they were willing to die for the cause, and that made them real heroes. Texans to the core.

"... even if it isn't true," Willard finished up.

Oh, for fuck's sake. It wasn't true? Willard had to be smoking crack. Where was he getting these so-called facts? Red had had enough.

"Way I heard it," Red said, "not only did Bill Travis draw that line, but Jim Bowie, who was in bed, sicker'n crap, asked to be carried across the line. Those were the kind of men that fought and died for Texas independence. Good men. Honorable. Not like a lot of people these days."

"Well, sure," Willard said, "nobody's saying they weren't good men, but there's no solid evidence the line in the sand ever happened. That's the only point I'm making. Nobody even wrote that story down until nearly 40 years later, and that guy heard it second-hand, and later he admitted he made some of it up."

"So you're saying it's bullshit?" Red asked, starting to get a little red-faced. "Then why did they tell us about it in Texas history class in junior high?"

"Actually, I never heard it in school, because I'm from Oklahoma. I moved here when I was nineteen."

Red had to laugh. "Good lord, you're a Sooner. Well, that explains it."

"Explains what?" Willard asked.

Explains why you're an ignorant, Alamo-bashing, Okie pinhead, Red thought.

Fortunately, before Red could say it out loud, Billy Don said, "Now they're saying the cops've got a helicopter hunting for the meat man in an F-350."

"What? Where?" Red asked.

"Off Miller Creek Loop," Billy Don said, checking his laptop. "Which makes sense, because that's where we left—"

"Whose truck is he driving?" Red said, to shut Billy Don up before he shared too much information.

"Doesn't say."

"Where are you getting this stuff?"

"The sheriff is warning everybody on Facebook, because they're saying he's armed and dangerous and everybody should be on the lookout."

Red was having trouble processing this new information. What the hell was going on?

"Does it say anything about his Tacoma?" Red asked.

"Not that I can see."

"Who is this meat man?" Willard asked.

"Some salesman that's been ripping everybody off," Red said. "And he might've been the guy who killed Hank Middleton."

"I heard about that," Willard said.

Red didn't know what to think, but one thing was for sure: If Lightfoot was on the loose around Blanco County, armed, crossing fence lines and such, there was a real good chance he wouldn't live long enough to get arrested.

The furrow wound on the side of Titus Steele's head was fairly nasty, but his skull was intact. An inch or two to the right and he likely would have been killed. The impact, even from a grazing shot, had been enough to knock him unconscious, and he'd woken up in a bed of fire ants. Talk about bad luck. If he hadn't come to fairly quickly, he might very well have died from the allergic reaction. But he'd received treatment for it—a shot of epinephrine—and Marlin was amazed at how quickly the swelling had subsided. Steele was recognizable again.

Marlin and Lauren were now standing beside his bed in a room at Blanco Memorial Hospital. A lot had changed in the past two hours. For the better. Progress in the investigation.

"Mr. Steele," Lauren said, "why don't you tell us what happened on that ranch earlier today?"

Steele hesitated, which was not a good sign.

So Marlin said, "After the paramedics picked you up, we went back onto that ranch and found a truck owned by a man named Cody Brock. You know him?"

Steele nodded slowly. Reluctantly. "He's my nephew. My sister's boy."

Outstanding. A critical piece of information had just fallen into place. Marlin did his best to conceal his surprise, but now they had a possible connection between Cody Brock and Sean Hudson. As Marlin and Lauren had discovered, Brock hadn't knocked on Hudson's door, trying to sell meat. Instead, the Walz ranch was the common ground. Hudson had been there on the survey crew, and Brock's uncle worked there.

Marlin said, "We found your bloody clothes just a few yards away from your nephew's truck, along with blood on the ground, so that appears to be where you got shot. Our crime scene tech is currently processing the scene, but it would be helpful if you would tell us what happened."

Lauren added, "Obviously, the big question we have right now is, who shot you? Was it your nephew?"

Judging by Steele's expression, he was a man torn, struggling to decide how to respond. He finally said, "I don't think I'm quite ready to talk about it." He sounded as if his tongue were still slightly swollen.

"But you remember what happened?" Lauren asked.

"Sort of."

"Any reason you aren't willing to discuss it?"

He grinned, then winced. "Well, I got shot in the head," he said. "So I can't guarantee my recollections would be all that accurate. Best if we give it a day. Let all my marbles settle back into place. That's why they wanna keep me overnight. Because I'm still kind of loopy."

Steele seemed perfectly coherent to Marlin, and he could sense Lauren's impatience when she said, "Maybe you know this already, but we've been looking for Cody for the past few days. So we need you to be straight up with us. Tell us what happened."

"Yes, ma'am," Steele said. "Tomorrow morning. That'll have to do."

"Right now we have a chopper in the air looking for your truck," Lauren said. "That *was* your truck out there today, right?"

"Yep."

"And it was Cody behind the wheel?" she asked.

Steele shook his head. He wasn't saying no, he was simply indicating that he wasn't going to answer.

Marlin had an idea why Steele was reluctant to talk. Marlin said, "I understand it isn't easy to rat out a family member, even one who shot you in the head. Maybe you're hoping he feels bad about what he did and will give himself up."

Steele shrugged. *Maybe so, maybe not.*

"You might even be thinking it was an accident," Marlin said. "He didn't mean to shoot you, he was just trying to scare you, right? That's why he didn't park another round in your head when you were on the ground."

"I really need to get some rest," Steele said. "So if you—"

"What did y'all argue about?" Lauren asked.

Steele kept quiet.

"Did Cody tell you how he wrecked his truck and why he was on that ranch?" Marlin asked.

"Come back tomorrow," Steele said.

"Where is Cody right now?" Lauren asked.

"I got no idea."

"Have you seen Cody carrying a Smith and Wesson .44 Magnum lately?" Marlin asked.

Less than three hours earlier, a reserve deputy named Homer Griggs had taken a report of a revolver stolen out of Rodney Bauer's truck. Turned out Cody Brock had visited Rodney the day before Rodney had noticed that the gun was missing.

Rodney occasionally did some target shooting with the big revolver around his ranch. Henry Jameson, the crime scene technician, was out there right now, hoping to find a spent bullet that he could compare to the bullet that killed Hank Middleton, which they already knew was a probable match to the bullet found in Marlin's door frame.

"You'd have to ask him about that," Steele said.

"So you haven't seen Cody with a .44?" Marlin asked. "That's what you're saying?"

"No, what I'm saying is my recollections ain't all that great right now. I'm doing y'all a favor by keeping my mouth shut until the fog clears."

An obvious dodge. Marlin's frustration was growing.

"How long has Cody been in the area?" Lauren asked. "Surely you can remember that."

Marlin knew where she was headed, and it was a smart move. If Steele wouldn't answer questions about the day's events, maybe he would unwittingly answer questions that would help them firm up the connection between Brock and Sean Hudson.

"Couple of weeks," Steele said.

"Where's he been staying?" Lauren asked.

"My place."

"Meaning your house on the Walz ranch?"

"Yeah."

Perfect, Marlin thought.

"Did Dr. Walz know he was staying there?" Lauren asked.

"I think I told him at one point. He wouldn't care about that sort of thing. I could have visitors."

Marlin was wondering why Walz hadn't mentioned Cody Brock during his interview. Had Steele really told him? Had Walz forgotten? When you were being questioned about a murder that might've taken place on your property, most innocent people would readily name every person that had been on that property recently—especially when you knew that you were a possible suspect yourself.

"Did Dr. Walz ever meet Cody?" Lauren asked.

"Not as far as I know."

"So he could have?" Marlin asked.

"Anything's possible, I guess. Cody comes and goes as he pleases. He might've run into Dr. Walz at some point."

This was a bizarre conversation. Why was Steele willing to answer some questions but avoid others?

"Does Cody have other family members in the area?" Marlin asked. Brock was on the run now, and it would be helpful to know if anyone might provide him with a place to stay.

"Just me."

"How about friends?" Marlin asked.

"He don't have friends anywhere," Steele said. "He's more of a loner, mostly because he can be a bit of an asshole, and he's got a mean streak."

"You know if he ever travels to Arizona?" Marlin asked, thinking back on the old man who had surprised two burglars in his home and gotten punched for his troubles.

"He travels all over the damn place," Steele said.

"That's a vague and useless answer," Lauren said.

"Best I can do," Steele said. Then he grinned again and said, "You really got a chopper in the air?" He was amused by the idea.

"We do, yeah," Lauren said, "and we're alerting the public that we're looking for Cody. Right now, we're assuming he shot you, and we're considering him armed and dangerous. If we got that wrong, you need to tell us right now. Otherwise, my deputies will respond accordingly when they find him."

"Gotta do what you gotta do," Steele replied. "I'm done talking. My head hurts."

An hour before sundown, Jacob Daughdril, the helicopter pilot, spotted the white Ford F-350 parked deep in a dense grove of cedar trees at the end of a narrow caliche road that ran through a small, rustic subdivision. Marlin knew that area well. There were a handful of small cabins nearby, each sitting on five to ten acres, but no homes with full-time residents. The perfect hiding spot. Quiet. Remote. Hovering low, Daughdril managed to read the license plate with binoculars and confirm that it was Titus Steele's truck.

Marlin, Lauren, and several additional deputies converged on the area, but the driver—whether it was Cody Brock or someone else—was nowhere to be found.

35

Red woke up Saturday morning with a hangover that was about a six on a scale of ten, but he was otherwise in a great mood.

He went into the living room and his heart dropped for a moment. Sitting there on the cable-spool coffee table—totally unguarded—were stacks and bundles of cash. Damn. Now he remembered. After Willard had left around midnight, Red had removed all of his cash from the safe in his bedroom closet and brought it out here to count it. It had been a while since he'd tallied it up, and he wanted to know how much he could afford to sink into his new home.

He'd started with more than $142,000 after the trip to Vegas. Now he had about $127,000. Less than he was expecting. Made him realize how easy it was to blow through cash when you weren't working steadily, and when you were eating out once or twice a day, and going to bars almost every night, and buying several hundred dollars' worth of lottery tickets every week—just basic necessities like that. No problem. He still had plenty—more than enough to build his dream tree house. He grabbed a Mexican blanket off the couch and tossed it over the cash. He'd put it back into the safe later.

He filled an enormous Bubba mug with black coffee and stepped onto his back porch.

For this time of year, it was an unusually cool and crisp morning. The sun was just rising. Birds were starting to hop around in the trees. A cluster of does and fawns ate corn from underneath the feeder near the back fence line.

A great start to the day, after the evening that had turned out surprisingly well.

After several more beers, followed by a bottle of Irish whiskey, he and Willard had managed to set aside their differences regarding the history of the Alamo—and Willard's Okie heritage—and focus on the tree house. And Willard had brought a great idea to the table.

Why not carry the Alamo theme throughout the interior of the home, too? That's what Willard had asked.

"How so?" Red had asked.

Willard's answer? Alamo memorabilia. Alamo artwork. Alamo furniture and Alamo hardware.

"Go all the way with it," Willard said. "Carry the theme everywhere, from the rugs on the floor to the lights on the ceiling. You can buy all sorts of stuff online without spending a fortune."

"Like what?" Red asked.

"Alamo commemorative dinner plates," Willard said. "Alamo drinking glasses. How about a big bedspread with a picture of the Alamo on it?"

"Sounds cheesy," Billy Don said.

"Sounds classy," Red said. "And who asked you?"

"Point is," Willard said, "once someone climbs up the steps and comes inside, it shouldn't feel like just any other tree house. It should feel like an *Alamo* tree house, top to bottom."

"That makes absolute sense," Red said, getting into it now.

"You need a couple of wooden ladders outside with dead Mexicans hanging on 'em," Billy Don said.

Red frowned at him.

"You know," Billy Don said. "Like they was trying to climb the walls and they got shot before they—"

"I get it," Red said. "It's friggin' sick. Nobody wants to see that." Red actually thought it might be a nice touch around Halloween, at which point he would claim the idea as his own.

Red and Willard had continued brainstorming well into the night, and although Red wasn't necessarily willing to go completely overboard with the Alamo theme, it did open up his imagination to the possibilities.

The excitement of it all had woken Red up early, and now he stepped down from the porch and walked toward the rear of his property, where the big oak trees would cradle his tree house. He wanted to picture it all in his mind—to *see* the front of the Alamo, right there, in the trees. It would be so damn awesome.

The deer trotted away nervously when Red approached, and as

he lifted his Bubba mug to his lips, he heard a dry twig snapping behind him. Another deer? That didn't make sense. Not *behind* him, where he had just walked.

Red turned slowly—and there was the meat man, pointing a big revolver.

"You've got to be fucking kidding me," Red said.

The meat man smiled.

"I'm going to record this conversation," Marlin said. "Just so you know."

"That's fine," Titus Steele said.

"You're going to be discharged later today?"

"That's what they tell me."

"You're feeling okay right now?"

"Can't complain."

"You aren't on any painkillers or sedatives?"

"No, sir."

"Any other medications?"

"Blood pressure meds, but that's all. My mind is crystal clear, if that's what you're wondering. As opposed to yesterday."

"And you're ready to talk?"

"That's why I called. Where's the pretty lady from yesterday?"

"That pretty lady is the chief deputy of Blanco County—second in command at the sheriff's office," Marlin said.

"I didn't mean no disrespect."

Marlin took a seat in the padded visitor's chair beside Steele's hospital bed. He placed his phone—with an audio recording app running—on the arm of the chair.

"Right now, she's coordinating a search for your nephew," Marlin said. "We found your truck late yesterday evening. We haven't found your nephew yet, but we will eventually. Right now I need you to tell me what happened yesterday afternoon."

"Yes, sir, I will, and a lot more. This goes back further than that, and I figure I might as well tell you every last bit of it."

"That would be good," Marlin said. "But one question before you start, since we currently have more than a dozen deputies, two search dogs, and a helicopter looking for your nephew. Was he the one who shot you yesterday?"

"He was, yeah," Steele said. "Sorry son of a bitch, really. His daddy—my brother in law—was pretty rough on him as a boy. Used to beat him pretty good. But that ain't no excuse, is it? Anyway, it looked like a .44 Magnum, just like you was wondering yesterday. Big ol' revolver."

No surprise there. Henry Jameson had found a spent bullet at Rodney Bauer's ranch, and had then made a positive match with the bullet that killed Hank Middleton. Cody Brock had stolen the gun from Rodney, killed Hank, shot at Geist, and then tried to kill his uncle.

"Any idea where he is now?" Marlin asked.

"Probably hiding in the woods somewhere."

Marlin had a lot of questions, but he always found it more effective to let the subject tell his story first, and then Marlin could follow up on any loose ends later. So he said, "Go ahead and start at the beginning."

"Okay," Steele said. "Well, like I said, he shot me, but he did more than that. He also killed that kid—Sean Hudson."

Marlin felt that familiar rush of adrenaline any cop feels when you're about to take a giant step forward in a case.

"How do you know?" Marlin asked. "He told you about it?"

"Better than that," Steele said. "I saw it happen."

"Billy Don!" Red called out, starting to sweat. "Come out here for a second!"

He was sitting in his recliner, where Lightfoot had told him to sit. Lightfoot was standing beside the flat-screen TV, which was mounted on the wall that formed a 90-degree angle with the long hallway that ran to the far end of the trailer. Billy Don wouldn't be able to see the meat man until he stepped into the living room, and then it would be too late.

"Again," Lightfoot said quietly.

Red didn't know what to do. He didn't see any way out. He had no choice but to comply. "Billy Don!"

If Billy Don responded to Red's call, Lightfoot would have both of them at gunpoint. Then he could do whatever he wanted to them. Red figured it wouldn't be pretty. This guy had probably killed Hank Middleton, and what would stop him from adding two more corpses to that list?

Red was kicking himself for walking around unarmed after learning that Lightfoot was on the run. Miller Creek Loop was several miles from Red's place, but Lightfoot had had all night to make the journey on foot, probably following dark county roads, ducking into the roadside brush whenever a vehicle passed. He could have gone anywhere, but he chose to come here. Bad sign. He wanted revenge for the way Billy Don had treated him after he'd wrecked his truck.

"Again," Lightfoot said.

"Billy Don!" Red yelled. Then, quieter, he said, "He's sleeps like a goddamn drunk mule."

Lightfoot shook his head, meaning he wasn't going to let Red give up.

"His hearing is shot," Red said. "Too many rounds from a deer rifle."

Lightfoot whispered, "Wake. Him. Up."

"You should take my truck and go," Red said. His heart was thundering. "It runs great. I won't call the cops. I was gonna replace it anyway. Or, hey, take Billy Don's Ranchero. Even better."

Lightfoot raised the revolver and sighted down the barrel. "Get him in here."

"Billy Don!"

Then Red remembered the stacks of cash forming a hump under the Mexican blanket. *Oh, good Lord, don't let him notice that hump.*

"You were there when Cody killed Sean Hudson?" Marlin asked.

"Yeah, I was," Steele said. "Now I'm gonna tell you the full story. Won't leave nothin' out."

"I appreciate that. And I'd like to hear what you have to say."

"Okay, so, I met the kid, Sean, when he was out there surveying the ranch. Seemed like a decent guy. He'd found an arrowhead—just lying there on the ground—and he gave it to me. Said it was worth about a hundred bucks. Later on, he asked if he could come out and look for more arrowheads and other stuff. Of course, you know how Dr. Walz feels about that kind of thing. He wouldn't want any amateurs screwing everything up. But then I started thinking about the feral hogs and the damage they do with all their rooting around. Hell, when you compare it to that, what would it hurt if a couple of people poked around in the dirt a little? It wasn't like they'd be coming in with a backhoe."

Steele was rationalizing. No surprise.

"So, yeah, I'm not proud of it, but I made a deal to let him on the place. He said they'd be digging mostly down by the river, which was fine by me, because that's the most remote part, where Dr. Walz wasn't likely to see 'em. Not that he got out on the ranch much, because he didn't. Never made much sense to me. Why would you own a place like that and then sit inside your house all day?"

Marlin was tempted to ask who Sean was digging with, but he resisted for the moment and let Steele continue.

"Of course, I ain't an idiot, so it occurred to me early on that they could cheat the hell out of me," Steele said. "I mean, I couldn't watch 'em all day, so how was I supposed to know what they found or what each piece was worth? So what I did was, I'd show up unexpectedly every now and then and ask 'em what they'd found. Surprise 'em, so they'd think I might pop up at any minute. Then I found this great little spot off the main road where I could park above the river and watch 'em through binoculars. Not hiding—they knew I was up there, and that was the whole point, being visible. Plus, I kept track of the Facebook page where they sold the pieces, so I had a pretty good idea what things were going for."

Marlin continued to sit silently, but he was compiling some questions for later.

"So then Cody calls and says he's coming over from New Mexico," Steele said. "Wanted to know if he could bunk at my place for a week or two. What am I gonna say, because he's kinfolk, you know? I didn't really want him around, but he'd be gone most of the day anyway, making sales calls. The day after he got here, I showed him around the ranch, and we ended up in that spot above the river.

Sean and that girl, Avery, were down there, so I was telling Cody about my sweet deal—they dig the items up, they sell 'em, and I get a third. The thing is, while we were sitting there, watching 'em, they looked like they was arguing about something, and it got pretty intense."

Steele grimaced.

"Then Sean hauled off and slapped Avery across the face."

36

Finally, Billy Don answered back, hollering, "I'm sleeping, asshole!"

Red looked at Lightfoot and raised his eyebrows. *What now?*

Lightfoot made an impatient gesture with the barrel of the revolver. *Yell again.*

"Well, come look at this!" Red called back. "Hurry up!"

No answer. Thirty seconds passed.

"You've got one minute to get him in here," Lightfoot said.

"Get your fat ass out here!" Red yelled. He was starting to panic.

Again, Billy Don didn't answer. There was no sound of movement from that end of the trailer.

"Thirty seconds," Lightfoot said.

Then Red had an idea—a way to send a secret warning and let Billy Don know that something wasn't right out here.

"There's a cougar behind the trailer!" Red yelled. "It just killed a deer! Hurry up, before it leaves!"

Red snuck a look at Lightfoot to see how he reacted. All he said was, "Fifteen seconds."

That meant Lightfoot hadn't picked up on it. There weren't any cougars in Blanco County. Hadn't been in decades. But that didn't stop plenty of people—especially the non-hunters—from thinking they'd seen one. Red and Billy Don always got a good laugh from those stories, because the "cougar" in question usually turned out to be a housecat, a bobcat, a ringtail, or even a fox.

The question was, would the warning work?

"Five seconds," Lightfoot said, raising the gun again. At this point, Red had no doubt that Lightfoot would shoot him dead in cold blood.

"Billy Don!" Red yelled one last time, and his voice had a noticeable quiver in it.

"Hang on, goddamn it!" Billy Don yelled back. "I'm coming!"

"Now, I don't know how you was brought up," Steele said, "but where I come from, you don't raise a hand to a woman, don't matter what she's said or done. So Cody and I piled out of the truck and went down the hill, and by then, Avery was trying to smack him back. She wasn't putting up with that shit, and who can blame her? Well, Cody was ahead of me, and he walks up and hits Sean with a left hook that knocks him to the ground, because let me tell you something, Cody knows how to throw a punch."

Marlin glanced at his phone to confirm that it was still recording. This was good stuff. The punch from Cody Brock was supported by the abrasion that had been found on Sean Hudson's face.

"Cody says something to him—calling him a little bitch or something—and Sean just stays down, rubbing his face. So then both of us—Cody and me—we turn to go see if Avery is all right, but she's already storming off, on her way up the hill."

Steele paused for a moment and shook his head, as if the memory was painful.

"We hadn't taken three or four steps when I heard Sean moving behind us. So I spin around and see that he's coming for Cody, and he has that little pickaxe in his hand—I forget what you call it, but they use it for digging."

"Wiggle pick," Marlin said.

"Right. Wiggle pick. Well, Sean's got that wiggle pick in his hand, and his face—man, I don't think I've ever seen anybody that angry. He was in a rage. Cody turns around just in time, because Sean takes a big swing with that pick and Cody jumps out of the way. Then he wraps Sean up in a bear hug, and they're wrestling hard, and the next thing I know, they come apart and Cody has the pick. I figure it's over then, you know, because Sean won't keep fighting. And he doesn't. Matter of fact, he starts to back off. But Cody has a hell of a temper, and he don't always think straight.

Instead of letting that be the end of it—no harm, no foul—he rushes toward Sean, and—"

Steele paused again, staring at the far wall. He was obviously replaying the scene in his mind, and it unsettled him.

Marlin waited.

Steele said, "Sean had his hands in front of him—I remember that part very clearly—that he was backing up, trying to get away, but Cody swings that pick sideways and nails him right in the side of the head." Steele looked down at his hands. "It was pretty damn bad. Sean sort of staggered around for about three seconds like some kind of goddamn zombie, and then he dropped without so much as another twitch. He was stone dead, no question about it. I stepped up and felt for a pulse, but I couldn't find nothin'. No breathing, either."

So it had been a senseless killing. No planning. No big conspiracy. No motive except anger. Unfortunately, those types of murders were all too common.

Obviously Cody Brock couldn't claim self-defense—not if Sean Hudson no longer had a weapon and was trying to back away. Marlin could understand why Steele had been reluctant to provide incriminating evidence against his own nephew, despite the fact that Steele didn't seem overly fond of him.

But what about Avery? Why hadn't she been willing to tell the sheriff's office what had happened? It was time to start asking questions and get the details nailed down.

"Where was Avery at this point?" Marlin asked.

"She was already halfway up the hill."

"So she didn't see Sean get killed?"

"No."

"Did she ever see the body?"

"Nope."

"Would you be able to show me the exact spot where Sean died?"

"Sure, no problem. It was under a big cypress tree. Except—well, I killed a pig and bled it out over that spot."

"Why did you do that?" Marlin asked. He knew the answer, but he wanted Steele to admit it on recorded audio.

"To screw up your DNA tests," Steele said.

"When was this?"

"Earlier this week. Wish I hadn't done it, but it's too late now."

"Okay, tell me what happened immediately after Sean died. What did you say? What did Cody say?"

"I can't remember word for word, but I said something like, 'I can't believe you just did that.' He said, 'Hey, he was coming after me! You saw it!' I didn't exactly feel like arguing the point, seeing as how he still had a crazy look in his eyes. So I just let it go, for the time being."

"Do you know what Sean and Avery were arguing about?" Marlin asked.

"Yep. Apparently Avery wasn't seeing Sean exclusively."

"She was cheating on him?"

"Guess you could put it that way. Sean sure did."

Red could hear Billy Don grunting and groaning as he hoisted himself out of bed, and then he could hear the squeaky hinges on the bedroom door, followed by the familiar vibrations as Billy Don began to lumber down the narrow hallway.

Red's heart fell. Apparently Billy Don hadn't picked up on Red's warning.

Joseph Lightfoot had his back pressed tightly against the wall, and now he raised the revolver again, ready for Billy Don to enter the room.

Red was terrified. Lightfoot was going to kill them both. That was why he was here, wasn't it?

There was only one remaining option. Red had to shout a warning to Billy Don, knowing that Lightfoot would immediately turn and shoot Red. Could Red jump out of the way?

He opened his mouth, preparing to yell his lungs out—and right then the vibrations stopped. Total silence followed for ten seconds.

Then Billy Don said, "I'm looking out the window in the junk room and I don't see nothing."

The junk room was on the other side of the wall Lightfoot was leaning against.

Red didn't know what to do. Should he answer? He looked at Lightfoot, who appeared equally at a loss. Had Billy Don understood the warning? Or was it just pure luck that he had stopped in the junk room?

"Red?" Billy Don said.

"Yeah?"

"Where's the cougar? You yanking my chain?"

Was Billy Don really looking for a cougar? Or was he playing along?

"It's still out there," Red said. "Probably the same cougar we saw last weekend. Remember that one?"

Would Billy Don get it? Lightfoot was the cougar! Red was trying to tell Billy Don that Lightfoot had come back.

Another long silence followed. Red was holding his breath. Lightfoot remained against the wall, waiting, as stiff as a dead possum.

Then Red heard a wonderful noise from the junk room—the unmistakable sound of a shell being racked into a shotgun.

37

"Who was Avery seeing?" Marlin asked.

"That I don't know," Steele said.

"How did Sean find out?"

"Don't know that either."

"Well, how do you know that she *was* cheating?" Marlin asked.

"Avery told me."

"When?"

"When I got up to my truck. See, I went up there to call the sheriff, and Avery was up there, and when I asked her if she was okay, she starts crying and telling me what an asshole Sean is. Tells me he was real controlling. That's the word she used—controlling. Said he basically forced her into a relationship she didn't want. And now, after that slap, she was angry as hell. I asked why he slapped her, and she said he found out she was seeing somebody else, but it wasn't any of his damn business and she could do whatever she wanted."

"And she still didn't know at that point that Sean was dead?" Marlin asked.

"Nope. I was just about to tell her, and I know she's gonna freak out, but that's when Cody shows up. I'm ashamed of what happened next. I truly am. Because I sat right there and let Cody lie to her. He said the same thing he said to me—that it was self defense—and I didn't say a word, even though it was bullshit."

Steele appeared authentically remorseful.

"Why did you go along with it?" Marlin asked.

Steele didn't answer for a long moment. Then he said, "Looking back on it, it was a bad decision. Stupid. But I was looking at this beautiful young girl whose face was still red from where Sean smacked her—and he *did* try to hit Cody with the pickaxe—and the truth is, I decided a guy like that had it coming."

Steele grabbed a plastic cup of ice water on the table beside his bed and took a long drink. Marlin waited quietly.

Steele said, "And then I thought—what's gonna happen now? Cody would get in trouble, for sure, and I had no problem with that at all. But what about Avery? She'd been trespassing, stealing artifacts—probably felony level, when you add 'em all up. Did she deserve to go to jail for that, after the way Sean treated her? She probably never woulda set foot on that ranch if Sean hadn't badgered her into it. Did she deserve to have her life ruined?"

More rationalizing.

"How did Avery respond when you told her Sean was dead?" Marlin asked.

"'Bout like you'd expect," Steele said. "Screaming and crying, but to be honest, I think she was mostly just scared that all three of us would be in deep shit because of it. She kept saying, 'What're we gonna do?'"

"She didn't want to call the sheriff, either?" Marlin asked.

Steele took another drink of water. Was he stalling? Choosing his next words carefully?

"I can't remember if she ever brought that up or not, but I know she wasn't thinking straight. It was like she was expecting us to figure out a solution."

"Okay," Marlin said. "Then what happened?"

Steele said, "We decided the best thing to do, considering the circumstances, was to move him. I mean, it wasn't like we could take back what had happened. And I went along with it for Avery's sake, to keep her out of trouble. Like I said earlier—stupid."

"Who first suggested moving the body?" Marlin asked.

"Cody. No question. All his idea."

"How did Avery react to that?"

"She really didn't say much at all. I think she would've agreed to whatever we decided. She was pretty out of it."

"How so?"

"Just dazed. Almost like she was in shock."

If that was true, a defense lawyer would play that up for all it was worth—to the point of suggesting that Avery Kingsberry was temporarily insane after learning that Sean Hudson had died, so she certainly couldn't be held accountable for her actions.

"How did you move the body?" Marlin asked.

"My truck," Steele said.

"In the cab or the bed?"

"The bed. Hosed it out real good afterward, because of DNA."

Simply hosing the bed out almost certainly wouldn't have removed all traces. Forensic tests would likely be able to confirm or discredit Steele's story.

"You moved it the same day?" Marlin asked.

"That night, right after sundown."

"All three of you moved it?"

"Just Cody and me. We told Avery to go on home."

"How did you decide where to dump the body?"

"I'd been on that ranch once before, hunting with a buddy of mine. I figured the buzzards and critters would get it before anyone found it, but I guess I was wrong."

"Walk me through it," Marlin said. "Step by step."

Billy Don's voice came from the junk room. "Hey, Lightfoot...I've got six rounds of double-ought buckshot with your name on it. Brand-new Maverick 88. Been looking for a reason to try it out on something warm-blooded."

Lightfoot didn't speak. Didn't budge. Neither did Red, except for the grin that slowly formed on his face.

Billy Don said, "I'm real tempted to start blasting through the wall. Oh, and before you decide to do the same, you should know I'm standing behind an 800-pound gun safe."

It was a lie. The gun safe was in Red's bedroom closet. But Lightfoot didn't know that.

"Lightfoot?" Billy Don said.

Lightfoot didn't respond.

"Red?" Billy Don said.

Red waited for Lightfoot to look his way and give him some kind of sign, but he didn't.

"Yeah?" Red said.

"Where is he?"

Now Lightfoot moved—just enough to point the revolver at Red. Red kept quiet.

"He's aiming at you, huh?" Billy Don said.

Red didn't answer.

Billy Don said, "Lightfoot, your best bet at this point is to walk out the door and start running. I'll give you a 30-second head start. Seeing as how I weigh twice what you do, I'd say your odds are pretty damn good. I get winded walking to the refrigerator."

Again, Lightfoot didn't answer. Smart, because if he did, Billy Don could estimate his location and deliver a round of buckshot through the wall.

"Hey, while we're having this little visit," Billy Don said, "we was wondering...are you an Indian or not? Excuse me, I mean Native American."

Red almost laughed in spite of the situation.

Billy Don said, "By the way, if these walls were any thinner, you could see through 'em. Just something to keep in mind. Have you made up your mind about that 30-second head start yet? Because I'm losing my patience. It's the best offer you're gonna get."

Lightfoot looked at Red. Then he looked toward the front door. Red was starting to get his hopes up.

Red said, "He's thinking about it," which caused Lightfoot to grip the revolver with both hands, as if he were about to fire.

"Billy Don, do me a favor," Red said. "If this asshole shoots me, make him suffer for as long as you can."

"You bet," Billy Don said. "Anything for a friend."

Surely Lightfoot understood that he had no realistic options.

Billy Don said, "Lightfoot, I figure you're afraid to move, because I'll be able to hear you. But I'm not waiting much longer. And the thing is, I'm pretty sure I know exactly where you're standing, because I know where *I'd* be standing if I were you. So my first shot is gonna go right—"

"Okay," Lightfoot said. "I'll leave. But I want my cash back."

"Not a chance," Billy Don said. "We gave it to all the customers you ripped off."

Stretching the truth, but it was kind of accurate.

"You're in no position to bargain," Red said.

"Shut up," Lightfoot said.

"Just get out," Red said. "While you can."

For one long moment, Lightfoot stared down the revolver barrel at Red. Then he said, "You'd better not come after me, even after 30 seconds."

"Fair enough," Billy Don said. "You got my word. As long as we never see you again. Not here. Not anywhere."

Lightfoot stepped slowly and softly away from the wall, past Red in the recliner, still aiming the revolver at him. Then he moved behind the recliner, where Red couldn't see him, and Red heard him open the front door.

"You guys are fucking idiots," Lightfoot said, pausing in the doorway.

"Hit the road," Billy Don said from the junk room.

Red sat perfectly still, his back to the crazy meat man, hoping Lightfoot wouldn't blast a parting shot. After a long moment, the door closed.

Red exhaled. Jesus. So close.

For a moment, there was silence.

Then Red felt it again. The trailer began to vibrate again as Billy Don rumbled down the hallway, hurrying for the door at the other end of the trailer.

"Billy Don!" Red yelled.

Why chase after an armed psychopath?

Red heard the back door open and slap hard against the outside of the trailer, so Red hopped out of the recliner and ran down the hallway. Before he reached the open back door, he heard a shot—a round from the revolver—followed by a blast from Billy Don's shotgun.

Then three more shotgun blasts in quick succession.

38

"There's not a lot to it," Steele said. "We waited until sundown, and then we came back to get him. The body. We couldn't drive my truck down there—too rough—so we carried him up the hill. Then we put it in the bed of my truck and put a tarp over it."

"How did you secure the tarp?"

"I had a couple of bags of corn in the back. We put one on either side."

"Okay, what next?"

"We drove over to that other ranch and—"

"Who drove?"

"I did. It was my truck."

"What route did you take?"

"All back roads, considering what we was hauling."

Marlin asked Steele to identify the specific roads, and he readily named them.

"What happened when you got to the other ranch?" Marlin asked.

"We kept it simple. Just pulled over on the shoulder—there ain't any traffic along there, especially at night—and we, well, dumped him over the fence. Then we climbed over and drug him into the brush."

"Did anyone drive by while you were there?"

"Nope." He waited to see if Marlin had more questions, then said, "Cody tried to pull the pickaxe out of his head, but it was stuck like a son of a bitch. Reminded me of a time I jackhammered too deep into limestone and got the bit stuck. He kept tugging at it, but I told him we had to go. He wiped the handle down with a bandana, and then we took off."

In this case, Marlin already knew that the quick wipe-down

hadn't been enough to remove the DNA. Henry Jameson had managed to pull three DNA profiles from the pick, and it was highly probable that one of those profiles would match Cody Brock.

"Did you go straight home?" Marlin asked.

"We stopped at El Charro to get some supper."

What kind of person was hungry after disposing of a corpse?

"What did you have?" Marlin asked.

"Enchilada plate. What I always have."

"What'd Cody have?"

"Same."

"What time was it?"

"About nine forty-five. They was just about to close up."

That would be easy enough to check. The restaurant would have saved the checks for each table.

"Who waited on you?" Marlin asked.

"I think her name is Veronica. Short, dark-haired gal. Mexican. She's only worked there a few months."

"How'd you pay?"

"Cash."

"Then what?"

"Swung by the reservoir and got rid of his phone."

Finally, that question was answered. And it gave credence to Steele's story, because he would have had no way of knowing Hudson's phone had never been found.

"Where, specifically?" Marlin asked.

"Parked right by the boat ramp and Cody heaved it as far as he could. Probably 50 yards out. He turned it off first, and smashed it with a rock."

"Was anyone else parked in the area?"

"Nope."

"What next?"

"We went back to the ranch. Next morning, I hosed out the bed of the truck."

"We'll need to take some swabs. You okay with that?"

"Be my guest. As long as I get the truck back without a bunch of bullshit."

"What about the tarp?"

"Hosed it off, too, and put it back in the shed."

More DNA. More support for Steele's story, if it was true and accurate. But Steele had lied during his interview on Wednesday, and he could be lying again now. That's why it was so important to force Steele to commit to his story—even the smallest details—so Marlin or Lauren could pick it apart later and note inconsistencies or factual errors, if there were any. They could also compare Steele's account to Cody's and Avery's, if either of them ever agreed to talk.

Marlin decided to branch out in his line of questioning. "Has Cody ever told you about an incident in Sanders, Arizona?"

Titus Steele grinned. "I can probably help you out with that, too—but first, maybe we should talk about the deal I'm gonna get if you ever want me to repeat any of this in court."

Red froze when he heard the shotgun blasts. Waited for more. Nothing. Instead of going out the back door, he ducked into his bedroom instead. Grabbed his Colt Anaconda .45 from underneath the mattress. Then he ran outside to see what was happening.

The revolver hung heavy in his hand as he peeked around the corner of the trailer. He spotted Billy Don 40 yards away, moving slowly through some cedar trees on the west side of the property, studying the ground as he went. He had the shotgun cradled in his arms. The meat man was nowhere to be seen.

Red gave a quick, sharp whistle. Billy Don looked back at him, then waved him over. The coast was clear. Red covered the space in a quick jog, and when he reached Billy Don, he said, "Where's Lightfoot?"

"Hauled ass," Billy Don said, still moving slowly along a deer trail through the trees. "That dude can run. Shoulda broken his legs the other day. I knew we went too easy on him. Now it's coming back to bite us in the ass."

"Think you hit him?"

"Don't know. Moving target. Limbs and shit in the way."

"Guess he didn't hit you," Red said.

"I don't think he even aimed," Billy Don said. "Probably figured the shot would scare me enough to back off."

There weren't any houses in the direction Lightfoot had run. Just a couple of small, empty tracts, and then a large cattle ranch beyond that.

"You saved my ass," Red said.

"Yup."

"Thanks."

Billy Don grunted, like *No big deal.*

"Glad you figured out my secret message," Red said. "I knew Lightfoot wouldn't know there ain't any cougars around here."

Billy Don stopped for a moment and looked at him, grinning. "That was the secret message?"

"Huh?"

"I thought the message was when you called me a fat ass. I knew you wouldn't've said that unless sumpin' weird was going on. Figured it had to be Lightfoot coming back."

Red didn't want to be annoyed—he really didn't—but he couldn't help himself. "Well, why would I have said all that shit about cougars?" he asked.

"I dunno," Billy Don said, continuing on the trail again. "Didn't make any sense."

"*Exactly*," Red said, following behind him. "That's why it was such a perfect secret message."

Billy Don took another step forward, and then another, easing along slowly, as if he were tracking a deer.

"That fat ass comment was meaningless," Red said. "It didn't even have nothing to—"

"Check it out," Billy Don said, pointing.

On the ground was an oblong splatter of bright-red blood about the size of a quarter.

Marlin had been worried that Steele would eventually clam up and ask for a deal, but he was glad the conversation had lasted as long as it had. He hated the possibility that Titus Steele might avoid prosecution, but that was the cold reality of the situation. Yes, Steele had just given an in-depth statement, all recorded, but if he didn't get a plea bargain, he could simply recant. Say he'd made it all up. Say he was still loopy from being shot in the head. Or refuse to repeat it in front of a jury. Happened all the time.

Of course, Marlin wasn't going to give up just yet.

"Any potential deal would be up to the county attorney," Marlin said. "And I'll get her over here. But if you talk about the thing in Sanders, you'd probably have an even greater—"

"Forget it," Steele said. "I just solved a murder for you."

"I understand, but the more you cooperate right now, the more—"

"I've cooperated plenty," Steele said. "When have you ever had it so good?"

Lightfoot was hit. How badly? Flesh wound? Something worse? How far could he go?

Billy Don stepped over the large drop of blood and began looking for more.

"What're you doing?" Red said.

"Going after him. I still got two more rounds, and three more in my pocket."

"Forget it, Billy Don," Red said.

"Look. Another drop."

"You've gotta let him go. So far, you ain't done nothin' wrong. But if you track him down and finish him off, cops'll give you a hard time—maybe even arrest you for it—especially if you do it on somebody else's land."

"But he was in *our* house. With a gun."

"Yep, but now he ain't. Ain't even on my property, so it's a whole new ball game. Different laws apply."

Red was almost positive he was right. Plus, he knew that if Billy Don went after Lightfoot, Red would have to go along, too—and he didn't see the upside in it. He wasn't nearly angry enough at Lightfoot to risk his life. He preferred to call the sheriff, let them handle it, and then forget the meat man once and for all.

"You sure?" Billy Don asked.

"Yep. You'd be placing yourself in legal jeopardy by crossing a property line with a gun, and then a second time if you used it on Lightfoot. It's what they call double jeopardy. It's in the

Constitution."

Billy Don appeared disgusted. "You been taking the fun out of everything lately."

Marlin said, "I can tell you right now—any deal you might get is going to be based on you telling the complete story. So if you've left anything out..."

"I've told you everything," Steele said.

Marlin stared at him for a long moment. Steele didn't flinch or look away.

Marlin said, "And if you've tweaked the truth a little, or even if you think you might be remembering something incorrectly, you need to be clear about that."

"Truth is, I'm doing you a favor here," Steele said. "And we both know it. If you'd rather I didn't—"

"No," Marlin said. "I just want to be up front with you about what the county attorney will expect. No surprises that way for either of us."

"Then let's get the ball rolling," Steele said.

The recording app continued to run, but a text message from Lauren popped up on the screen.

Plz call ASAP. Brock possibly wounded in shootout with BD Craddock.

39

If a man like Cody Brock had gone on the run from the law in rural Texas 40 years earlier, or 30, or even just 20 years earlier, he would have had a rough time evading capture for more than a few days.

But today, he had a better chance, because he had a world of modern technology in his pocket.

Compass.
Maps.
Flashlight.
Aerial photographs.
Police scanner.
Radio.
TV.
Weather radar.
Even a phone.

He could use those tools to avoid populated areas and forge a path most likely to allow him to escape. He could monitor radio transmissions from the sheriff's department, read breaking news updates, or check Facebook for the latest rumors regarding his whereabouts. He could research various types of plants and berries to determine which were safe to eat, or search for a reliable source of clean water. And, yes, he could make phone calls or send text messages—and possibly arrange for someone to pick him up in an out-of-the-way spot on some quiet county road.

Making matters worse, according to Titus Steele, Brock was a reasonably active outdoorsman, with the skills necessary to get along just fine for several days, even in the Texas heat. Brock had been wearing the same outfit he always seemed to wear: jeans, a long-sleeved denim shirt, and a sturdy pair of hiking boots. Better than shorts, a tank top, and flip-flops.

In less than three minutes after receiving Lauren's text, Marlin was in his truck and on his way to join her and the search team. Of course, now their focus had shifted several miles away from Hidden Valley Ranch Road, where Cody Brock had stashed Steele's Ford F-350, to Red O'Brien's place.

He called Lauren, who answered on the third ring, saying, "Hang on," and then he could hear her having a discussion with some of the search team members. Marlin waited patiently, and then Lauren came back on the line and gave a quick update on the situation. Early that morning, Cody Brock had accosted Red O'Brien outside his trailer. Billy Don Craddock had come to the rescue, shotgun in hand, and now it appeared Brock was wounded.

"No way of knowing how badly," Lauren said. "We found about a dozen drops of blood going about forty yards, and then nothing."

Marlin knew that didn't mean the wound wasn't serious. Brock might've applied a makeshift tourniquet, or perhaps the blood had coagulated enough to stop flowing on its own. But he could be gravely injured.

"How long since the shot?" Marlin asked.

"About forty minutes now."

Not good.

Assuming a speed of four miles per hour—not running, but walking quickly, or perhaps even trotting at times, if he could—Brock could've already covered nearly three miles. Problem was, that was three miles in almost any direction. A circle with a radius of three miles would cover more than 28 square miles, if Marlin remembered the formula correctly. Also, with every minute that passed, that circle became larger.

"Got a perimeter working?" Marlin asked.

There was no practical way to secure the entire circumference of the search circle—that would require literally hundreds of deputies—but they could create checkpoints at strategic places on the roadways leading out of the circle. Stop each vehicle leaving the area. Ask the occupants if they'd seen a man matching Brock's description. Request permission to check the trunk or any other potential hiding spot. Even if they didn't find Brock that way—and Marlin doubted they would—the checkpoints would provide useful information. They'd know whether he was still on foot.

"As quick as we can," Lauren said. "I might set you up at an intersection. I'll let you know in the next few minutes."

Marlin could hear a search dog barking in the background, and more voices. Arranging a search was usually a chaotic scene, and you felt the pressure to get things rolling as quickly as possible.

He said, "I'll let you go, but FYI, Titus Steele just named Brock in the murder of Sean Hudson. Steele was an eyewitness."

"Outstanding."

"Okay, more later. Let me know where you want me."

"Will do," Lauren said, and she disconnected.

Marlin then quickly made a phone call to Deborah Timms, the county attorney, to discuss the situation with Titus Steele. She didn't answer, so he left a brief voicemail.

Then he called Nicole. She was working from home, but she didn't answer either. He said, "Hey, Cody Brock is still on the run—last seen over by Red O'Brien's place. That was nearly an hour ago, so he could've covered quite a bit of ground since then. Just a heads-up. Text me when you get a chance."

He hung up. No reason to be concerned. Marlin's house was more than three miles from O'Brien's place. Probably five or six miles. Which meant, theoretically, that Brock could arrive there sometime in the next hour, even moving at no more than a brisk walking speed.

It wasn't out of the question. Brock had obviously covered a lot of ground to reach O'Brien's place. Would he have the guts to go after yet another customer who had made him mad? Could he do it in the daytime, injured? Or was he hunkered down somewhere, waiting for nightfall?

Marlin took a left off the highway and headed west.

Cody Brock was drenched with sweat, thirsty as a son of a bitch, and out of breath, but he maintained a steady pace toward his destination, which was now less than a quarter-mile ahead.

The important thing right now was to keep a cool head. Don't panic. Just stay calm. Think straight. Make the best of a bad situation. He should've taken off last night, but he could still find a way out of this. One step at a time.

His left forearm ached, almost as bad as his nose, but the wound wasn't that bad. The bleeding had stopped. He'd have to dig the buckshot out later. Just one piece. That's all that had caught him. Talk about a stroke of luck. The big hillbilly had unleashed four rounds from a 12-gauge, and somehow Cody hadn't been torn to pieces. Sure, he'd been running, and there'd been trees in the way, but still, good luck. No denying it.

It was bad luck, on the other hand, that he hadn't been able to shoot both of those rednecks right in the chest and watch them suck for air until their eyes went still. That had been his plan—take care of those two idiots, then blaze a trail for parts unknown. Now he'd have to leave without getting that satisfaction.

He came over a small hill and there it was 80 yards below. The house. He had a great view into the fenced back yard, which was still and quiet. No people. No animals. There weren't any neighbors close enough to worry about. But was anybody home?

He eased up next to the trunk of a large cedar tree and stood perfectly still. Waited. Watched. Let his breathing slow and his heart rate decrease. Twenty minutes passed. He saw no movement anywhere around the house. What about inside? Only one way to know for sure.

He began a slow descent down the hill, with the revolver hanging in his right hand as he went.

Marlin's phone chimed with an incoming text from Nicole. He slowed down—no traffic coming—and took a quick peek at his screen.

All good here. Plz don't worry. G is inside with me.

That made him feel better. Nicole could handle anything thrown her way. She was smart enough that she'd have the doors locked, the blinds closed, and her handgun strapped to her hip. Plus, the security cameras would send her a motion alert if anybody approached from any side of the house. If Brock was dumb enough to show up, he'd be a sitting duck.

Marlin put his phone away.

He hadn't heard anything more from Lauren, but by now the search would've continued, with more than a dozen deputies, several tracking dogs, and a helicopter. It would be a smooth, well-organized effort, but that didn't mean Brock couldn't slip through the cracks. A full hour had passed since Cody Brock had run from Billy Don Craddock. The radius of the search circle was now four miles. More than fifty square miles. And there were variables. What if Cody Brock was capable of jogging for a full hour without stopping? He was young. An average jog would be about five miles per hour. A circle with a radius of five miles created a circle containing 78 square miles. That was an area more than three times the size of Manhattan. Needle in a haystack.

Where would Cody Brock go? How far ahead had he planned?

He'd had the chance to get away the previous night, but instead he had gone to Red O'Brien's place, obviously intending to do some harm. He chose to walk directly into the lair of two heavily armed rednecks—confronting them where they lived. He must've known there would be risk involved. Had he had a back-up plan? Had he known where he would go if things didn't go as planned?

The answer had to be yes.

But where?

Now that Brock was implicated by an eyewitness in a murder, the search would become even more intense. Deputies from neighboring counties would join in. More game wardens. State troopers. Texas Rangers. Brock would know that. He might decide that it would be too hard to slip away, and instead he would need a place to hide for several days.

Oh, man.

An idea came to Marlin, and he tried to tamp down the adrenaline rush he felt running up his spine and through his chest.

It was just an idea. Was it possible? The distance was right. It made sense. He had to check it out, didn't he?

He pulled to the side of the road and quickly sent a text to Lauren.

Long shot but i'm gonna check hank middletons house.

40

Cody Brock moved from tree to tree, stopping every few minutes to wait and watch. Still no movement around the house. No sounds. Not even the hum of an air conditioner unit. What about inside? Blinds were closed on every window. Hard to tell if any lights were on. Someone could be watching him right now—peeking out. Unavoidable.

Fuck it.

He gave up all pretense of stealth and walked directly toward the home. When he reached the five-wire fence on the rear property line, he climbed over it, slowly and carefully, but it made the buckshot in his forearm flare with pain and begin to trickle blood again.

Thirty yards from the back door now.

Twenty yards.

He slowly crossed the yard and stepped onto the concrete porch, near the back door. Stood dead still for a minute. Listened. Heard nothing from inside the house. No voices. No TV. No stereo.

To the left of the door was a spigot. He could almost taste the sweet well water that would come out of there, but he couldn't risk it yet. He had to make sure there was nobody home first. Once inside, he could relax a little. Drink some water. Hell, drink some beer, if he was lucky enough to find any in the fridge. Cool off in the AC. Take a shower. Watch the news and keep tabs on the cops. Then he'd know when it was safe to clear out for good.

He reached for the doorknob, and that's when he heard a vehicle coming up the driveway in front of the house, gravel crunching under the tires.

Under different circumstances, Marlin would have parked a good distance from Hank Middleton's house and approached on foot, concealing himself as much as possible. Even better, he would've waited for back-up.

But in this case, time was critical, so Marlin eased up the driveway to the house, watching for any movement near the house or in the trees surrounding it. He stopped his truck at an angle 20 yards from the house and killed the engine. He could see the orange warning sticker on the front door. The house was still considered an active crime scene. No admittance.

One hour and twelve minutes had passed since Red O'Brien had called the sheriff's office about Cody Brock's shootout with Billy Don Craddock. According to Google maps, O'Brien's trailer and Middleton's house were 4.4 miles apart. Which meant, if this had been Brock's destination, there was a reasonable possibility he hadn't arrived yet. Marlin was betting on it, and that's why he had risked driving up to the house. Every minute—every second—counted. He wanted to be here, waiting, when Brock arrived, which could be at any moment.

If Brock arrived.

Marlin knew it was unlikely. A long shot, as he'd said in his text to Lauren. He quickly checked his phone. She hadn't responded yet. Too busy.

So Marlin thumbed his mike and let Darrell, the dispatcher, know that he would be out of his vehicle at this address.

Then he put his phone on silent mode and stepped from his truck.

Brock fought the urge to panic. That's what got men killed. Freaking out and losing your shit.

He tried the doorknob. It rotated, but the deadbolt above it was locked, so the door wouldn't give. Now what?

Who was out front?

Brock had read a couple of articles about the man he'd killed—

Hank Middleton—and none of them had mentioned a wife or any kids. But the dead man was bound to have some kin. The person out front could be a nephew or cousin, coming around to check on the place.

The sound of crunching gravel came to a stop. The low drone of the engine went away. Brock waited to hear a door closing, but the sound didn't come. Maybe it simply wasn't loud enough.

He knew he had to make a decision quickly. Haul ass back up the hill? What if the person in the vehicle saw him before he reached the trees? What would they do?

He could wait right here and play it by ear. But what if the person in front walked around to the rear of the house? Brock wouldn't have much of a choice at that point. Open fire. Not good, because someone would report the gunshots, given that a manhunt was taking place.

But hold on a second. He'd been overlooking the obvious.

He could take the vehicle. That might be the best solution yet. Maybe tie the person up and leave them inside the house. Or bring them along; make them do the driving. Cops would be less likely to stop a car with two people in it, right?

All of these thoughts crossed Brock's mind in less than three seconds, and then he stepped off the porch and began to make his way along the rear wall of the house. He moved toward the southeast corner of the house, with the revolver raised in his right hand, ready for action.

Marlin crouched low beside his truck and remained perfectly still, listening. He heard nothing but birds, his ticking engine, and some traffic noise from the highway several miles away.

He drew his .357 and held it in the low-ready position—gripped in both hands, just below his line of sight, but ready to raise and fire rapidly, if necessary.

He wanted to get to the rear of the house as quickly as possible, because Brock would arrive from that direction. But Marlin had to be cautious. Had to allow for the possibility that Brock was already inside the house, or that he might arrive at any moment.

The four windows at the front of the house were covered by blinds that were drawn shut. Marlin slowly came around the front of his truck—feeling more vulnerable now that he had no cover or concealment—and walked toward the house as quietly as possible. Ten steps, then twenty, and as he got closer to the front porch, he veered to the right, toward the two windows on that side, and came to a stop between them, with his body no more than 12 inches from the house. Close, but not touching. Scraping the siding with any part of his body or clothing could give a warning to anyone inside. They could fire a shot right through the wall.

He waited again. Listened. Nothing.

He was beginning to suspect that he was wasting his time—chasing a dead-end lead when he should be joining Lauren and the other deputies in the search, miles away.

But now that he was here, he had to clear the premises.

Taking slow, careful steps, he moved counter-clockwise toward the northwest corner of the house. Not a random choice. He was right-hand dominant, so it was advantageous to round corners with his right arm leading.

He reached the first corner and stopped. Listened some more. Nothing.

He did a quick peek—a search technique in which you bob your head around a corner for a glimpse, then pull it back in a fraction of a second, before you can even register if you've seen anyone. That way, if anyone is waiting and watching, they don't have time to react before your head is gone from view. If you do see someone, and you decide to take a second quick peek, you never do it at the same height.

In this instance, Marlin saw nothing. So he rounded the corner, .357 still in the low-ready position, and continued down the west side of the house.

Cody Brock turned the corner and started walking along the east side of the house. The windows on this side of the house also had the blinds closed. He passed the HVAC condenser unit, which was not running. He reached the northeast corner and slowly stuck his head around to check the front of the house.

He saw nobody.

But a green Dodge truck was parked diagonally in the driveway. From Cody's position, he was looking directly at the front grille. Strange, because it looked a lot like the green Dodge truck he had seen yesterday, after he had nearly blown Uncle Titus's stupid head off. If it *was* the same truck, what did it mean? Surely it was a coincidence. Had to be a different green Dodge truck.

Where was the driver?

Cody turned and looked back the way he had come, just in case. Nobody sneaking up on him.

Had to be one of two possibilities. Either the person from the green truck had gone around the other side of the house, or, more likely, he had gone inside. Which meant he didn't know Cody was here. So he wasn't a threat—unless Cody accidentally revealed himself.

Cody could stay put and hope the person left soon. Or...

Marlin reached the southwest corner, waited, and then took another quick peek.

Nobody around back. No movement. No Cody Brock.

Was Brock on his way here right now, still crossing the ranch behind the house? Maybe.

Or was he inside the house? It was possible. Could be asleep. Or taking a shower. He'd been on the run for a full day, in the heat, without an easy food source, so it was likely he'd want to eat, shower, then sleep.

Marlin pulled his phone out and checked for a text.

Lauren had replied: *No luck here. Anything there?*

Marlin said *Not yet*, and he put his phone away.

Time to rule out the possibility that Brock was inside.

Marlin moved slowly to the back porch and gently twisted the knob on the back door. It turned, but the deadbolt above it was locked. Good. That's the way the deputies would've left it after searching the place. If the deadbolt on the front door was also locked, Brock wouldn't have been able to enter without leaving some evidence of a break-in.

Marlin continued to the southeast corner to check the east side of the house and circle around to the front. He did a quick peek, expecting nothing, but instead saw movement—a man, black hair, blue denim shirt, raising a large revolver with one hand, firing a shot just as Marlin pulled his head back out of sight.

Marlin didn't hesitate. Didn't weigh the odds. He simply reacted, at lightning speed, because he sensed an advantage—an opportunity for an immediate counterstrike.

When he came around the corner a second time, crouched low, less than half a second after his quick peek, Marlin's instincts paid off, because, just as he'd suspected, the revolver in Brock's hand was still high in the air, pointing skyward, recovering from the recoil—

—and Marlin's first shot caught Brock dead center in the chest.

The second shot caught him a little higher—in the soft spot at the base of the throat.

The .44 Magnum fell to the ground just as Marlin's third shot busted through Brock's rib cage.

For two more seconds, Brock stood with his arms hanging loosely, body swaying, eyes unfocused.

Then his knees buckled and he fell forward, face down onto the hard-packed soil. He didn't so much as twitch. There was no sound of breathing, except for Marlin's own, which was fast and ragged. He felt a bit lightheaded. His peripheral vision was cloudy.

Marlin stood in place, his gun still raised, watching for any sign of life from Brock. There was none. The .44 Magnum was several feet from Brock's closest hand. No need to move it.

Marlin carefully slipped his .357 back into his holster, with the hammer resting on a spent shell.

41

It wasn't the first time Marlin had killed a man, and even though he knew from experience the emotional roller coaster that awaited him in the immediate hours, days, and weeks after the shooting, there was no avoiding the ride.

Relief, at first. Even exhilaration—simply because he had survived the encounter. The elation was almost intoxicating.

Then, on the other extreme, guilt would occasionally set in. Or maybe it was just remorse. Despite the fact that Cody Brock had proven himself to be a murderous sociopath through and through, Marlin couldn't help wondering if there might have been a way to take Brock alive. What if he'd tried to talk Brock into giving up? What if he'd called for back-up? Would Brock have gotten away again? Doubtful.

But that was nonsense. If Marlin *had* refrained from firing back, Brock would've run. The search would've continued. And later—an hour or a day—a deputy or even some innocent civilian might've been killed as a result. Marlin had done the right thing. He had potentially saved a life. Maybe several.

And he'd settle on that, until the next sudden twist in his thinking.

For instance...had he behaved selfishly by killing Brock? An odd way to look at it, but had he robbed Brock's victims of justice in the courtroom? Maybe Sean Hudson's and Hank Middleton's surviving family members would've preferred to see Brock rot away in prison for the rest of his life. Marlin had taken away that opportunity, right? Then again...what if Brock had been tried and found not guilty? Slim chances, but not impossible.

And on it would go.

The shooting had to be investigated, just like any other shooting.

Less than two hours later, Marlin sat in the conference room at the sheriff's office and gave a full statement to Brad Anderson, a Texas Ranger out of nearby Llano County. Since Marlin was a state employee, Anderson would lead the investigation, working closely with the sheriff's office.

Over the years, Marlin had spoken with various law-enforcement officers involved in shootings who said the resulting investigation made you feel as if you were being treated like a criminal. Fortunately, despite the ruminations inside his own head, Marlin didn't feel that way.

Anderson impounded Marlin's .357, which was standard.

Marlin's supervisor, a captain from Austin, arrived and placed Marlin on administrative leave—also standard. Then he reassured Marlin that the department had always had the utmost confidence in him, and nothing had changed in that regard. His way of saying he had no doubt the shooting was a good one.

Then he provided Marlin with a back-up service weapon—a nine-millimeter semi-automatic. It felt a little odd in Marlin's hand, but he'd get used to it. The fact that the captain had issued him a back-up was, in itself, another show of support.

The captain asked if Marlin wanted to talk about the incident with someone, meaning a mental health professional. Marlin declined. The offer would be available later, too, if he felt the need for it.

The captain also pointed out that the Blanco County grand jury was currently in session. With luck, Marlin could be cleared and back in the field in a week or two. Marlin said that would be fantastic.

Then he went home.

"You awake?" Nicole asked.

It was nearly one in the morning. Of course he was awake. He hadn't slept yet. Too restless. Mind racing. Replaying the shooting again and again. This was normal. It would be unusual if he *were* able to put it out of his mind.

He reached over and placed his hand on Nicole's hip. She snuggled in closer.

"I'm just so glad it's over," she said.

He could hear Geist snoring softly on her pillow in the corner. The hole in her ear was healing just fine.

"Me, too," he said.

He had received dozens of calls, texts, and emails over the course of the evening—friends and area residents checking in on him. Wishing him well. Saying they'd pray for him. Asking if he needed anything. Phil Colby had been the first to get in touch, saying, "The good guys win again. Glad you're okay."

Marlin was tempted to get up and go into the living room. Watch some TV in there until he could fall asleep. But he didn't want Nicole to worry.

It wasn't bad—lying here in the dark, a beautiful woman by his side. Comfortable. Safe. Secure. He'd done his job to the best of his abilities, despite any misgivings or second guesses.

Sleep would come.

"Wouldn'ta bothered me for a second," Billy Don said. "I guarantee that. I woulda fed him to the hogs and felt like I was doing a public service."

Red had asked Billy Don how he would have felt if he had managed to kill the meat man with the shotgun.

"We ain't got no hogs," Red pointed out.

"Well, I woulda found some hogs," Billy Don said, "or an uncapped well, or, hell, I coulda just sunk his body in a lake. Or cut him into a hundred pieces and scattered 'em from here to Fort Worth."

"Hard to do that and not get caught," Red said.

"Don't matter anyway, because if I *had* kilt him, the cops woulda given me some kind of medal and a pat on the back."

They'd been drinking beer all night out on the back porch, every now and then raising a tall boy to toast the meat man's demise. Was that harsh or cruel, to celebrate a person's death? Maybe, but so what? The man had been a menace to the core.

On the other hand, Red knew from experience that it could shake you up to kill a man. Red had done it once. He'd made an amazing long-distance shot to hit a crazed taxidermist who was threatening the game warden and a little boy. Technically speaking, nobody could be positive that Red had killed the man, but they knew for sure that Red's shot had hit him, and that he'd bled a lot, and then, several days later, they'd found part of his corpse, which also had some fang marks on it, which may or may not have been from a real-life chupacabra, or possibly a hyena. Weird story that Red still told occasionally in beer joints and honky-tonks, or even in feed stores and doctors' offices. Or anyplace where anybody would listen, really.

Every so often, Billy Don would spend a few minutes looking at his iPhone—keeping track of all the gossip about the killing of the meat man by John Marlin. Earlier, somebody said Marlin had shot Lightfoot eighteen times, unloading his Glock on him. Total bullshit, of course, because Red knew for a fact that Marlin didn't carry a Glock. Red had instructed Billy Don to set the record straight, because he figured commenters on Facebook would be willing to accept new information and admit that they were mistaken without any further argument.

Someone on a different thread said they had it on good authority that the cops knew for sure that Lightfoot had killed Hank Middleton, and he'd done it with a .44 Magnum he'd stolen from Rodney Bauer earlier in the week. Same gun Billy Don had taken from Lightfoot's truck, so it was a damned good thing they'd returned it later. Nobody knew. Nobody would ever know.

Some dude from Austin claimed that Lightfoot was a "false flag operation" arranged by the government. He said Lightfoot was an actor and the victims were fake, but the whole thing was supposed to appear real and create panic, which was intended to result in stricter gun laws. The dude ranted about "sheeple" and "libtards" before he got banned from the page. Weird.

Then someone else added that Lightfoot was being blamed for the murder of the guy who'd been found in the western part of Blanco County the previous weekend. Some kind of arrowhead hunter or something. Red wondered what that kid had done to piss off the meat man. Probably wouldn't have taken much. Joseph Lightfoot had proven that he was one of those evil bastards that just walked around making life miserable for as many people as he could. Who knew why there were men like that in this world? Good thing he was dead. That was the bottom line.

"Where do you think we go when we die?" Billy Don asked out of nowhere. "You believe in Heaven and Hell and all that?"

It was the deepest question Billy Don had ever asked, as far as Red could remember.

Red thought about it for a few minutes. "I guess nobody knows for sure. Plus, you gotta be real careful how you answer that sort of thing, because a lot of folks'll think you're some kind of heathen if you don't believe the exact same thing they do—which is tricky, considering there's about a hundred and eighty different breeds of Christians."

"Sure enough. But if you *had* to answer, between you and me..."

The night was warm, but comfortable, with low humidity. A gentle breeze was blowing from the south.

"I figure when you're gone, you're gone," Red said. "That's all she wrote."

"Nothing comes after?"

"Don't know, but I ain't counting on it. Which is why we gotta have fun *now*. Every day. In case this is the only run we get."

"Makes sense," Billy Don said.

"It's an old philosophy I just made up," Red said.

"Guess that explains your Alamo tree house," Billy Don said. "'Scuse me, I mean elevated housing."

"How so?" Red asked.

"It'll make you happy," Billy Don said. "Right?"

"Yeah, I guess."

"So if it's what you wanna do, who cares what anybody else thinks? Build your Alamo. I think it'll be pretty damn cool."

"Yeah?"

"Yeah, but that don't mean I won't make fun of it. Call it a waste of money."

"'Bout what I'd expect," Red said. "And I'll say your tiny brain isn't capable of appreciating creative architecture."

"Fair enough," Billy Don said. He shook his empty beer can. "Want another? I'm buying."

"How are you buying?" Red said. "It's my beer."

"We shouldn't get hung up on the details," Billy Don said.

42

For the next several days, Marlin wished that he—or one of the deputies—could sit Avery Kingsberry down and question her at length.

Would her answers support Titus Steele's account? What if she had seen more than Steele thought she saw? Marlin couldn't help thinking Avery might have witnessed the killing of Sean Hudson, perhaps from halfway up the hill. Or perhaps closer. Maybe Titus Steele was lying about that part—trying to keep Avery from being dragged into it.

Marlin was still on leave, so he couldn't actively participate in the investigation, but Lauren kept him up to date, and what she told him made it obvious that Avery Kingsberry had no intention of speaking with law enforcement. She didn't answer her phone. Didn't return calls. She either wasn't home or wouldn't answer the door on the two occasions when Lauren sent a deputy to her place. Finally an Austin attorney called Lauren and said, "Please do not contact Avery Kingsberry again. I'm representing her, so you can call me, but it will be a waste of your time. She has nothing to say."

Marlin and Lauren agreed that it would be satisfying to charge Titus Steele with something—failure to report a felony, or tampering with or fabricating evidence, or even filing a false report—but they had nothing on him except his own statement, which he'd now recanted. He had nothing to gain from it, with Cody Brock being dead. A competent defense attorney could get the statement tossed in a heartbeat because of Steele's head injury. The lawyer would claim that Steele had been confused. It had all been a fantasy in his head, see? The county attorney would have no interest in pursuing a flimsy case like that.

Lauren called one morning while Marlin was sitting in a chair on his front porch, reading a Billy Kring novel. Geist was snoozing in a sunny spot on the grass.

"Walz won't let us search the ranch," she said. "Says he doesn't want a bunch of deputies digging around and tearing the place up."

Marlin wasn't surprised. Walz had struck him as a highly intelligent man, but the type who doubted the competence—or the dependability—of everyone around him. For a man like that, it was easier to deny access than to trust that the deputies wouldn't leave his property with gaping pits and scarred furrows. Ironically, Walz would've let them search the house where Steele had been living, but he didn't have the authority to let them in. Walz owned it, but it had been Steele's residence, so the deputies would need a warrant, which they probably couldn't get.

Where was Steele now? Nobody knew for sure. Walz had been livid when he learned that Steele had been allowing a couple of diggers onto the ranch, and he had fired Steele immediately. Steele had left town the next day in his F-350. He was under no obligation to tell anyone where he was going.

Lauren had been hoping to process the crime scene near the river and collect samples of the soil beneath the cypress tree where Sean Hudson had allegedly died. The blood from the pig that Steele had gutted over that spot would present a challenge, but it would still be worth a shot.

"Gonna try for a warrant?" Marlin asked.

"Yeah, but don't hold your breath," Lauren said.

The same circumstances that were preventing them from charging Titus Steele—namely, his head injury and the fact that he was no longer standing behind his statement—would likely prevent a judge from granting a warrant. Without the statement, they had no evidence whatsoever that Sean Hudson had been killed on Walz's ranch.

The same circumstances applied to Avery Kingsberry. They did not have probable cause for a warrant to search her house or obtain her phone records.

"Unless something changes soon, Steele and Kingsberry are

going to walk away scot free," Lauren said.

Out on the grass, Geist stood up, turned a circle, and lay down in the sun again.

"I can live with that," Marlin said.

"Yeah, I guess so," Lauren said. "The important thing is, Cody Brock won't be bothering anyone else. You did the world a favor. If that sounds callous, I'm sorry, but that's how I feel."

Marlin didn't reply. He wouldn't sum it up in those same terms himself, but he didn't blame her for doing so. He hadn't heard anything more from Brad Anderson, the Texas Ranger, after the initial interview, but Marlin had no qualms about that. The shooting would be ruled justified and he'd be back on active duty before long.

After that first restless night, he hadn't been particularly disturbed by the shooting. No nightmares. No depression or anxiety. No more second-guessing. Brock was a murderer, and he'd shot at Marlin first, so he'd sealed his own fate. Why should Marlin have had more regard for Brock's life than Brock had had for it himself?

Marlin could see an old Ford truck pulling up to his gate, Red O'Brien driving, Billy Don Craddock in the passenger's seat. What did those two bumpkins want? "I've gotta go," he said to Lauren. "Talk to you soon."

Two hours earlier.

Red was sitting at the small dinette table in the kitchen—a notepad in front of him, calculating how much lumber he'd need for the first stage of his Alamo tree house—when Billy Don joined him, looking glum.

"First that .44 Magnum, and now this," he said, sitting down across from Red. The flimsy chair held.

"Huh?" Red said.

"I'm gonna have to give that laptop up," Billy Don said. "To the cops. They're gonna take it from me. Five hundred bucks, down the drain."

"What are you babbling about?"

"You ready for this?" Billy Don asked.

"Ready for what?" Red said.

"You're not gonna believe it," Billy Don said.

"Well, I'm not gonna have an opinion either way if you don't spit it out."

"Okay," Billy Don said, and he pulled his iPhone from his pocket. "You 'member that girl from the video?"

"Yeah." How could Red forget? He still watched that video a dozen times a day.

"Well, check this out."

Billy Don turned his phone around so Red could see the screen, and there was a Facebook photo of the blond hottie. Just a regular photo—she wasn't naked or anything—like she was outdoors somewhere and somebody said, 'Hey, look this way,' and then they took a picture. She still looked great, even with her clothes on.

"The kid that got killed was her boyfriend," Billy Don said.

"Hang on, what?"

"That arrowhead hunter guy? She was his girlfriend. And now everybody's saying she saw him get killed. That's the rumor."

"No friggin' way," Red said.

"That means the guy who wanted to run away to Costa Rica with her in the video is the dead guy," Billy Don said.

Which was true. And the blond hottie would get drug into the investigation most likely. And Billy Don was right that the cops would want the laptop.

"That's what you get for buying used electronics," Red said.

Marlin walked out to the gate, Geist trotting ahead, and by the time they reached it, O'Brien and Craddock had already gotten out of the truck and were waiting on the other side.

"Need to show you something," O'Brien said.

Craddock had a laptop computer in his hands.

"What's up?" Marlin asked.

"Weird to see you out of uniform," O'Brien said, grinning.

Marlin waited.

"Anyway," O'Brien said, and he looked at Craddock.

"Okay, well, last week I bought this laptop from a woman up in Round Mountain. She had an ad on Craigslist, and it looked pretty good, so I paid her five hundred bucks, and took it home. Later on, I started poking around on it and came across a video."

"Go ahead and tell him what kind of video," O'Brien said.

"It's a naked lady. Not like some high-dollar porn, but just a naked lady swimming in a river."

"Looks like the Pedernales," O'Brien said.

"That's right, it does," Craddock said. "And so she's swimming, or more like wading, and then she gets out, and—"

"It's some guy filming her," O'Brien said. "Probably with a phone."

"Yeah, and they're talking back and forth," Craddock said, "and the thing is, I'm pretty sure the lady is the girlfriend of that guy that got killed and dumped on that ranch west of town. That arrowhead hunter guy, Sean Hudson."

"Her name is Avery Kingsberry," O'Brien said. "The girlfriend, I mean. But you probably already know that. We found it all inline."

"Online," Craddock said.

"What I meant," O'Brien said.

"Yeah, I found it," Craddock said, "and while they're talking, at one point, the boyfriend—this Sean guy—he says something about going to Costa Rica, because they'll have a lot of money soon."

"That's down there below Mexico," O'Brien said. "We checked a map."

Marlin was wondering if Billy Don Craddock had bought Sean Hudson's missing laptop. That would be a tremendous step forward in the case, but Marlin didn't get his hopes up yet.

"Let's see the video," Marlin said. He was still on administrative leave, and he really should've referred them to the sheriff's office, but he couldn't resist.

O'Brien grinned again. "You're a lucky man. Not everybody gets to look at naked ladies as part of the job."

Marlin stared at him until his grin faded.

"Okay, well," O'Brien said. "Billy Don?"

Craddock punched a button on the laptop, and then he turned it around so Marlin could see the screen.

It was Avery Kingsberry, no question. She was in the river up to her bare shoulders. Based on the surroundings, it did look like the Pedernales, just as Craddock and O'Brien had said.

A few seconds later, Avery Kingsberry stood up, revealing her naked torso.

"There we go," O'Brien said.

There was no denying she had a nice body—toned and shapely. Now she walked onto the river bank, toward the camera, revealing that she was totally nude. She grabbed a towel draped over a low-hanging cottonwood branch and began to dry off. Her clothes were in a pile on the ground. She slipped her panties on, and then some khaki shorts, and then her bra, and then she finally noticed she was being filmed.

"What're you doing?" she said. "I told you to stop doing that." There was a hint of a smile on her face, but that didn't necessarily mean she was okay with it.

A male voice said, "Can't help myself. Just look at you. You're a freakin' goddess."

Marlin recognized the voice, and it wasn't Sean Hudson.

It was Jordan Gabbert.

43

Four days later, Lauren and the deputies had built the case as solid as they could build it—but everyone involved conceded that it still had some holes in it. They also agreed that it was time to roll the dice and move forward anyway. By then, the Blanco County grand jury had cleared Marlin in the shooting and he had returned to active duty.

Five days after Red O'Brien and Billy Don Craddock had come forward with the video of Avery Kingsberry, Marlin and Lauren caught up to Jordan Gabbert as he walked from his car to his apartment. It was nearly seven o'clock in the evening and Gabbert had spent a long day working on the surveying crew.

"Jordan," Marlin called out, approaching from behind just as Gabbert slipped his key into the doorknob.

Gabbert turned and appeared mildly startled. "Oh. Hey. What's going on?"

"Got a minute?" Marlin asked.

Gabbert's eyes were bloodshot, but Marlin suspected it was from working outdoors all day. Gabbert was wearing a faded tank top, dirty cargo shorts, and a pair of hiking boots. He had a slight sunburn.

"Uh, for what?" Gabbert asked.

"Just a few more questions. Won't take long. Have you met Chief Deputy Lauren Gilchrist?"

He shook Lauren's hand and said, "Well, honestly now isn't a real good time."

Marlin could guess why Gabbert was reluctant to invite them inside. He probably had pot or paraphernalia in plain view. That was the least of his problems, but he didn't know that yet.

"Yeah, you probably want to wash up," Marlin said. "How about we come back in, say, 20 minutes?"

"Uh..."

"Then we'll be out of your hair."

"Yeah, okay."

Twenty minutes later, they sat in Gabbert's sparsely furnished living room, Lauren and Marlin on a tattered couch, Gabbert in an upholstered chair. His hair was still wet from the shower, and the apartment smelled strongly of recently sprayed air freshener. A nearby sliding glass door looked out onto a wooded area behind the apartment complex. It was a fairly typical living arrangement for a single guy his age.

"Thanks for talking to us," Marlin said. Lauren had suggested he lead the interview, since he'd already spoken with Gabbert twice. She would chime in as necessary. "I just have a couple of follow-up questions that might help us nail down some details."

"I'll help however I can," Gabbert said. "Same as last time."

"That's great," Marlin said. "We appreciate it. First, let me ask if you've seen Avery lately."

Would Gabbert's answer remain consistent?

"The girl Sean was seeing?" Gabbert asked.

"Right."

"Sorry, man, I've never met her. Don't know her."

Same thing he'd said in the first interview.

"Oh, that's right, and you told me you don't have her phone number. Correct?"

"Right."

"So you've never called or texted her, obviously."

"Nope. How could I?"

Marlin nodded. "Good point. You know what a wiggle pick is?"

"A what?"

"A wiggle pick. It's like a small pickaxe used for digging artifacts."

"Never heard of it."

"Hang on a sec." Marlin slipped a piece of paper from his breast pocket and unfolded it, showing Gabbert a photo. "That's a wiggle pick."

"Never seen one before."

"Sean had one," Marlin said. "You never saw it?"

"Nope."

"So you never handled it?"

"No."

"You're positive?"

"One hundred percent certain. Never touched it in my life."

"Okay, good. Last time we talked, you said you hardly ever go down to Blanco County. You said you couldn't remember the last time you'd been there. Was that accurate, now that you've had a little more time to think about it?"

Gabbert said, "I don't remember talking about that."

Not really an answer.

"Okay, then when *was* the last time you went to Blanco County?" Marlin asked.

"When I came to see you at the sheriff's office," Gabbert said.

"Oh, right. When you came to tell me Sean was your dealer."

Gabbert appeared uncomfortable. "I don't know if I'd say he was my dealer. He sold me pot a couple of times."

"Right. Your dealer."

"Whatever."

"Okay, so before that, when was the last time you'd been to Blanco County?" Marlin asked.

"I can't remember. A long time."

"Weeks? Months?"

"Probably months."

"You sure about that?" Marlin said. "Think hard."

"I don't understand what's going on," Gabbert said. "It's like you think I'm lying or something, and I don't appreciate it."

Lauren spoke up in a gentle tone. "Jordan, sometimes we run into a situation where a person is afraid to be totally honest with us because of things that have nothing to do with our investigation. For instance, a husband might say he was working late one night when he was actually at a girlfriend's house. He doesn't want to admit that to us, so he stretches the truth a little, and, well, that just causes problems for everybody. You understand where I'm going?"

"Not really, no."

"Okay, well, to be blunt, we've been wondering if you and Avery were hooking up behind Sean's back."

"Absolutely not."

"If you were, it would be best if—"

"I told you, I don't even know her." Gabbert was starting to sound distressed.

"There was no relationship there at all?" Lauren asked.

"No. Why would you think there was?"

He was wondering what they had on him. Wanting them to reveal information.

Marlin's instinct told him it was time to get more aggressive. He shifted impatiently in his seat and said, "Jordan, let's quit fooling around, okay? We have a copy of a certain video of Avery. I'm guessing you know exactly which one I'm talking about. She was swimming in a river. Ring any bells? It should, because you shot it."

Now Marlin saw panic in Gabbert's face. Fear.

"Jordan?" Lauren said.

"I don't know anything about a video," he said. His face was flushing. "I wasn't in a video with Avery."

"You're right," Marlin said. "You weren't in the video. But your voice was. And we'll be able to prove it. Voice identification software is pretty sophisticated nowadays."

Gabbert was rocking back and forth, his nerves fraying. He was no longer making eye contact.

"It gets worse, Jordan," Marlin said. "We know exactly where you were when you shot the video—on the Walz ranch. On the Pedernales River, right where Sean and Avery used to look for artifacts. We've been down there and we found the location."

Walz had been willing to let Marlin and Lauren scout the river, without a warrant, as long as they promised no digging or snooping around. Marlin gave Gabbert time to respond—to explain himself—but Gabbert had nothing to say.

"You familiar with metadata, Sean?" Marlin asked "The metadata for the video tells us *when* you shot it, too. It was the day before Sean died. I don't think that's a coincidence. I think Sean found out about you and Avery, and you got into a fight the next day—the day after you shot the video—at the same spot on the river."

It was an educated guess, but Marlin was fairly confident it was right.

Titus Steele had told the truth when he'd said Avery Kingsberry had been cheating on Sean Hudson. But Steele had tried to blame his nephew Cody Brock for the killing—payback that hadn't worked. That was the working theory now, and it was supported by facts.

"Just hold on," Gabbert said.

"We've *been* holding on," Marlin said. "You've been misleading me from the beginning and I'm not going to waste much more time with you."

Lauren made a gesture with her hands, like *Everybody calm down*. She said, "Jordan, now is the time to be totally honest with us. It's your best chance to stay out of trouble—but we have to know what happened out there."

Gabbert was shaking his head slowly. Still not ready to talk.

"Here's the kicker," Marlin said, leaning into Jordan's personal space. "Couple of days ago we got a search warrant for your cell phone. We know you and Avery called and texted each other a lot. But the warrant also included the location data for your phone, and it matches everything the video told us—the date and time and all that. It confirmed that you were on the Walz ranch, down by the river, on the day Sean died."

Marlin was making the location data for Gabbert's cell phone sound more precise than it was in reality. But in this case, they'd been able to compare the location data for the two consecutive days—the day Gabbert shot the video of Avery, and the day Sean died—and Gabbert's phone had pinged off the same tower for several hours on both of those consecutive days. It didn't prove conclusively he had been on the Walz ranch that second day—he could have been at some other location served by that same tower—but Marlin didn't think that was likely.

Gabbert finally spoke again. "The data is wrong, then."

"And the phone records?" Marlin said. "The calls and texts?"

"Man, I don't know what to tell you," Gabbert said.

"Could someone else have had your phone that day?" Lauren asked, again sounding gentle, even empathetic, but she was trying to keep Gabbert talking, so they could find flaws in his story.

"No way," Gabbert said. "My phone wasn't there and neither was I. You're trying to trick me."

"So the pings off the cell towers are inaccurate?" Marlin asked, trying to sound as disdainful as possible.

"That's what I'm saying," Gabbert said. "Sometimes technology doesn't work the way it should."

His voice quivered with desperation. Marlin had no question they had the right man.

"We talked to several other people that showed up in your cell phone records," Marlin said. "Know what they told us?"

Gabbert didn't answer.

"*You're* the guy dealing pot," Marlin said. "Not Sean. You were his dealer, not the other way around. You have a pretty nice little operation running.'"

Dealing pot was small potatoes compared to a murder charge, but Marlin wanted to rattle Gabbert as much as possible. Make him think they knew everything about him.

Marlin and Lauren both sat quietly for half a minute and let Gabbert stew. He was staring at the carpet and apparently had no intention of replying.

"What we're going to do next," Marlin said, "is get a sample of your DNA. We have a warrant for that. Then we're going to compare it to the DNA we found on the murder weapon—Sean's wiggle pick. Which you never touched, of course. But we all know you did. And when that match comes back—"

"Stop," Gabbert said.

Marlin waited. The only sound in the room was the hissing of air coming from the AC vent above.

"It was self-defense," Gabbert said.

Ten seconds passed.

"Okay," Marlin said.

"Tell us about it," Lauren said.

44

Jordan Gabbert thought he had been in love before, but then he met Avery Kingsberry. It started out as a crush and grew from there. He tried to resist it because she was seeing Sean, but he couldn't help himself. Couldn't stop thinking about her. Couldn't stop wanting her. Crazy, considering he'd only known her for a few months, and had only hung out with her and Sean a handful of times. But he felt some sort of spark between them. The way she looked at him sometimes. Was he imagining it? Of course he was.

Silly.

Stupid.

Then she texted him one day. Said she needed someone to talk to. She was confused. Upset.

So Jordan went over to her place. Gladly.

Avery told him she didn't know what to do about Sean. He was moving too fast. Wanting more of a relationship than she wanted. Then she admitted she had feelings for someone else. "And that person is you," she'd said. It was one of the happiest moments in Jordan's life.

They spent that night together. And several more afterward. When they were apart, Jordan thought about her all the time. Wanted to be with her every minute of every day. The only problem was, Avery was reluctant to break it off with Sean. Not just because she didn't want to hurt him, but because of the little operation they had going on. The artifact digging. She said she'd call it off with Sean as soon as they were done at the ranch. When would that be? Soon, she said. Soon.

Jordan promised to be patient, and in the meantime, they kept seeing each other. That meant Avery had to sneak around. Make excuses. Tell lies.

And then they got caught.

Avery offered to take him out to the ranch, to show him where she and Sean had been digging. They picked a day when the foreman was going to be out of town. It was hot. They went for a swim in a secluded spot. Then Jordan shot the video of Avery. He just couldn't help himself. She really was a goddess, just as he'd said. What guy wouldn't want to have a lasting memory of a moment like that? He might never have another like it.

It was a dumb thing to do, and he made it worse by keeping the video instead of deleting it. He figured it wouldn't be a problem. He'd be careful with it. Wouldn't show it to anyone. He'd be the only person who would even know it existed.

Yeah, right.

That night, Sean came over to Jordan's place to get some more weed and they ended up smoking a couple of bowls. Got really high. High enough that Jordan fell asleep while Sean sat there watching some sci-fi movie on TV.

That's when a text arrived from Avery.

"Sean had to have seen that text, which was unusually bad luck, because she'd sent it hours earlier and it hadn't gone through," Marlin said. "It had gotten hung up somehow, and that meshes with Gabbert's claim that his texting had been acting squirrelly in the month or so before Sean died."

Marlin and Lauren were in Bobby Garza's office, bringing the sheriff up to date on Jordan Gabbert's confession.

"Which is why Gabbert called Sean several times during that timeframe, instead of texting him," Lauren added.

"'Sometimes technology doesn't work the way it should,'" Garza said, repeating Gabbert's remark.

"Well, he's right," Lauren said. "And it totally screwed him in this case. We can only guess how it went down, but we figure Sean saw the text from Avery pop up on Jordan's phone, so he grabbed it and began to snoop around. Didn't take him long to find the video of Avery."

"I'm surprised he didn't confront Gabbert right then and there," Garza said.

"He was probably tempted," Lauren said. "But he came up with something a little more despicable."

"I woke up and Sean was gone," Gabbert said. "I didn't think much of it until I realized he'd taken a bunch of pot from me, plus about five hundred bucks. So I texted him—and he told me to fuck off. I knew something weird was up, so I called him, but he wouldn't answer."

Gabbert's phone records backed that up. He had called Sean Hudson late that night.

"Then I called Avery," Gabbert said. "She was freaking out because Sean had told her he knew about us, and he had a copy of the video I'd shot. I checked my phone and saw that it had been texted to Sean's phone, so it's obvious he did that while I was sleeping. Anyway, you wanna know what kind of scumbag Sean was? He told Avery he was gonna post it online unless she promised to quit seeing me. Can you believe that crap? I can understand why Sean was upset, but it didn't give him the right to threaten her like that. Some girls wouldn't care if anyone saw a video like that, but Avery wasn't that way. She was very private. The more I thought about it, the madder it made me."

Gabbert took a deep breath.

"The next morning, it got worse. Sean and Avery were supposed to dig at the ranch again, but of course she didn't want to go. At that point, she never wanted to see Sean again. When she didn't show up, he started texting her. Harassing her, really. She ignored him. Then, a couple of hours later, he texted her a photo of a point he had just found. She didn't believe it at first, but she also knew he couldn't be lying. He was holding the point up, and she recognized the location near the river. The lucky son of a bitch had found an Andice point, totally undamaged."

"What exactly is that?" Garza asked.

"An early archaic point, meaning about seven or eight thousand years old," Marlin said. "It's made from chert and has deep basal notches that give it a unique look, but they're fragile, so most of the specimens people find are broken. A complete one is very valuable."

"How valuable?" Garza asked.

"Well, it varies, but totally intact—no chips or breaks—a really good one could sell for 20 or 25 thousand. Keep in mind that we don't know the quality of the one Sean Hudson supposedly found that morning."

"Lot of money, especially for a kid Sean Hudson's age," Garza said.

"Yep, and he knew Avery Kingsberry would want her share. So he sent her the photo and said he'd split it with her—if she would come out to the ranch and talk to him about the situation with Jordan."

"Damn, he was a manipulative bastard, wasn't he?" Garza said.

"And it worked," Lauren said. "But not for the money. Her plan, according to Jordan, was to tell Sean it was over. Jordan didn't like the idea—he wanted her to do it over the phone—but she went anyway, so Jordan decided to go out there, too."

"He had to know that wouldn't go well," Garza said.

"And it didn't," Lauren said. "He and Sean immediately started arguing, and then Avery got between them, and that's when Sean slapped her. According to Jordan."

"Right," Marlin said. "We all know Gabbert can't necessarily be trusted. We'll want to interview him again in a few days and see if his story changes."

"And if we're lucky," Lauren said, "Avery will eventually agree to talk."

"That would help," Garza said. "So what happened next?"

"Here's where Gabbert's story and Titus Steele's story start to overlap a little bit," Marlin said. "Gabbert said he and Sean started to get into it then—both of them throwing punches, but neither of them doing much damage."

"Like most fights between men who don't know what they're doing," Garza said.

"Which seems to be the majority of them," Lauren said. Marlin and Garza both laughed. "And women, too," Lauren added. "Most people don't know how to fight, or how to defend themselves."

"That's for sure," Marlin said, "but—according to Gabbert—suddenly some other guy comes up from behind him and decks Sean."

"Cody Brock," Garza said.

"Right," Marlin said. "With Titus Steele hanging around, too. Apparently, just as Steele described, they had been up on the hill watching when the confrontation began, except Steele didn't mention that Gabbert was on the scene."

"How did Sean react?" Garza asked.

"I think Sean was just as surprised as I was," Gabbert said. "I mean, who *was* this guy? He looked like an Indian or something. Later on I saw in the news that his name was Cody Brock." He looked at Marlin. "The guy you shot last week."

Marlin nodded and said, "Go on."

"Okay, well, at first it looked like Sean was going to stay down, but then he jumps up with that little pickaxe in his hand. Only problem was, instead of going after Cody Brock, he came after *me* again. I thought I was dead for sure. How do you stop a guy when he's swinging a weapon like that?"

"Couldn't you have run away?" Marlin asked.

"No way. Sean was in great shape. He was a bicyclist and all that. He would've caught me in a second and buried that blade in my back."

"So what did you do?"

"I got lucky, that's what I did. He took a swing and I managed to jump out of the way. Then I rushed him and wrapped him up in a bear hug. We fell to the ground and Sean dropped the pickaxe at some point. I knew that because suddenly he had both hands around my throat, choking me. I tried to break free, but he was on top of me, and his grip was strong as hell. From all the digging, I guess. Anyway, I was just about to black out when one of my hands brushes against the handle of the pickaxe. I reacted without even thinking about it. I swung that pickaxe hard at the side of Sean's head."

Gabbert was starting to cry. Marlin and Lauren waited for him to gather himself.

"I couldn't believe how easily that blade sunk in. Sean let go immediately, and a few seconds later, he fell off of me. I'm pretty sure he was already dead, but I don't know for sure. He never moved again, I know that much."

"Where was everybody else at this point?" Lauren asked.

"Cody Brock and that other guy Titus were right there, nearby. They'd been standing around, watching. They could've helped me, but they didn't."

"What about Avery?"

"She was on her way up the hill. I think she took off as soon as Sean and I got into it. She didn't see what happened. She didn't know about it until later, when I told her."

Gabbert wiped his nose with the back of his arm. Lauren got up, went to a cabinet for a box of Kleenex, and placed it on the table in front of him.

She sat back down and said, "Why should we believe your version of events?"

Gabbert looked at her, surprised. "Why would I lie?"

"Because," Garza said, "there remains the very real possibility that Avery Kingsberry was the one who hit Sean with the wiggle pick."

"Yep," Marlin said.

"Sean had just slapped her," Garza said. "She would've been angry, or scared, or both."

"We asked Jordan why he never came forward and told the truth," Lauren said. "After all, if it happened the way he said it did, it *was* self-defense."

"What did he say?" Garza asked.

"That he was scared," Lauren said. "That he was afraid we'd charge him with murder anyway."

They all knew this was a realistic answer. Sometimes emotion trumped logic, and as a result, people made poor decisions.

Marlin said, "Gabbert caved when I said we were going to pull his DNA and compare it to samples from the wiggle pick. He had no way of knowing I was bluffing, because we have only three samples—Sean Hudson himself, an unknown female, probably Avery, and the unknown male that matched the burglary and assault in Sanders, Arizona. That's almost certainly Cody Brock, and that indicates he did actually try to remove the pick after they dumped the body. We were operating on the assumption that when Brock wiped it down, he managed to remove Gabbert's DNA."

"But in reality, we think Gabbert never touched it," Lauren said. "The idea of a DNA test concerned him because, if he's covering for Avery, he wouldn't want us to know his DNA *wasn't* on the murder weapon."

"Exactly," Marlin said.

"What did he say about moving the body?" Garza asked.

"That he had nothing to do with it," Marlin said. "Titus told him they would take care of it, and they should just keep their mouths shut or they'd all end up in prison."

"Steele had several reasons to keep quiet," Lauren said. "He didn't want to get fired, and he wanted to keep the money flowing from the artifacts. So, according to Gabbert, Steele pressured Avery to keep digging in the days after Sean was killed. I'm sure she didn't want to, but we suspect that Steele threatened to implicate either her or Jordan. So she cooperated."

"What about the Andice point?" Garza asked. "Where is it now?"

"I don't know," Jordan Gabbert said. "I never saw it. None of us were worried about that."

"What happened to Sean's stuff?" Lauren asked. "He usually had a backpack with him, right?"

"I don't know. You should ask Titus Steele."

Made sense. Steele and Cody Brock had disposed of the body, the clothes, and the phone. They must've ditched the backpack, too. And Steele would know to look inside first for artifacts. If he found the Andice point, would he even understand the significance of it? Surely he'd learned a little about artifacts from Sean and Avery over the course of their illicit partnership.

"Have you left anything out?" Lauren asked.

"No, that's it. That's the whole story."

"Have you lied about anything?" Marlin asked.

"No, I swear. Not this time."

Marlin glared at him, skeptical.

"Am I under arrest?" Gabbert asked.

"No, you are not," Lauren said. "But you'll need to come to the sheriff's office and tell the entire story again."

"You think his account is accurate?" Garza asked.

"Man, I don't know," Marlin said. "He's a good liar. We *know* that. He really could be covering for Avery. I don't think we'll ever be sure. I think he was there, just as he said, but he might've changed just that one detail—who actually swung the wiggle pick."

"The DNA results say it was probably her," Lauren said.

"If she killed Sean, that, too, might've been in self-defense," Garza said.

"Possibly," Marlin said. "I'm convinced Sean did slap her. And I feel fairly certain the fight unfolded as Gabbert said. It matches the abrasion on Sean's face. Cody Brock showed up out of nowhere and punched him. Titus was there, too."

"We'll go back at Gabbert in a few minutes," Lauren said. "Make him start from the beginning yet again. If he changes his story at all, we'll be all over him."

Gabbert was waiting in an interview room. This time the interview would be videotaped.

"And if it stays the same, we'll have to accept the fact that that might be the closest we'll ever get to the truth," Marlin said.

"Sometimes that's the best you can do," Garza said.

45

Four days later.

"I have gathered all of you here today," Red said, "to give you the chance to participate in something truly historic."

Ten men stood in front of him. Most of them were tradesmen—carpenters, electricians, plumbers—that Red and Billy Don had worked with over the years. They were all good men. Hardworking men. And Red was hoping to take advantage of that fact.

Billy Don, meanwhile, was sitting on top of a 165-quart Igloo cooler filled to the brim with ice and beer. Red knew full well he'd have to keep the cold beer flowing if he wanted his proposition to work.

"As most of you know—or you've heard through the grapevine—I intend to build, in the oaks behind me—"

"A tree house," Billy Don said, and everybody laughed. Red glared at him. "What?" Billy Don said. "Remember I said I was still gonna make fun of you."

Red shook his head and went back to his speech. "It will be an elevated home—but not an ordinary elevated home. This one, my friends, is gonna be a replica of the one structure that every true Texan holds near and dear to his heart. This one, my fellow patriots, is gonna be a model of the Alamo."

Red waited for applause, but none came. So he forged ahead. He had written the speech the day before and done his best to memorize it.

"What I am suggesting to you today is that any red-blooded God-fearing Blanco County citizen might like to take part in the construction of such a monumental and meaningful project."

Red had a long, dried stalk from a sotol plant in his hand, and now he stepped within a few feet of the loose line of men. Using the sotol stalk, he proceeded to draw a line in the dirt in front of them. Who cared what Willard Fisk said about the actual line in the sand? As far as Red was concerned, it happened back then and he was making it happen now.

"If you would like to be among the elite group of men who joins in this effort to honor our brave forefathers and commemorize the liberty they bought for us with their lives, I am asking you to step across this line."

Nobody moved. A couple of men were frowning.

"There will, of course, be plenty of beer and barbecue for all volunteers," Red said.

All ten men stepped across the line.

Lauren stopped in the doorway to Marlin's office and said, "Got some results back from Henry."

Marlin waved her in. She closed the door behind her and took a seat in the chair across the desk from him.

"It's confirmed that the unknown male DNA from the wiggle pick matches Cody Brock, and that means he's good for that burglary-assault in Arizona."

"What we expected," Marlin said.

"They'll be glad to close that case."

"I'm sure they will. Might even help them figure out who the other assailant was. Someone Brock was known to run with."

"Good point. Okay, the sample from the unknown female will just have to remain unknown, but it's gotta be from Avery Kingsberry, right?"

"Agreed. As you said before, it's reasonable to assume she used that pick when they were out there digging."

"That leaves the swabs from the back of Steele's truck and the tarp in the shed—and those match Sean Hudson."

"So Steele really did move the body, just as he said."

"Yep."

"I'm not sure what to make of that."

"Me neither, but with that and testimony from Gabbert, we can probably prosecute Steele for it."

"If we can find him," Marlin said.

"We will. Sooner or later."

"Hope so."

"And the last thing, not 20 minutes ago, I finally got a return call from Desmond Langman's lawyer."

It took Marlin a moment to place the name. Then he remembered—Langman was Sean Hudson's landlord.

"Oh, yeah?" Marlin said.

"Just like we guessed, he wants to talk about a deal. He didn't get specific, but you know Langman's gonna cop to stealing the artifacts from Hudson's apartment."

"And the laptop," Marlin said.

"Right, and the laptop."

Deputy Ernie Turpin had come up empty when he'd scoured the laptop for more of Hudson's files, which meant that Langman had attempted to obliterate any trace of the previous owner. But Turpin had simply compared the serial number to a receipt found in Hudson's apartment and it was a match. Then Turpin had spoken to the woman who'd sold the laptop to Billy Don Craddock. She confirmed that she'd bought it from Langman for $200 after he'd tacked an ad to a bulletin board at his church.

"Funny that Langman might be the only person who gets charged with anything," Marlin said. "And by 'funny' I mean disappointing and ironic."

Lauren laughed. "They can't all be slam dunks."

"I guess not."

"I have to say, I've really been enjoying working with you these past few months. It hasn't been weird at all."

That was typical Lauren—saying exactly what was on her mind.

"Thanks. Me, too," Marlin said.

"How does Nicole feel about it?" Lauren asked.

"About us working together?"

"Yeah. You know—the former girlfriend and all that. A lot of women wouldn't like that arrangement. Men, too. Am I being too nosy?"

"Not at all. And Nicole isn't bothered in the least. That's how she is."

"That's what I've gathered. Of course, it probably doesn't hurt her confidence to look the way she looks."

"She is a knockout, isn't she?" Marlin said.

"Pretty much," Lauren said. "And a nice lady. You done good."

"Thanks."

"I'd better get back to work," she said, rising from the chair. "I have a reputation to uphold as the chief deputy around here."

He was still grinning after she'd left.

Titus Steele stepped outside the small café, his belly now full, and walked to his truck. It was hotter than hell out, but the air was dry. Much drier than in central Texas. He liked the area. Was even considering sticking around, rather than continuing on to Montana, which was his original plan.

He started the engine and sat there in the parking lot for a moment. Checked his phone. It appeared the cops had given up on him. No more calls. He figured they'd dug deep enough by now that they knew the truth. What could they do about the lies he'd told? Not much, really.

He lifted the hatch on the center console and grabbed the small box inside. Removed the lid and studied the arrowhead resting on a bed of cotton. Okay, yeah, he guessed he could admire the beauty of it. The craftsmanship required to create it. The fact that it had survived in pristine condition for nearly 10,000 years.

And, once more, with regret, he had to acknowledge that he couldn't do anything with it. Couldn't sell it—not without leaving a trail that could get him busted. The Andice wasn't his—and the value of it placed the theft well into felony territory. He'd been lucky so far. Why push it? Wasn't worth it.

He shifted into drive and pulled onto the highway.

When he was five miles out of town, he tossed the box out the window.

Want to know when Ben Rehder's
next novel will be released?

Subscribe to his email list
www.benrehder.com

Have you discovered Ben Rehder's
Roy Ballard Mysteries?

Turn the page for an excerpt from

GONE THE NEXT

GONE THE NEXT

1

The woman he was watching this time was in her early thirties. Thirty-five at the oldest. White. Well dressed. Upper middle class. Reasonably attractive. Probably drove a nice car, like a Lexus or a BMW. She was shopping at Nordstrom in Barton Creek Square mall. Her daughter—Alexis, if he'd overheard the name correctly—appeared to be about seven years old. Brown hair, like her mother's. The same cute nose. They were in the women's clothing department, looking at swimsuits. Alexis was bored. Fidgety. Ready to go to McDonald's, like Mom had promised. Amazing what you can hear if you keep your ears open.

He was across the aisle, in the men's department, looking at Hawaiian shirts. They were all ugly, and he had no intention of buying one. He stood on the far side of the rack and held up a green shirt with palm trees on it. But he was really looking past it, at the woman, who had several one-piece swimsuits draped over her arm. Not bikinis, though she still had the figure for it. Maybe she had stretch marks, or the beginnings of a belly.

He replaced the green shirt and grabbed a blue one covered with coconuts. Just browsing, like a regular shopper might do.

Mom was walking over to a changing room now. Alexis followed, walking stiff-legged, maybe pretending she was a monster. A zombie. Amusing herself.

He moved closer, to a table piled high with neatly folded cargo shorts. He pretended to look for a pair in his size. But he was watching in his peripheral vision.

"Wait right here," Mom said. She didn't look around. She was oblivious to his presence. He might as well have been a mannequin.

Alexis said something in reply, but he couldn't make it out.

"There isn't room, Lexy. I'll just be a minute."

And she shut the door, leaving Alexis all by herself.

When he first began his research, he'd been surprised by what he'd found. He had expected the average parent to be watchful. Wary. Downright suspicious. That's how he would be if he had a child. A little girl. He'd guard her like a priceless treasure. Every minute of the day. But his assumptions were wrong. Parents were sloppy. Careless. Just plain stupid.

He knew that now, because he'd watched hundreds of them. And their children. In restaurants. In shopping centers. Supermarkets. Playgrounds and parks. For three months he'd watched. Reconnaissance missions, like this one right now, with Alexis and her mom. Preparing. What he'd observed was encouraging. It wouldn't be as difficult as he'd assumed. When the time came.

But he had to use his head. Plan it out. Use what he'd learned. Doing it in a public place, especially a retail establishment, would be risky, because there were video surveillance systems everywhere nowadays. Some places, like this mall, even had security guards. Daycare centers were often fenced, and the front doors were locked. Schools were always on the lookout for strangers who—

"You need help with anything?"

He jumped, ever so slightly.

A salesgirl had come up behind him. Wanting to be helpful. Calling attention to him. Ruining the moment.

That was a good lesson to remember. Just because he was watching, that didn't mean he wasn't being watched, too.

2

The first time I ever heard the name Tracy Turner—on a hot, cloudless Tuesday in June—I was tailing an obese, pyorrheic degenerate named Wally Crouch. I was fairly certain about the "degenerate" part, because Crouch had visited two adult bookstores and three strip clubs since noon. Not that there's anything wrong with a little mature entertainment, but there's a point when it goes from bawdy boys-will-be-boys recreation to creepy pathological fixation. The pyorrhea was pure conjecture on my part, based solely on the number of Twinkie wrappers Crouch had tossed out the window during his travels.

Crouch was a driver for UPS and, according to my biggest client, he was also a fraud who was riding the workers' comp gravy train. In the course of a routine delivery seven weeks prior, Crouch had allegedly injured his lower back. A ruptured disk, the doctor said. Limited mobility and a twelve- to sixteen-week recovery period. In the meantime, Crouch couldn't lift more than ten pounds without searing pain shooting up his spinal cord. But this particular quack had a checkered past filled with questionable diagnoses and reprimands from the medical board. My job was fairly simple, at least on paper: Follow Crouch discreetly until he proved himself a liar. Catch it on video. Testify, if necessary. Earn a nice paycheck. Continue to finance my sumptuous, razor's-edge lifestyle.

You'd think Crouch, having a choice in the matter, would've avoided rush-hour traffic and had a few more beers instead, but he left Sugar's Uptown Cabaret at ten after five and squeezed his way onto the interstate heading south. I followed in my seven-year-old Dodge Caravan. Beige. Try to find a vehicle less likely to catch someone's eye. The windows are deeply tinted and a scanner antenna is mounted on the roof, which are the only clues that the driver isn't a soccer mom toting her brats to practice.

Anyone whose vehicle doubles as a second home recognizes the value of a decent sound system. I'd installed a Blaupunkt, with Bose speakers front and rear. Total system set me back about two grand. Seems like overkill for talk radio, but that's what I was listening to when I heard the familiar alarm signal of the Emergency Alert System. I'd never known the system to be used for anything other than weather warnings, but not this time. It was an Amber Alert. A local girl had gone missing from her affluent West Austin neighborhood. Tracy Turner: six years old, blond hair, green eyes, three feet tall, forty-five pounds, wearing denim shorts and a pink shirt. My palms went sweaty just thinking about it. Then I heard she might be in the company of Howard Turner—her non-custodial father, a resident of Los Angeles—and I breathed a small sigh of relief. Listeners, they said, should keep an eye out for a green Honda with California plates.

Easy to read between the lines. Tracy's parents were divorced, and dad had decided he wanted to spend more time with his daughter, despite how the courts had ruled. Sad, but much better than a random abduction.

The announcer was repeating the message when my cell phone rang. I turned the radio volume down, answered, and my client—a senior claims adjuster at a big insurance company—said, "You nail him yet?"

"Christ, Heidi, it's only the third day."

"I thought you were good."

"That's a vicious rumor."

"Yeah, and I think you started it yourself. I'm starting to think you get by on your looks alone."

"That remark borders on sexual harassment, and you know how I feel about that."

"You're all for it."

"Exactly. Anyway, relax, okay? I'm on him twenty-four seven." Crouch had taken the Manor Road exit, and now he turned into his apartment complex, so I drove past, calling it a day. I didn't like lying to Heidi, but I had a meeting with a man named Harvey Blaylock in thirty minutes.

"Well, you'd better get something soon, because I've got another one waiting," Heidi said.

I didn't say anything, because a jerk in an F-150 was edging over into my lane.

"Roy?" she said.

"Yeah."

"I have another one for you."

"Have scientists come up with that device yet?"

"What device?"

"The one that allows you to be in two places at the same time."

"You really crack you up."

"Let me get this one squared away, then we'll talk, okay?"

"The quicker the better. Where are you? Has Crouch even left the house?"

"Oh, yeah. Been wandering all afternoon."

"Where to?"

"Uh, let's just say he seems to have an inordinate appreciation for the female form."

"Which means?"

"He's been visiting gentlemen's clubs."

A pause. "You mean tittie bars?"

"That's such a crass term. Oh, by the way, the Yellow Rose is looking for dancers. In case you decide to—"

She hung up on me.

I had the phone in my hands, so I went ahead and called my best friend Mia Madison, who works at an establishment I used to do business with on occasion. She tends bar at a tavern on North Lamar.

Boiling it down to one sentence, Mia is smart, funny, optimistic, and easy on the eyes. Expanding on the last part, because it's relevant, Mia stands about five ten and has long red hair that she likes to wear in a ponytail. Prominent cheekbones, with dimples beneath. The toned legs of a runner, though she doesn't run, but must walk ten miles a day during an eight-hour shift. When Mia gets dolled up—what she calls "bringing it" —she goes from being an attractive woman you'd certainly notice to a world-class head turner.

On one occasion, she revealed that she has a tattoo. Wouldn't show it to me, but she said—joking, I'm sure—that if I could guess what it was, and where it was, she'd let me have a look. Nearly a year later, I still hadn't given up.

"Is it Muttley?" I asked when she answered.

"Muttley? Who the hell is Muttley?"

"You know, that cartoon dog with the sarcastic laugh."

"You mean Scooby Doo?"

"No, the other one. Hangs with Dick Dastardly."

"I have no idea what you're talking about."

"Before your time, I guess. Are you at work?"

"Not till six. Just got out of the shower. I'm drying off."

"Need any help?"

"I think I can handle it," she said.

"Okay, next question. Want to earn a hundred bucks the easy way?" I said.

"Love to," she said. "When and where?"

3

Harvey Blaylock was maybe sixty, medium height, with neatly trimmed gray hair, black-framed glasses, a white short-sleeved shirt, and tan gabardine slacks. He looked like the kind of man who, if things had taken a slightly different turn, might've wound up as a forklift salesman, or, best case, a high-school principal in a small agrarian town.

In reality, however, Harvey Blaylock was a man who held tremendous sway over my future, near- and long-term. I intended to remain respectful and deferential.

Blaylock's necktie — green, with bucking horses printed on it — rested on his paunch as he leaned back in his chair, scanning the contents of a manila folder. I knew it was my file, because it said ROY W. BALLARD on the outside, typed neatly on a rectangular label. I'm quick to notice things like that.

Five minutes went by. His office smelled like cigarettes and Old Spice. Rays of sun slanted in through horizontal blinds on the windows facing west. As far as I could tell, we were the only people left in the building.

"I really appreciate you staying late for this," I said. "Would've been tough for me to make it earlier."

He grunted and continued reading, one hand drumming slowly on his metal desk. The digital clock on the wall above him read 6:03. On the bookshelf, tucked among a row of wire-bound notebooks, was a framed photo of a young boy holding up a small fish on a line.

"Boy, was I surprised to hear that Joyce retired," I said. "She seemed too young for that. So spry and youthful." Joyce being Blaylock's predecessor. My previous probation officer. A true bitch on wheels. Condescending. Domineering. No sense of humor. "I'll have to send her a card," I said, hoping it didn't sound sarcastic.

Blaylock didn't answer.

I was starting to wonder if he had a reading disability. I'm no angel — I wouldn't have been in this predicament if I were — but my file couldn't have been more than half a dozen pages long. I was surprised that a man in his position, with several hundred probationers in his charge, would spend more than thirty seconds on each.

Finally, Blaylock, still looking at the file, said, "Roy Wilson Ballard. Thirty-six years old. Divorced. Says you used to work as a news cameraman." He had a thick piney-woods accent. Pure east Texas. He peered up at me, without moving his head. Apparently, it was my turn to talk.

"Yes, sir. Until about three years ago."

"When you got fired."

"My boss and I had a personality conflict," I said, wondering how detailed my file was.

"Ernie Crenshaw."

"That's him."

"You broke his nose with a microphone stand."

Fairly detailed, apparently.

"Well, yeah, he, uh — "

"You got an attitude problem, Ballard?"

"No, sir."

"Temper?"

I started to lie, but decided against it. "Occasionally."

"That what happened in this instance? Temper got the best of you?"

"He was rude to one of the reporters. He called her a name."

"What name was that?"

"I'd rather not repeat it."

"I'm asking you to."

"Okay, then. He called her Doris. Her real name is Anne."

His expression remained frozen. Tough crowd.

I said, "Okay. He called her a cunt."

Blaylock's expression still didn't change. "To her face?"

"Behind her back. He was a coward. And she didn't deserve it. This guy was a world-class jerk. Little weasel."

"You heard him say it?"

"I was the one he was talking to. It set me off."

"So you busted his nose."

"I did, sir, yes."

Perhaps it was my imagination, but I thought Harvey Blaylock gave a nearly imperceptible nod of approval. He looked back at the file. "Now you're self-employed. A legal videographer. What is that exactly?"

"Well, uh, that means I record depositions, wills, scenes of accidents. Things like that. But proof of insurance fraud is my specialty. The majority of my business. Turns out I'm really good at it."

"Describe it for me."

"Sir?"

"Give me a typical day."

I recited my standard courtroom answer. "Basically, I keep a subject under surveillance and hope to videotape him engaging in an activity that's beyond his alleged physical limitations." Then I added, "Maybe lifting weights, or dancing. Playing golf. Doing the hokey-pokey."

No smile.

"Not a nine-to-five routine, then."

"No, sir. More like five to nine."

Blaylock mulled that over for a few seconds. "So you're out there, working long hours, sometimes through the night, and you start taking pills to keep up with the pace. That how it went?"

Until you've been there, you have no idea how powerless and naked you feel when someone like Harvey Blaylock is authorized to dig through your personal failings with a salad fork.

"That sums it up pretty well," I said.

"Did it work?"

"What, the pills?"

He nodded.

"Well, yeah. But coffee works pretty well, too."

"You were also drinking. That's why you got pulled over in the first place, and how they ended up finding the pills on you. You got a drinking problem?"

I thought of an old joke. *Yeah, I got a drinking problem. Can't pay my bar tab.* "I hope not," I said, which is about as honest as it gets. "At one point maybe I did, but I don't know for sure. Probably not. But that's what you'd expect someone with a drinking problem to say, right?"

"Had a drink since your court date?"

"No, sir. I'm not allowed to. Even though the Breathalyzer said I was legal."

"Not even one drink?"

"Not a drop. Joyce, gave me a piss te—I mean a urine test, last month, and three in the past year. I passed them all. That should be in the file."

"You miss it?" Blaylock asked. "The booze?"

I honestly thought about it for a moment.

"Sometimes, yeah," I said. "More than I would've guessed, but not enough to freak me out or anything. Sometimes, you know, I just crave a cold beer. Or three. But if I had to quit eating Mexican food, I'd miss that, too. Maybe more than beer."

Blaylock slowly sat forward in his chair and dropped my file, closed, on his desk. "Here's the deal, son. Ninety-five percent of the people I deal with are shitbags who think the world is their personal litter box. I can't do them any good, and they don't want me to. Most of 'em are locked up again within a year, and all I can say is good riddance. Then I see guys like you who make a stupid mistake and get caught up in the system. You probably have a decent life ahead of you, but you don't need me to tell you that, and it really doesn't matter what I think anyway. So I'll just say this: Follow the rules and you can put all this behind you. If you need any help, I'll do what I can. I really will. But if you fuck up just one time, it's like tipping over a row of dominoes. Then it's out of your control, and mine, too. You follow me?"

After the meeting, I swung by a Jack-In-The-Box, then sat outside Wally Crouch's place for a few hours, just in case. He stayed put.

I got home just as the ten o'clock news was coming on. Howard Turner had been located in a motel in Yuma City, Arizona, there on business. Police had verified his alibi. He had been nowhere near Texas, and the cops had no reason to believe he was involved.

So Tracy Turner was still missing, and that fact created a void in my chest that I hadn't felt in years.

ABOUT THE AUTHOR

Ben Rehder is an Edgar, Shamus, and Barry Award finalist. His novels have made best-of-the-year lists in *Publishers Weekly*, *Library Journal*, *Kirkus Reviews*, and *Field & Stream* For more information, visit www.benrehder.com.

OTHER NOVELS BY BEN REHDER

Buck Fever
Bone Dry
Flat Crazy
Guilt Trip
Gun Shy
Holy Moly
The Chicken Hanger
The Driving Lesson
Gone The Next
Hog Heaven
Get Busy Dying
Stag Party
Bum Steer
If I Had A Nickel

Made in the USA
Lexington, KY
31 July 2016